International Pr

Super skilled graft of fiction onto history...an authentic winner.
Sunday Times

Unusual, exotic and tantalising.
Irish Times

Has the rancid strength of a distillation of the best of Le Carré
and Deighton: an authentic winner.
Sunday Times

In the top flight of thriller writers.
Natal Mercury

Smashing action scenes...superb entertainment.
New York Times Book Review

Espionage in the le Carré class
The Observer

Brierley's style is first class, and his evocation of external
bleakness...is superb.
The Jerusalem Post

One is definitely hooked from the first page
BBC French Service

Also by David Brierley

Novels
Cold War
Blood Group O
Big Bear, Little Bear
Shooting Star
Czechmate
Skorpion's Death
Snowline
One Lives, One Dies
On Leaving a Prague Window
The Horizontal Woman
The Cloak-and-Dagger Girl
Death & Co
Dead Man Telling Tales

Short Stories
To El and Back

Budapest Hand

David Brierley

SAFE HOUSE BOOKS

www.safehousebooks.co.uk

Safe House Books Ltd
London, England
www.safehousebooks.co.uk

Published by Safe House Books, 2023

BUDAPEST HAND

Cover design by Stuart Polson

A catalogue record for this book is available from the British Library

9781739754020 (paperback)

Typeset using Atomik ePublisher from Easypress Technologies

To Maggie, Mike, Clare and Anna

'I can't write this story,' I said.

In my voice I hear the echo of a boy protesting to his mother and stamping his little foot. Jozsef could hear it too. He rubbed his knuckles along his chin as if it was tender from a punch.

'You can write it,' he told me.

'I can't. They'll find a way to stop me.'

'You can write it,' he said again, more force this time. 'You'll find a way.'

Jozsef stared at me, Jozsef my cousin, the cop, the killer, the cuckold, the survivor.

All right. I took a deep breath.

'This is a true story. Only the facts have been changed.'

Jozsef's smile was slow to come but worth the wait.

'Isn't that the Hungarian way?'

CHAPTER 1

Have you ever seen with your own eyes something that is impossible? I have.

Date: Thursday 8 April 2010. Time: 6.19 pm. Location: Oxford. My life is about to change forever.

See how precise I am. The facts are absolutely clear. It's important you know that. I glance at my watch as I press the button on the television. It's tuned to BBC One, coming up to the final stretch of the national news. I am standing in the centre of the sitting room, glancing at a couple of pieces of junk mail. Got it? Then it happens.

Out of the corner of my eye I see her. Eve. On the TV screen. My wife.

She's been dead for four months.

My name is Bazil and I am a journalist.

They use that formula at AA meetings. Let's face it, it's not a bad comparison. Working in newspapers is an addiction. Highs when you've got a scoop. Your pulse races. Your blood sings. Then the lows when you are disgusted by the job. Doorstepping. Phone hacking. No need to spell that out. There's a hunger, a dependency, a need. And maybe, just maybe, it will kill you.

So here I am, Bazil Potter, this journalist who's finished his shift at the wordface, standing in his living room, staring at his wife who was dead and is now alive. She's changed a bit, hair cropped, furrow between her eyes. I don't care. It is her. A man *knows* his wife. There is no disguising the spirit, the soul, the self. But her hands… Damn it, her hands are hidden.

I pick up details. That's the reporter in me. Eve is standing at the shoulder of, but a step behind, a man I have never seen before. You wouldn't say they were a couple, an 'item' to use the jargon. The man is wearing a charcoal grey suit. Expensive? I'd say so but I only caught a glimpse. White shirt. Interesting about his tie – a snake with an apple in its mouth. So he's got a wild side. The camera is focused on him. My wife is not the story, this man is. Is he angry? More irritated, I'd say, with a snappy answer to some question. Look at that hard stare he gives the camera. Don't mess with me, those eyes say. He turns and walks out of frame. The camera is hand-held and whips round. The man gets in the front passenger seat of a black Mercedes. My wife gets in the back and the car moves off while she is still closing the door. It joins traffic crossing a bridge and disappears.

All in silence.

How long did that snippet last? Twenty seconds, maybe less. Of course there was more of the story before I switched on… I stand still, shocked. Then I unfreeze, cast round for the remote control. Last night I'd muted the sound to cut off a politician. Where's the bloody remote? I find it in the fruit bowl. By now the news has moved on.

I grab the phone and stand in the centre of the room with an eye on the television in case there is a recap. I punch in Josh's number.

'Josh? It's Baz. I've just seen Eve. Have you got the news on?'

Josh Banner, friend, colleague, shoulder to cry on. He has helped me through the bad times of Eve's death. News of her resurrection troubles him. He thinks my sanity has finally cracked. 'Eve? Seen her?'

'I just bloody said that. On the six o'clock news.'

'Baz…' Blown it, haven't I? My obsession has become a bore.

'Listen. Her. Alive. On the news. Five minutes ago.' In my urgency I am speaking like a tabloid. No verbs. Short sentences in case the reader's attention span can't stretch to the end of the line. 'Josh, she's done her hair differently, but it was her.'

'You do mean Eve? Not…'

'Eve.'

'Well, er, that is…amazing.'

'What do you mean amazing? It's wonderful, fantastic. Well. Isn't it?'

But Josh is silent. I cut the connection.

Think, I order my brain, think. What was the story? Wife of journalist rises from the dead? No, she wasn't the story, the snappily dressed man was the focus. If she'd been the story my editor would have been shouting at me to follow it up.

I've got to tell you about my editor. Name of Dexter Lincoln. Dexter has buzz words and one of them is 'real'. Get real. Is this for real? A real drink. That is what is in my hand: a real drink. It's a tumbler of Scotch, darkish. 'We print real news or we are nothing.' Dexter stabs his desk with his finger. Get the message. We're fighting a never-ending war against lies, mush, spin doctors, official secrets, no comment, the old boy network, Freemasons, PR, PC, deep background, deep shit.

I nurse my Scotch and hop between the channels.

Dexter is not a dwarf but he's not tall and wears a bow tie as short men often do. He has the habit of slipping his hand inside his shirt while he is concentrating on something. 'It's his Napoleon complex,' Josh says. Dexter would read your copy and say, 'Order of the Golden Spike. Get round to the Council offices and ask awkward questions. Trouble about living in Oxford is that it's become a one-party state.'

Why is ITV ignoring the real news? My wife who was dead is now alive. I have seen her with my own eyes. God damn it, she was there, behind some unknown man. Twenty seconds. That was how long that clip lasted. I replay it in my head. Camera whipping round to follow him. Eve coming into frame, hurrying. She had to. Scrambling into the car. The car driving off. All in silence. What was it all about? If only I hadn't muted it.

My glass is empty. Someone has stolen my whisky.

* * *

The telephone rings and I wheel round. *Darling, it's me, I'm alive, I'm at the airport. I almost didn't make it – some crazy TV crew thought I was a film star.* That voice of hers, the rush of her way of speaking, a certain impatience, excitement, happiness.

'I watched the news, the whole menu.' The telephone is in my hand and it's not Eve, it's Josh. 'Eve didn't put in an appearance.' So he has taken me seriously. I think. Silence for a bit. 'Let's meet for a drink.'

'Got a drink,' I tell him.

'It'll do you good to get out. You're alone too much.'

'I can't. Speak to you later.'

I can't because of the flow of news. Six: BBC1. Six-thirty: ITV. Seven: Channel 4. Early evening is a news junkie's heaven. I leave it on all the time, Dexter said, it's the air I breathe. He's younger than me, only thirty-three. Editing a provincial daily is his stepping-stone to London. One of the Sundays, most likely. There's always one in trouble. A Sunday gives you the luxury of time to get the real story, like the great Harry Evans did with the *Sunday Times*.

I sip and stare at the TV. I'm waiting for my next fix. I'll tell you about me and Dexter.

'I'm giving you a column, Fridays only, op-ed, so you've got a week to dig out the facts. Under the Carpet, we'll call it. Look under the carpet and what you'll find among the dirt is the truth they tried to hide – that's how we'll trail it.'

'Which particular "they" is this?'

'Anybody who thinks they are our masters, our superiors, our guardians, our jailers, our censors. While we are just plebs, proles, grockles, cannon fodder, *Untermensch*.'

Hold on a minute. That little exchange between us makes him seem the caped crusader, which was never the whole truth. I was to be the means to his end. 'All journalists are investigative journalists,' Dexter declared, 'or they are nothing. Your job is to add bite. You'll need a name.'

'Got a name.'

'Your byline. That's what I'm talking about. Not the Man They Couldn't Gag. Not *Custos*.'

'Dexter, I've got a name.'

'Bazil Potter? No.' He shook his head. 'Cross between Basil Fawlty and Harry Potter. The ungodly won't tremble in their socks. More sparkle, more punch, more – '

I cut him short. 'Baz Faz.'

He frowned. You see politicians doing that. What's the trap?

'Explain.'

'Baz – OK?'

'And Faz?' he asked.

I kept quiet, smiled, the man of mystery.

'Baz Faz. Baz Faz.' Dexter rolled it round his tongue. Was it to his taste? Will it be the Order of the Golden Spike or a magnum of champagne? He shrugged. He was reserving judgement. 'Could be stupid enough to intrigue. Give it a whirl.'

So I'm Bazil Potter, also Baz Faz.

Channel 5 ignores the story about Eve too. What's wrong with everybody?

The phone rings. Do I want to listen to Josh hectoring me? I don't answer and wait until I hear his voice on the speaker while his message is taped.

'Baz, me old mucker.' Note how chummy he is now. 'Nothing on Channel 4 news or 5 either. Er…' Don't hesitate, Josh, out with it. You think I'm unhinged. 'Are you one hundred per cent sure it was the real Eve? Even the Queen has a double. See you. Cheers.'

Dear God, why has he brought the Queen into it? Have I been married to the Queen? Taken the corgis for a royal wee? It's Eve, I shout at Josh. In my head. I am married to her. I know her. She has the kind of allure that draws men's eyes. She doesn't relish it as a power over men. But she doesn't belong to that branch, correction, that little twig of women's lib which argues that it is degrading when a man sees a woman as a woman. Or that Dracula's blood-sucking was a revenge on women for menstruating. No, I'm not making that up. Eve is an achiever, a strong character. But you cannot pretend that you do not react to her as a woman. I never could. Other men felt the same draw to her. And I have seen her.

There's a lasagne in the freezer. I am giving it the kiss of life in the radiation box when the telephone rings. I have discovered that glaring at a telephone makes it shut up. No one leaves a message. Bastard. Who was it? I punch in 1471 for caller-ID. It was Mary Monroe. Do I want to speak to her? She works for the *Oxford Herald* too, a snapper. Now there aren't many women press photographers. You can hear a dozen explanations: they're not aggressive enough, too cautious, not tall enough in a crowd, not visual. I've even heard their mammary equipment gets in the way of their technical equipment. Blah-blah-blah. OK, Mary is short but she's full of energy, bustling. Also, busty. Oh yes. Round the office she's known as Two Boobs. Just don't say that in her hearing.

'Mary, you rang,' I say.

'And you didn't answer.'

'And you didn't leave a message.'

Pause. Jesus. This exchange is veering towards a marital tiff. Why are people so difficult tonight? Give me a reason. She breaks the silence.

'Josh told me? About Eve? About your saying you saw her on TV?'

Why the questioning tone? Come straight out and say it. I'm deluded.

'I did.'

'Baz, Baz, Baz, that is simply not possible. Eve died four months ago. Accept that. You've got to. Josh watched ITV news and she wasn't on that. I watched Channel 4 and *nada*. It couldn't have been her. You saw someone who looked like Eve. It just ain't her. Facts are facts. You've got to move on, Baz.'

Move on. Life is a dance floor? Time to change partners? Life is not like that. Life is playing poker with God. How can you win? He knows what's in your hand, knows when you are bluffing.

'Mary, I've got to go. My lasagne is cooling. I'll speak to you.'

'When?'

Hanging up is my answer.

I'm in the trade – print, TV, radio, it's all reporting the news. I know how it goes. Whatever it was has stopped being 'real news'. It could have been a filler in the early evening slot, cut when something big came up. It was one of the pains of working on a national paper. First editions come out. Shit, the competition has an exclusive. Thirty minutes to do a rewrite. Rejig the front page. Some other story gets the elbow to make space. It happens on TV too: vote in parliament, a bomb, plane crash, whatever. Out with Eve Potter, in with the biggie. I know that. In my head I know that. But in my guts…

The doorbell rings.

Eye to the spyhole. It's Josh, head tilted, trimmed black beard, puckered brow. Think Toulouse-Lautrec. He is not so much frowning as trying to peer back at me through the little glass eye.

'Are you alone?'

'No. You're here.'

'Smarty pants.' Josh stares at me, searching for signs of madness. 'We're going out for that drink.'

'I'm waiting for …'

The telephone cuts in. We both go still, listening to it. Why? It's just a telephone.

'I bet that's her,' Josh says.

'Her? Eve?' I look at him and see his grin. The answerphone kicks in and I hear a familiar voice. I pick up my coat from the hall chair and we go out.

'Two Boobs,' Josh says. 'That husky croak, courtesy of a hundred thousand fags. Is romance in the air? I can just see the movie: *When Two Boobs met* – '

'Shut up and walk faster.' I don't want to see her. She's too much. I lengthen my stride. 'Where are we going?'

'The Temporary Sign.'

'As if I need ask.'

The pub, a block and a half away, is a victim of profit-seeking in the brewing industry. It has been a plaything of Big Beer. Here's its story. Sold from one multi-national to another, sign taken down and replaced. Next a change of marketing strategy meant a fresh sign was painted. Then subject to a management buy-out. New sign needed. Finally sold to one of those thrusting new chains – you know, the Dog and Bone, the Bull and Shit, one of those. Somewhere in the midst of this turmoil despairing workmen hung up a board reading Temporary Sign. Good enough name, sticks in your memory better than whatever it's called today. I like the pub in moderation. It's not city centre so it misses out on tourists and the university buzz. It's a pub. That's all it is. A pub.

From a back room comes the clack of bar billiards, a darts match is in progress in this bar and there is that defining mark of the traditional English boozer: people standing with their pints. But we take our drinks to a corner table.

'Sexy Dexy called me in,' Josh begins as if recounting this was the whole purpose of his coming round to my bijou non-des res. 'When he first arrived to sit on the editorial throne he had that five year plan: pick the *Old Hag* up, shake it until its teeth rattle, make waves, get noticed, get a reputation as being a hot 'n' happening editor, move on to the metropolis as the conquering hero. Remember that plan?'

'Strikes a faint tinkle.'

'Right. Two years have flitted past so it's become a three-year plan. More urgent, right?'

He pauses to drink some beer. The *Old Hag* was Dexter Lincoln's name for the *Oxford Herald* when he rode to the rescue. Sexy Dexy is our name for him, though not to his face, no more than Mary is called Two Boobs when she is around.

'Truth is,' I say, 'the boss doesn't have plans. He has a few drinks and goes wild.'

'He brainstorms.'

'Brainstorms,' I echo. That's about it. There's a Hollywood B movie streak in Dexter. He paces the room, throwing off ideas, and minions run in all directions. That's not the modern style. He should be cool, computer-literate, no alcohol, able to chop logic better than the house lawyer.

'All right, the Sexy one says to me – just this pm – we need to make national news,' Josh goes on. 'Note that – make news, not report news. He says we have the most prestigious university in the solar system squatting in the middle of town. He says it's stuffed with retired diplomats and government ministers. He says they have a hundred secrets, scandals and bombshells waiting to be exposed – if you can expose a bombshell. Think big black headlines and screams from the government. Think threats of prison for the brave reporter. Which is me.' He steadies his nerves with a swig of beer. 'So as of this evening I am officially sniffing round for a bombshell.'

'Eve,' is my response. There's a quiver in his beard.

'Baz, can't you put that to rest?'

I lean in to Josh as you do when you want to say something important, something urgent, something private.

'The whole scenario is very, very weird. It's one of Dexter's bombshells. I can smell it. Journalist's nose.' I tap mine for extra emphasis.

'A disfiguring disease.'

'I saw her. I *did*. She was on the news with some unknown man. It was in Budapest.'

'Budapest?' Josh straightens in his chair. 'How do you know?'

'How do I know? For God's sake. The car drove away across the Chain Bridge. In the background, other side of the Danube, was the parliament building. Of course I bloody know.'

'Baz, our parliament is on the river too. Don't they look alike? Gothic monsters.'

It's in some people's nature to act devil's advocate. I can't be cross. I shake my head.

'The Palace of Westminster is like a village hall. Believe me, there's no comparison. What I want to know is what the news story was, why my wife was there, how she rose from the dead and where she is now.'

Josh is staring me straight in the eyes. Then, by degrees, his eyes drop until he is focussing on his tankard, tipping it from side to side, watching foam slide down the glass. He can no longer hold my gaze so I know that what is coming is painful.

'Bazil, excuse me but I have to ask.' Using my full name - now he is really intense. 'Could you see her hand? I mean…' He swallows. 'her left hand?'

Between us there is silence. There are the usual evening pub noises in the Temporary Sign, voices raised, laughter from the darts players, clack of billiard balls. But I hear other sounds. Have you ever woken at night in a terrified sweat, sounds echoing inside your head, tyres screeching, metal rending, a single voice screaming, screaming? God, I have. The sounds don't exist so why are they so real?

'Listen, bloody listen.' I take a breath like a sob. 'Eve was standing behind the unknown man, part hidden by his body. Then I had a back view of her scrambling into a car in a flurry. So no, I didn't see her left hand. I couldn't have. It was never in shot.'

'Bazil,' he says again, then seems to lose heart.

Because, you see, the wreck of Eve's car was found in the Danube on the outskirts of Budapest, a bit to the north of Margit Island. But my wife's body was never recovered. Only her left hand.

CHAPTER 2

Back home, mind racing. *Where is she? What is she doing? Who with?* Everything is in turmoil. Things I don't understand. Things I wasn't expecting.

Me, me, me. Stop it. I turn over in bed.

My life has been too easy I decide. Just think of my parents.

The year is 1956, war clouds stacking up. We can't focus on two crises at the same time. It's too much. Suez grabs the lion's share of headlines, the drama in Hungary playing to a distracted audience. Imre Nagy – a Gorbachev figure thirty years before his time – tries to reform the system, go neutral, invite the Soviets to kindly leave the stage. That was like trying to stroke a tiger. Krushchev may have denounced Stalin but he isn't going to be ordered about by some jumped-up economics professor. Besides he has certain generals with faces like the back end of a truck he needs to keep sweet. The Red Army smashes its way back into Budapest, thousands are killed, teenage boys hurl cobbles, Molotov cocktails and insults at Russian tanks, and when the uprising is crushed tens of thousands escape the country. Among them are the newlyweds Istvan and Judit Fazekas.

They fled the capital and headed west on foot, by bus, in farm carts. Stolen bicycles got them as far as the suburbs of Sopron. The Austrian border was so close they could – as Istvan put it – 'almost smell the *apfelstrudel*.' Twenty-four hours they lay up in the Lövér hills to the south of the city. They hid, they watched, they listened. They learnt. This was a red alert area. Roadblocks, police, army and the hated AVO secret police. So they made a detour to the east and circled round Sopron. Fields, woods, signs warning of mines, barbed wire, trembling at the distant baying of dogs. They arrived on the shore of a lake. It was Lake Fertö, a refuge for geese and herons, out of bounds to common folk but where high-ups in the party came to enjoy the shooting. They hid again, watched, waited until nightfall. They cut the rope securing a fowler's punt. They poled through reeds, paddled a bit and broke through wire. Dear God, a searchlight switched on. It swept across the water and they flattened themselves. Paddled some more. Told startled ducks to hush. They crossed right over the lake which changed nationality and became Neusiedlersee. They waded ashore. A boathouse hid them. A frosty dawn saw them making a flitting progress along a track. They came to a crossroads. There was a sign: Wien one way, Neusiedl the other. They were in Austria.

I tell you, those were the days when plain ordinary people had to act like James Bond.

A police patrol picked them up. The change was startling. No curt questions, no threats, no accusations of ill-defined crimes against the state. Two tired middle-aged officers took them to Neusiedl – an overgrown village, at least it was then. They sheltered in a wooden building like a barn right there in the main street. A dozen other refugees stared at them. Talk was in murmurs. Where are you from? Did they shoot at you? Who have you left behind? What will happen to us? A couple of students from Oxford were going round handing out cigarettes and taking down details of family in the West they could contact. Istvan and Judit had none. Next it was a camp outside Vienna run by the Red Cross and here there was a disaster. Judit was pregnant. Fear, stress, fighting, escape - it was too much. The foetus aborted. What to do? When they were next interviewed Istvan remembered those two kind students and invented a cousin in Oxford.

In six weeks' time, after the usual bureaucratic song and dance, they found themselves in Oxford where a puzzled Social Services cared for them. They had changed countries so they changed their names too: Istvan became Steven, Judit became Judy. Fazekas in the Magyar language means Potter, so that was the surname they adopted. When in four years' time a son was born, Steven thought long and hard. He wanted a name as far removed as possible from the horrors of communism they had suffered. Something royal. King was not a first name. Prince sounded too much like a title, Earl like a jazz pianist. How about Basil – that came from the Greek and meant royal. A spasm of nostalgia made him use the Magyar spelling Bazil though the name is rare in Hungary.

So I made my bawling entrance on the world stage: Bazil Potter. Now you get the byline Baz Faz.

Enough family history. Just understand there is stubbornness in my genes.

One more little story.

My dad got a job at the car factory at Cowley. He shifted boxes of parts. Assembly line work paid better but he was turned down. 'Why?' 'Safety reasons, Steve. You need to speak better English.' Same thing next year. What was going on here? Was the union stopping Johnny Foreigner taking a good job from one of our own lads? Finally Dad said – this is his version - 'I've listened to the boys on the line. They don't say, "Kindly pass me the monkey wench." They say, "Here old son, shove that fucker over my way." You think I can't eff and blind like they do?'

Monkey wench. Don't you love it? Perhaps the shop steward did too because my dad was moved onto the line.

How did I grow up? Nearly done.

Language unites people and divides nations. In the outside world - factory, shops, school - English was spoken. The council house where we lived was Hungary: music, cooking smells, rows, the Magyar language. It's what I grew up speaking. When you're a kid it's easy to chatter in two languages so it was English at school. Stepping inside our front door I crossed a frontier and became Hungarian. Believe me, it's a tricky language. It's like nothing you know. Even Russian is closer to English. Imagine the scene. You're in some country inn. Pick up the menu and peer at it. You understand nothing. Truly. So you stab your finger at something towards the top of the menu and something half way down. You are quite surprised when the waiter puts down gherkins and dumplings. You need a drink. Forget that all-purpose word *vino*. You want *bor*. By now you need a *szilvapalinka*. Find that one out for yourself.

Were they happy together? Lying awake tonight I ask myself that question. What child can answer for his parents? I have heard my father quote a line from the poet Ady – don't worry, I shan't baffle you with the original. 'Because I am Hungarian, my life is tragic and absurd.' Despite this he seemed happy. He was quick to learn English and always ready with a joke. 'How are things going, Steve?' I heard a neighbour ask. 'Worse than yesterday,' my dad replied, 'but let's look on the bright side: better than tomorrow.' Does that remark leave you puzzled? Then you'll never get along with Hungarians.

But my mother…She loved my father, she loved me, she loved the baby she miscarried at three months in that Red Cross camp. But she wasn't happy. I don't think so. All her life she was an exile. She was homesick for a land which had rejected her with great violence.

I was nine when we first went to Spain. Package holidays weren't big business then. It was more of an adventure. We went all the way by coach to Torremolinos. Then it was Benidorm. Next year a plane to Majorca. Then Tossa del Mar. They loved the sun, the outdoor life, the sea – though they swore Lake Balaton in August was warmer. When I left home to work in London they tried Rhodes but Spain was their true love. 1985 was the year Gorbachev came to power in Moscow and the ground began to tremble under the feet of the old communist war horses. But no, they wouldn't visit the mother country. They went to Almeria, middle of June, before the school holidays. 'Bit cheaper, you see. Save a bob or two'. My dad was quite tenacious about holding on to the shillings and pence he had learned when he first arrived.

Funny the snippets you remember about your parents. But this isn't funny. Not at all.

Seventeenth of June it was. I was young, living in London, working on the *Daily Mirror* – a pup like me, a reporter on a national paper, but that's another story. Ten-ish in the morning, coffee and yawn time. The story came in from Reuters: coach crash in Spain, twenty-eight German tourists killed. It had been an all-day excursion from a coastal resort to Granada. On the return, driving through the Sierra Nevada in the dark, the bus left the road at a nasty corner, and rolled over and over down into a ravine not far from Fiñana. Only Krauts, the copy taster sniffed, fewer towels on the sun-loungers, story will play well in Bavaria but not here. No interest.

Forty minutes later came a correction, or update as they called it. The driver of the bus and the female guide had been Spanish, twenty of the passengers had been German, two Dutch and six British. Aha, things were looking up. *Brits in holiday tragedy.* Three-quarters of an hour later they sent names of the dead. The holiday company was called Sunburst, or maybe Sunfine, something bright and sunny anyway. Here's one for you, young Baz, see what you can make of it. Get the addresses from the Sunny-off people, go and do the interviews, neighbours, family, workmates. Mind you don't forget the dog, get the name of the dog. I ran my finger down the print-out with the names. Steven and Judy Potter.

The room went silent. Or possibly it was only in my head.

Tell me you know of a good way to learn of the death of your parents and I'll call you a liar. I can still reach into myself and conjure up those moments of silence in my head.

When I was told of Eve's death it was different: a pain in my throat, a sob that wouldn't come out. No, not possible. But the facts, Baz, you've got to accept them. What facts? There was no body, you see. Just a hand.

Now I've seen her alive I'm going to track her down. I have to. Knowing that, I find sleep at last.

* * *

It is morning. Breakfast with the *Times* and the *Guardian*. No mention of Eve. TV news is no better. Don't tell me I am obsessed. I want my wife back. Or I want *something*. The truth would make a good start. The BBC will tell me.

I telephone and could be trying to contact Mars. The 6 o'clock news broadcast on BBC One last night, I say. There was a 6.19 pm item I need to know more about. Idiot switchboard. I'm put through to some studio in the news department. They are actually live on air. No idea who I am speaking to but he swears at me and cuts the connection. I dial again and have a runaround with current affairs, multi-format brands (don't ask me), public relations. What do I want with PR? They are the ones who put up a smokescreen around real news.

I catch myself eyeing the bottle of Johnnie Walker – and it's not yet 9.15. Then I think of Mike Simmons. Mike and I go back to *Mirror* days. His beat is entertainment. That includes television, right? He keeps different hours from normal humanity and when I telephone him at home his wife Gloria is doubtful about disturbing his sleep.

'Tell him he's getting a world exclusive,' I encourage her.

'Oh Lordy, not again. He gets such terrible hangovers after a world exclusive.'

In the end Mike is roused and I explain.

'Are you out of your tiny little mind?'

'I saw Eve,' I say doggedly. 'I did.'

'Yeah, and I saw Elvis on a number 11 bus.'

'You know people at the Beeb,' I point out.

'Not everyone,' he says cautiously.

'Look, find out about Eve and you could be in for a hero's hangover.'

'Jesus, Potter,' he whispers, 'you're crazy.'

'Crazy as a loon,' I shout back at him. 'I want to know.' But he's already put the phone down.

He'll do it, I know he'll do it, not because he's a pal, not because it's a world exclusive (every event of every day is an exclusive when you think about it), not because his editor will send him a Jeroboam of Dom Perignon. Mike will do it because he lusts after Eve.

One of Oxford's many church bells is striking ten o'clock when the telephone rings.

'Hello,' I say. 'Yes? Anybody there?'

'What can you see out of the window?' It is Mike.

'What are you talking about?'

'Tell me what you can see out of the window.' His voice has a quiet soberness to it. 'Just do it.'

I swing round to the window, finger a parting in the net curtains and squint at the outside world. A little old lady is making her way along the pavement with one of those trundly shopping bags on wheels that trip you up in Sainsbury's.

'Nothing out of the usual.'

'No strangers arguing over a map? Man tying his shoelace?'

'I'm not in the mood for games, Mike.'

'Not a game.' Brief pause. Can I hear him swallowing? 'I spoke to a contact at the place you're interested in, asked about that news item from last night. You didn't tell me the details but I gave him Eve's name. He said he'd ring back. So he rang back and his voice had changed. He sounded as if he was speaking from the bottom of a well. By the way, has my voice changed?'

'What the hell are you trying to tell me?'

'There is no tape of the 6 o'clock news.'

'There has to be. They tape everything. They have to. There could be questions in parliament, law suits, so on…' I stop. Mike knows this so he must also know something else. 'What is it? Stop playing silly buggers.'

'The tape's been wiped.'

'That's bloody careless.' I think a bit. 'Is it careless?'

'No. My contact wanted to know why I was interested and I let your name drop, the grieving husband bit. That was before I knew that the tape had wiped. Sorry about that.'

We are both silent for a spell. I am trying to make sense of what he has told me. 'I want to be sure I have this straight. A tape was made of the news, right?'

'Right.'

'Then on someone's orders it was destroyed. We're talking about a deliberate act. Is that it?'

'Yes.'

Mike is making me work for this. He volunteers nothing.

'All right, on whose orders?'

'Ah well, that's what we newshounds try to sniff out and my contact got shifty. He'd asked the same question of their morgue, whatever they call it.' Morgue is newspaperspeak for files on every news story you can think of. 'For an answer the engineer – so my contact called him – jabbed a finger upwards. Department head? No. Director-General? No, higher. God? No, higher still. Then who? Government. In whatever shape or form, ministry or department, civil servant or politician or secret policeman – no information given. Just government.'

More silence.

'You still there?' Mike asks.

'No,' I tell him, 'just a husk. The real me has flown.'

'Well yes…' He trails off. 'Listen, I don't understand what's going on. Sounds weird. But if everything turns up roses and you track down the lovely Eve, make sure I get the glad news, hear me?'

He's gone.

I find I have swung back to face the window. The net curtains haze the street scene. Now a car is parked opposite, a man bent low over the steering wheel speaking into his mobile. Listen, I am no more neurotic than the next fellow but I find I am holding my breath. Eve who was dead is alive. The tape has been deliberately wiped. Big Brother is outside watching me. But then the car door opens and it is only the neighbour across the street, Sam the Smuggler. He does a regular run to Calais and loads up the back of his Volvo estate with whatever goodies Her Majesty's Customs hold to be reasonable for personal use. He is contacting one of his customers arranging the drop in some supermarket carpark. But just for a moment…

Yes, I'm paranoid. So would you be.

I'm a journalist, right. Journos cultivate a lot of people. I met Jacobson at a party, my first philosopher. This is Oxford, remember. I have no idea how the subject came up but he explained Aristotelian syllogisms to me this way: all swans are white; this bird is not white; therefore it is not a swan. OK, got it. Then black swans were discovered in Australia. Therein, my philo friend tut-tutted, lies the danger of basing logic upon empirical premises.

Have I got that right? Close enough for now.

Forget Aristotle. My own logic runs like this: my wife Eve is dead; I saw my wife alive last night; therefore something freaky is going on.

Call that a Potterism.

Plan A. I'll move on to Plan B but you have to start with Plan A.

'Hi, Dodo, it's Baz. I'm not coming in today. If his Holiness asks, say I'm following a hot lead.'

Dodo is Doris, Dexter's secretary. She favours black leather miniskirts but has legs like farm gateposts. This way to make hay.

'Who is she?' Dodo asks at once.

I open my mouth, then hesitate. This is not a time for confiding.

'It's something personal.'

This doesn't deter Dodo. 'What is it - a job interview? Going to edit *Old Moore's Almanack*? You can trust me. Tell Dodo.'

It's about Eve. But I don't tell Dodo.

I cancel my haircut and lunch date with Peter.

'Sorry, got to see a man about a dog.'

'Bitch more like.'

We swap friendly insults and agree to fix something next week.

Then it's the big one: Lovegrove. There's a name to cherish. I've seen it on a funeral parlour in Reading and I wonder if by any chance they are related. It takes some time to make contact, through mysterious crackles, electronic hums and even a snatch of Vivaldi's Spring to lighten the mood.

'Lovegrove.'

How does he do it? Just one word. His voice says it all. I have disturbed him in some work of national importance. I take a breath.

'Potter,' I bounce back at him.

He says nothing.

'It's about Eve.'

There's another pause. There are always these silences when I speak about my wife because it embarrasses the other party. Is Lovegrove thinking, consulting a file, waiting for me to commit myself further?

'Oh really?'

'She's alive,' I tell him. 'I saw her on the news last night. I want to come and see you.'

'Well now,' he says.

Is this significant? Lovegrove is the first person not to tell me that what I saw is impossible.

'So I'm coming to see you,' I tell him again. 'This afternoon.'

'Well, yerrs,' he says. You won't find that word in any dictionary. It means: I hear you, I disapprove of your lowly presumption, I doubt the usefulness of what you suggest, I have loftier things to do but I will accede with ill grace. To deliver *yerrs* in the right tone you have to cultivate a Foreign Office drawl. That is where Lovegrove works though I don't know what he does. He was the one who broke the news to me about Eve's death.

You see, Eve also worked at the Foreign Office. Does the name Eve Potter ring a bell now? One of the weighty Sunday papers called her a diplomatic high-flier. She was furious.

Lovegrove is burbling but I miss what he is saying.

'That club of yours where we met before. I'll be there at two-thirty.'

I put the phone down. Rude. I don't care. Bugger him.

CHAPTER 3

That voice of Lovegrove puts my back up. I'm not sexist or racist but maybe I'm *voiceist*. I can live with that. It is a superior voice, a privileged voice, a well-fed voice. That voice makes you think of a fat man but he's not. Picture him: hollow cheeks, lips pressed so tight they disappear. That voice lunches at his club and that is where we are meeting. I met him there when the news was broken to me that Eve's car had been found in the Danube with just the aerial above water.

A day later I met him again. This time he told me her hand had been recovered. Just a minute. Surely they knew that when the car was hoisted out of the river? The journalist in me woke up. Curious. It's as if they were making this up as they went along. Sorry Potter but that hand means she must be dead. When I returned from her funeral in Budapest I met him again. Why? Now I think he just wanted to see if I swallowed the story.

What does he do in the Foreign Office? The journalist in me made me ask and the journalist in me noted his blink. He hesitated – not long but I picked it up. See that airy wave of his hand. 'Oh, I just beaver away at the Middle Europe desk.' Hang about. There's another thing. *Mitteleuropa* is a German concept. We don't say it. We say Central Europe. So is his work a little…different?

We've always met at this club. I've never got to see his office in that grand pile in Whitehall – if that is where he works.

The club has a name but it didn't register. 'At the club, you know the one,' he said. I know how to get to it. It is in a cul-de-sac off Curzon

Street near where it bumps into South Audley Street. That's in Mayfair, in case you're a stranger in those parts. The mellow brick wall has nothing so vulgar as a sign. If you don't already know what's behind the loden green door they don't want you inside. A well-polished brass plaque proclaims simply: 10. Isn't that wonderful? No, I'm afraid Mr Lovegrove is not available, he has an urgent meeting at Number Ten. Oh, seeing the prime minister you assume. End of probing.

A brass bell-push advises: Press and enter.

'Mr Potter, sir, you *are* expected. Mr Lovegrove is in the Grenfell room. If you would be so kind as to proceed along that passage…'

'I know the way.'

I know the room. It is a chamber where gentlemen can conduct whatever business they don't want other gentlemen to overhear. Two tall windows look out onto a light well, dark oil portraits of fellows in naval uniform, leather-cushioned easy chairs that are not easy to sit in, a French-polished round table with silver coasters and a ship's decanter and glasses. I count the glasses: three.

Lovegrove pushes himself up from one of the chairs. He lays aside a magazine which hides itself from idle gaze behind auburn leather covers. Is it *Investor's Chronicle, Horse & Hound, Jane's Fighting Ships?* I'm curious. I can just make out cracked gilt lettering: *Private Eye.* Now there's a surprise.

'Potter,' he says, 'well done.'

Well done? I've travelled from Oxford to London. Another thing. I've never taken to his habit of addressing me as Potter, not Basil or Mister. He is part of that vanishing world where chaps call other chaps by their surname. Only the grocer is called Mister.

When he shakes my hand he bends forward. It's not a little bow; it is part condescending, part intimidating. For the first time I notice his eyes - very pale blue with no laughter lines. When he blinks it is a camera shutter clicking. I have been captured in his brain, each grubby detail, my grey suit and blue tie specially worn because we are meeting in a gentlemen's club, my hair that needs its cut, my complexion with the dark half-moons of tension under my eyes.

'Good journey?' he asks. Does he think I have flown in from Shanghai?

'I took the Tube.'

'What? I thought you were coming from Oxford.'

Now comes a little interplay. I explain that the Oxford Tube is the name for the bus service that runs every twelve minutes. He knows that, everybody does because the buses run through the centre of London and the name is in huge letters along the side. His show of amusement is just to put me in my place: a member of the bus-travelling class. He turns away to the table, lifting the decanter.

'I thought we might refresh ourselves. Certainly, if you travelled by "Tube",' and I can hear the inverted commas as he brings out the word, 'you'll be in need of it.' There is reverence in the care he takes filling two of the three glasses. He hands one to me. 'Good health.'

We drink.

'It's Fonseca, the '77.' His eyes slide to my glass. 'Mortally little left, I fear.' This is spoken as a warning: sip, do not gulp. 'Shall we make ourselves comfortable?'

We lower ourselves into the unergonomically designed chairs. So, we are to wait for a third person, whoever he is.

'Tell me about it again,' Lovegrove suggests. 'Our telephone conversation was a tad, how shall I put it, confused.'

'Our conversation was not confused,' I tell him. He gives a little frown. 'I told you exactly what happened. I switched on the 6 o'clock news, BBC1. It was towards the end of the programme. There was an item – I don't know what it was about because the sound was off. A man being was being interviewed or possibly refusing to be interviewed. Behind him was my wife. They both got into a car and were driven off across the river. It was in Budapest. The river was the Danube. I recognised the Chain Bridge and the parliament building.'

'Yerrs.' Why does he frown at his glass? He tips it back and forth, watching the port as it flows down the side. 'And when you say "wife" you do refer to Eve? Not some other lady?' He looks up over the glass at me. 'For instance, your first wife?'

'I mean Eve. Why do you think I'm here seeing you?'

'Quite,' he says.

What did he expect me to do? Smack my forehead, struggle to my feet and mumble: Silly old me, I do feel an ass, dashed sorry to have troubled you, Lovegrove.

'It was Eve I saw. If it had been Moira – my ex – I wouldn't have contacted you. Moira made her decision years ago and that was that. Finis.'

His eyes have fixed on me, sensing weakness. Moira was BE, before Eve as I think of it. When Moira left me I was angry and bewildered. One reason for moving out of London, returning to the town where I had grown up, starting again. Lovegrove is still staring. Why?

'Yerrs, of course,' he says and takes a miser's sip of port.

Hold on a minute, I say to myself, he brought up Moira, my first wife, so he's been running a check on me. Before I can challenge him on this he is on a new track.

'Tell me – I hope you don't mind one asking – fill me in on the, ah, other conditions surrounding this sighting on television.'

What's he talking about? I stare at him.

'Well, the light in your sitting room, for instance. Gone past six, darkish outside. Curtains were open if you'd just come in? Streetlamps shining in. How about reflections on the TV screen?'

'I wasn't fumbling around in the gloom. I flicked on the lights when I came into the room, went to the TV, switched that on, I was standing and looking through my post when I noticed what was on the screen. It was perfectly clear. All right? Answers your questions? Who are we waiting for, by the way?'

His eyes dart to the third glass on the table, then back to me. He doesn't answer my question.

'And you – again, don't take offence, Potter, I know you are under strain, have been these past months. What sort of condition were you in? Chap does tend to console himself a bit.'

My glass is empty and his gaze has fixed on it.

'Booze, you mean? I'd had a drink with a couple of colleagues. End of the working day.'

'*A* drink? Each bought a round possibly?'

His eyes rest on me, judging my reaction. Ah, got it. He wants to make me angry enough to stomp out.

When I don't answer he says, 'Help yourself, by the way. I see your glass is empty.'

He thinks I won't so I do.

'I could see perfectly well. And even if I got cockeyed I'd never be so blind drunk I couldn't recognise my own wife.'

'Quite so,' he says and sighs.

Silence falls.

High-fliers in the Foreign Office are called mandarins. Another Potterism forms in my brain.

All mandarins know best. This mandarin does not know best. Therefore he is not a mandarin.

So what is he?

Lovegrove tires of the silence and carries on. 'And work, how is that going?'

'You mean, am I falling to pieces?'

'*Oxford Gazette*, isn't it?'

'*Herald*.'

'Editor's got an odd name, if I'm not mistaken.'

'Dexter Lincoln.'

'Dexter, yerrs. Well, better than…'

I know, just know, he is going to make a stale joke about Dexter being better than Sinister but I am spared. There is a knock at the door. Enter the third man.

'Ah, *Gray*.' Lovegrove says it with such emphasis it's obvious the man's name is something else. 'Well done. I was just beginning to wonder.'

Wonder what?

How old is Gray. Early thirties? Life doesn't seem to have touched his features. His pale skin is unlined. His hair is dark brown. You'd never pick him out in a crowd except he has a strange widow's peak and a pointy nose. Know what he reminds me of? Some small animal that comes out at night and snuffles through the undergrowth. His eyes dart past me to settle on Lovegrove.

'You know those people who say "no problem"?' he blurts out. 'I just ran into one who said "problem".'

For a moment, just a moment, I like Gray. He is oblivious to me and why I have come.

'What?' Lovegrove gives a little grunt. 'I told you to get hold of Whatsisname.' He waves a hand in exasperation.

'Indeed you did, sir. Unfortunately he is off for a long weekend in the country on a bonding course.'

Lovegrove's expression is baffled. Is it necessary to say he is middle-aged and always has been?

'A bonding course? No one has ever suggested I go to one. Whatever do they do?'

'It varies.' Gray stops but more is expected. 'Go into the woods and engage in mock combat with paintballs, then in the evening get drunk together and, well, bond.'

'Our licence fee goes on romps in the woods?'

Gray doesn't answer.

'Yerrs, well.' Lovegrove decides to end this little sideshow. 'All right, this is Potter, come up to town by Tube. And *Gray*, who has been undertaking certain tasks on my behalf.'

Gray's attention switches to me. I am putting out my hand to shake when he nods his head. That's it. Social formalities are done with.

'So what happened?' Lovegrove asks. 'You ran into difficulties?'

It may be my wife we are concerned with but it is Lovegrove he reports to.

'The person you told me to see wasn't there. That always trips you up. When it's the usual channel, there's an understanding, a few quiet words and things get done. That's the way of the world, right?'

'What are you trying to tell me?' Lovegrove sounds peeved. 'You had no success?'

'No, no, no, just that there was what you might call a fumble, sir, a certain amount of telephoning, fixing things up. Everything was smoothed over in the end.' Gray turns his head towards me. 'You said you saw your wife on the news last night.'

'At 6.19,' I say.

'Now, while I didn't get to see a tape of the news – '

'Because it's been deliberately wiped.'

Gray frowns at the interruption. 'I was given a programming synopsis. Here.'

He thrusts a sheet of paper at me. What does BBC internal stationery look like? I have no idea. How can I tell if it is genuine? It is headed by the BBC logo, underneath is Directorate of Television, Channel 1, yesterday's date. The sheet is marked Page 14. It starts at the top *18.00.00 National News*, followed by a number of items, each with a time. My eyes run down the page until I reach *18.18.52 Hungarian Grand Prix*.

'What does it say? Dammit, do I have to…' Lovegrove is pushing himself up from the chair as Gray takes the paper back from me to read aloud.

'*Hungarian Grand Prix. Controversial changes defended by organiser Lörinc Gogl, interviewed with assistant Ibolya Borokai.*'

Ibolya Borokai? I shake my head. 'No,' I murmur. 'That is…' What? Ridiculous? No, it is a lie. But Lovegrove looks pleased, even relieved.

'Another glass. Potter? You do the honours, Gray.'

The programming sheet disappears inside Gray's jacket and he busies himself pouring the drinks. The ship's decanter is now half empty.

Lovegrove sips. 'Mmm, marvellously structured wine, don't you agree? Warre '63 has the reputation but for me it is verging on the baroque whereas the Fonseca has an elegance, a *strictness* almost, not a note out of place.' His eyes settle on me. 'So there we are, Potter, I think that clears the matter up quite satisfactorily. Straightforward case of mistaken identity. Your wife was a most attractive woman and doubtless this secretary – assistant they called her - you saw on the television reminded you quite irresistibly of her. Can so easily happen when one is grieving. Are you a golfer? I recommend you take it up. Fresh air, exercise, companionship. I recommend it. Golf,' he repeats in case I have missed it.

'Golf,' Gray says. 'What a super idea.'

That's it for me, the turning point, Gray trying to use charm on me. I came here as the bereft husband and it is time I stopped. Remember what Dexter said? All journalists are investigative journalists or they are nothing.

'Can I see that programming sheet again?'

It's as if the projectionist has stopped the film. They both freeze. For a moment it is silent.

'What for?' Gray wants to know.

'I want to have another squint at it.'

There is no good reason to refuse me so he draws the sheet from his inner breast pocket. I take it and hold it to the light of one of the windows.

'What are you doing, Potter?' Lovegrove asks me.

'Checking the watermark.'

'What do you mean – checking the watermark?' Gray asks.

'I want to see if the paper really is from the BBC or whether it is government issue, with the crown and crest of HMSO, as used in the Foreign Office.'

I am making this up. I have no idea what paper they use in the BBC or the Foreign Office. Doesn't matter. Lovegrove doesn't know either.

'What do you mean?'

'Seeing if it really came from the BBC or whether you ran it up yourselves.'

Lovegrove puts his glass down and both of them crowd close to peer at the paper held up against the light. *Gotcha.*

'There's nothing,' Lovegrove snaps. His face seems to remake itself as emotions come and go: worried, relieved, puzzled, aggrieved. 'There's no watermark at all.' His tone is peeved as he realises he's been tricked. 'This is just a piece of photocopy paper.' He straightens up to his full height. 'Hold on, where do you think you're going?'

'Out.'

'Out? What do you mean? Are you going back to Oxford? I must say you're being damned high-handed. You demand a meeting as if…' His voice acquires sudden urgency. 'Watch what you're doing.'

Putting on my coat I swing back towards him, an empty sleeve brushing the decanter.

'I'm getting out because it's a con. I don't know why, but I'll find out. Eve was on the news last night and you've tried to con me into believing I was mistaken.'

'Your wife is dead, Potter,' he says in a flat unemotional tone. 'It's upset you, quite naturally.' He turns to Gray. 'He's not being rational.'

'He should see a doctor.'

They talk about me as if I was not here.

'Somebody at the BBC said the tape of the news was wiped on orders, for all I know yours. Why?'

Neither of them answers. Gray's eyes flick towards the door. Cheeky bugger is thinking of locking me in. Then what?

'A con,' I repeat. 'Why? What's up? My wife's alive, isn't she, so why are you trying to hide it?'

Gray takes a step towards the door. I pick up the decanter in both hands and lob it to him in a gentle arc.

'Here, catch.'

And he does though he fumbles it, the stopper comes out and port splashes his jacket. I'm through the door into the passage when I hear Lovegrove's voice.

'Wait. It's not what you think.'

Not what I think? I don't know what to think. I turn back to face the pair of them framed in the doorway like hosts seeing off a guest. Two men are walking towards us and we stand like statues. One of the men is saying, '…and they've bought this absolute ruin near Ludlow – hello, Lovegrove, have a good weekend…' and they pass, releasing us.

'Tell me this. If my wife *is* dead, why aren't I getting a widower's pension?'

There is the faintest smile on Lovegrove's face. 'Well, yerrs, good point. And there may well be a special augmentation – if you follow my drift – when a diplomat has died *en poste* abroad, bearing in mind her extra responsibilities. Look into that on Monday, will you, Gray?'

'Sir?' Grey seems stunned by this but he rallies. 'Yes sir. Monday morning. I'll make a note of it.'

'Follow your drift?' Then I get it. For the first time I feel real anger. I take a deep breath but hold back. 'Yes, I follow your drift and there's a word to describe it.'

Let him choose it.

As I'm going down the passage I hear Lovegrove's voice. 'Potter, you simply don't understand.'

I will.

CHAPTER 4

The Oxford Tube is a double-decker. Most people go on top because it's a squeeze down below with the driver's cab, the stairs, the defunct coffee machine and the toilet for dwarfs. There are a dozen seats and I take one. I am alone with my thoughts.

I stare out of the window but what I see is Lovegrove and his dogsbody Gray. I relive that crucial moment: Lovegrove hauling himself out of the easy chair. That look on his face – is it shock, worry, disbelief, anxiety? There I was, sheet of paper in my hand, holding it up to the light. The BBC logo on top is there for show. But I said I was looking for the watermark. That worried him. He didn't know what watermark I'd find. Just that one action gave his con away. Why the lies? Why the forgery? Because Eve *is* alive. Why shouldn't I know? And how can her hand have been found?

Dexter lives off the Banbury Road, down a side street of late Victorian gloom. Glad I don't live there. His house rises out of a dank jungle of privet and berberis. Eve and I have been here for dinner and Dexter could barely keep his eyes off her.

The bell rings somewhere in the bowels of the house though I've heard nothing and no one has come to let me in. But the house is not empty – light escapes at the edge of curtains. My finger reaches out to ring the bell a second time and hesitates. The door opens a crack and my eyes drop to a naked foot. The door opens more. I see a pair of feet, female, naked, brown, toenails a watermelon pink. My eyes move up. Bare ankles, bare calves. A skirt starts just below the knees, then comes a long-sleeved blouse. Her hair is straight and black, brushing her shoulders. Her face is Asian. This happens in total silence. I am taller by a head and she takes a step back.

'I've come to see Mr Lincoln. My name is Potter. I telephoned earlier so he is expecting me.'

She stands aside to let me in, giving me a smile as warm as a lover's. 'Follow please.'

The hall is big with three doors off it, male voices coming from behind one. The girl leads me to another room and switches on the light. 'Mr Dexter – he come.' She leaves me alone, closing the door as softly as she opened the front door.

Two thoughts go through my head. One, there is an echo of 'Mistah Kurtz – he dead.' And the second, she didn't call him Mr Lincoln. The room I've been shown into is his study. There's a Sierra Club calendar on the wall. The desk has an old-fashioned Filofax, an electronic paperknife, a Baccarat paperweight, an ashtray from the Oriental hotel in Bangkok, an Apple Mac and printer, and today's *Oxford Herald*. On one wall is a framed certificate but before I can learn what this celebrates the door opens. Turning, I see Dexter and behind him not one but two Asian girls.

Noticing my eyes over his shoulder Dexter says, 'Anong and See.'

'Er, yes. I've already met Anong. Or it might have been See.' All right, tell me, what would you have said?

'Thai girls. From Phitsanulok. Heard of it? Town in the middle of the country with a famous *wat*. It's better to have two at a time then they don't get homesick. OK?'

Dexter is brisk, his voice with an edge of impatience. I recognise that tone from the times he has been about to give my copy the Order of the Golden Spike. He stays by the door as if he is expecting a short meeting. The hell with that. I pull out a chair from the wall to sit in front of his desk. He gives the door a push. It half shuts. Sounds from the hall still drift in: rumble of male voices, giggles of the Thai girls. Sexy Dexy I think for no particular reason. Well, except for the obvious one.

'You were out all day,' Dexter says.

'I called in and told Dodo.'

'You didn't tell me.'

'It didn't seem necessary. Why disturb you?'

'So that I know what the hell's going on. I run a tight ship. I need to know what the crew are doing.'

There you have the other part of Dexter's make-up. He may be the thrusting ambitious editor but he has a petulant side to him. I am the naughty boy caught playing truant. The office verdict is that he is good at his job but lacks the largesse of spirit to be one of the great editors. I don't intend to argue so I say nothing, just watch him. He nods: all right, let's move on. Finally he sits behind his desk.

'Dodo said you were on to a story. Under the Carpet? Something big?'

In my time I have done odds and ends of acting. Nothing remotely pro, you understand, just student reviews, enough to believe in bits of theatrical business. I make a point of leaning forward and raising both hands like a boastful fisherman.

'Bigger.'

Dexter goes still and our eyes meet and hold. Without speaking he gets up to close the door. He doesn't sit down again but lounges against the wall next to the certificate I cannot make out.

'Bigger is what we need,' Dexter says. 'I told Josh yesterday: think local, write national. A lead story in Fleet Street starts as a local story somewhere else. Do we imagine the Chancellor of the university is local? Look at his career – Westminster, Hong Kong, Brussels, Oxford. Suppose he lets slip some secret. Is that a local brick he's dropped or is it a national bombshell? Depends how you write it.'

Dexter begins to wander. Another man might pick things up, inspect them while he talks, but there is little here: no souvenirs, no photos, no gifts from the grateful. He does this at work, pacing his office. Have you gone to a zoo and seen a lion do that? What's the lion thinking? Get me out of this cage and let me loose on the big stuff.

'Josh told me you'd talked of unearthing a bombshell,' I say.

He stops to look at me, then starts pacing again, ending up at the window behind his desk. He stares at the glass. It's his own reflection he sees.

'You have a bombshell?'

'Yes.'

'Tell.'

'It's to do with Eve. You know I saw her on the news last night?'

Josh or Two Boobs will have gossiped but Dexter's face gives nothing away.

'Go on.'

'Journalist sees missing wife on the telly – that's local,' I say.

'Barely. More like parish magazine.'

'All right, try this. Dead diplomat is alive – mystery of Foreign Office cover-up. That's national, isn't it?'

'Is she alive?'

'I saw her.'

'You say.'

'She was on the news. A source at the BBC says the tape was wiped on orders from the government. This afternoon I had a meeting with two men from the Foreign Office. One of them whipped out of his pocket what he said was the programming sheet of last night's 6 o'clock news. It showed it was about someone else entirely.'

'But you insist it was Eve.'

'It was.'

'Your word against theirs.'

'You think I don't know my wife?'

Dexter turns away from the window to study me.

'If what you say is true,' his voice is quieter than I am used to, 'and she's been pretending to be dead for four months, I would say that no, you don't know your wife.'

Bloody cheek! I open my mouth…and then…I don't know what to say. Maybe it's true. Have I got our time together all wrong? Dexter is walking again but to a cabinet. He holds up a bottle of Glenmorangie.

'Scotch do you?'

I nod and he pours the whisky into squat tumblers, a real drink. Dexter believes water would be a crime, ice a sin.

With a warm glow spreading in my stomach I go on. 'Two more things. I held up the paper they said came from the BBC, pretending to look for the watermark. You know, was it perhaps government issued and not the BBC at all.'

'You know about these watermarks?'

'That's not the point. What happened was they hustled over to check for themselves. They didn't know what the watermark was and were worried in case they'd been found out that it was forged.'

'Nice one,' Dexter says. 'And the other thing?'

'The end of the meeting – I was actually on my way out – a thought popped into my head. "You say Eve is dead. So why aren't I getting a widower's pension?" Lovegrove – that's the senior man's name – took my query as an invitation for a bung.'

'A bribe to shut up?'

'Yes.'

'And?'

'He said they'd see about it. Plus an extra wodge of cash.'

Dexter smiles, giving a little shake of his head – can you credit it.

'What's the joker's name again?'

'Lovegrove. His sidekick was introduced as Gray.'

'Lovegrove and Gray. Great sitcom title. We'll check them out tomorrow. Do you know them?'

'Lovegrove I met when Eve's car was found in the Danube and she wasn't, except for a hand. Presumed drowned. Gray is younger, his gofer.'

'Eve.' Dexter pauses. 'I've met her twice. Dinner here and a Christmas party. She struck me as…' But he stops. It's my wife he is talking about. 'Tell me about her.'

All of it? The good, the bad, the dirty?

* * *

Oxford is my home town. Born here, brought up here, even went to university here for a while, started the English course, put off by Beowulf, switched to history and lost interest. Typical journalist, you say.

I left and went to the big city, worked for the big papers, got married, got hurt, got divorced. So I returned to the womb, or at least the place where I was born. My life in an eggcup: birth, copulation and death.

Four years ago I was working on the *Oxford Herald*, throwing away the first chapter of novels. Then I met Eve.

This is how it happened. Prepare yourself for some Hungarian tongue twisters.

Oxford means university, right? Live here and you tiptoe round it, colleges, surging students, sit-up-and-beg bicycles, tourists who come for selfies. The university is a fixture. I mean it's like a broken paving stone you step over every day without thinking. Then one day something changes and it trips you up.

The university has a society called the Magyar Klub. On the first Sunday of the month they show a film at the Phoenix.

So, 10.15 on a certain Sunday. I was at the Phoenix for a nostalgic rescreening of Miklos Jancso's *The Red and the White*. Bit early. I dawdled on the pavement across the road, autumn sun on my face, watching who came, who greeted who, who cut who. There was Professor Stumpf whose hairstyle was inspired by Einstein, a couple of what I took to be visiting fellows, students looking so serious they could be hungover. Everyone had to understand Hungarian because the film was not dubbed. No subtitles either. It was for serious language students or expats. My case was a little different. I'm the son of refugees. I know the language but that's not enough. I feel a voyeur in a different world. I watch a film – they'd shown Dettre and Szabo and Szomjas – and I see men and women on the screen. They walk. They talk. But for me the camera could have been smuggled on the starship Magyaroszag. It was sailing through space where gravity was lost and time ran backwards. I was a foreigner in those parts, that's all I mean.

Time to cross over to the cinema. Then the taxi arrived. This is not London. Taking a taxi to the cinema in Oxford is making a statement: I'm from the big city. The driver must have been in a tearing hurry. I was still crossing the road as he drove off. The passenger was bending over from paying him through the window then straightening upright. We faced each other. We were three steps apart.

Do you believe in love at first sight? Could you have a lifelong bond with someone you know nothing about? Scary stuff. But I felt we were linked already, maybe always had been. Is that love? Experience from other lives? Madness?

'*Jo napot kivanok,*' I said. How formal.

'*Jo reggelt,*' she replied. We stared a moment before she said, 'I'm English, you know.'

'But you speak Hungarian.'

'I'm learning. That's why I'm here.' She nodded at the cinema.

Is this how people normally meet? *Hello* and *Good morning*, that simple, as if we'd arranged a date to go to the film? Neither of us said: Are you waiting for someone? We just went into the cinema together.

Maybe it was something beyond love. Destiny?

Her beauty strikes you. Film star looks and more. She's a source of energy and life and movement. Do you understand? Perhaps I'm not making myself clear. A vibrancy, a daring.

She could have chosen any career provided it offered a challenge: investment banker, architect, actress. She would have done it. Why the hell did she choose the Foreign Office? Odd. Being a diplomat? Is that enough? I asked her and she fixed me with dark eyes.

'You think it's all cocktail parties and receptions on the Queen's birthday? Writing a report: Whither Europe?'

Part of me thinks that but I shut up.

'I am a woman,' she said. 'Women have been held back. Now the high-ups feel guilty so it is a good moment to be a woman provided you have ability and drive.'

Good looks don't hurt. But I didn't say that either. So, like a skilful diplomat, she deflected interest in what she actually did all day.

The Phoenix had roped off a section for our little band. Professor Stumpf in the row in front swivelled his bulk round to nod at Eve. He'd met me before. Maybe he'd forgotten because he ignored me. The absentminded professor is a cliché. Hungarian professors have taken this cliché to a higher level so you might call it rudeness. He was jealous, I think.

Two days later we met for a meal at the Jade Garden – now closed. How did she know Professor Stumpf, I asked. He's a sort of tutor. *Sort of?* Well, she wasn't a real undergraduate, not actually a member of the university at all. This was when I learnt that she was at the Foreign Office and was sent to do a year's study here. Stumpf was at St Anthony's, a college with a link – some say more – to the Foreign Office. He was guiding her in hoovering up Hungarian language, literature, society, customs, achievements and heroic struggles against Turks, Germans, Russians and other ill-intentioned folk.

'Viktor says that with your origin, you could give me an insight into *az aktos negyven ev*,' she said.

The Accursed Forty Years is how Hungarians refer to the communist dictatorship. That wasn't what surprised me about what she said. It was calling Stumpf by his first name and that he had noticed me after all at the Phoenix.

'He didn't see you,' Eve said. 'I asked him about you. In the end he said you might help me but at first he was quite – how shall I say – sniffy about you.'

She grinned and laid a hand on mine. Just for a moment.

'Of course he wants to sleep with me. Have you seen his wife? Need I say more?'

So had he?

At the end of the meal I said, 'Chinese restaurants serve atrocious coffee. They do it so people leave early and they can squeeze in another sitting. However…' I was nonchalant under her steady gaze. 'I have an espresso machine and some Lavazza at home. We can talk about life and the universe.'

'That sounds…' She made me wait for it. '…wonderful.'

Wonderful? I hoped so. We arrived at my non-des res and she laid a hand on my arm to stop me as I was about to go in the kitchen.

'Baz.'

I turned. She was so close. She had already dropped her coat on a chair.

'We don't have to bother with the coffee.'

I believe I could feel the blood pumping through her heart and the warmth of her breasts and belly. There was a pull like the current in a river or a sudden wind that rocks you on your feet. Forgive the purple prose. I wanted her.

'We can talk about life and the universe afterwards,' she said. 'One condition.'

What passed through my mind? I must kiss her toes, there must be candlelight, some nonsense.

'We speak only Hungarian in bed.'

Did that make me part of her intensive Hungarian course? Is that what you're thinking?

She left around 7 in the morning. I saw her off at the front door. No, of course I shouldn't escort her back to her digs. Did I think Oxford was bandit country? Was it a perverse chivalrous act to protect a helpless female? Some helpless female.

'*Szia,*' I said.

'See you soon,' she said, stroking my cheek with a finger.

She was leaving Hungary behind in the house and stepping back into England. When I was a child I'd done the same.

I thought I would go back to bed, to smell her on the sheets. The bed was cold without her. So I made coffee, the espresso we hadn't drunk last night, as strong as the coffee in Hungary. Cup in hand I went from room to room. This was the path she had taken, naked, taking measure of my life in the grey light of early morning.

* * *

After three months we married. It was a squeeze fitting the wedding into an intensive Hungarian course. We honeymooned in bed. Eve's days were full. I know she saw Stumpf because a couple of times I took curt telephone messages from him. 'Tell her I cannot do Tuesday.' 'Tell her only Balassi's love poems.' He spoke English to me as if jealous of my Hungarian link with her. She went to history lectures. She had long rambling talks with an old man who had come out of Budapest in '56, just as my parents had. She worked hours at the Bodleian library. Also there were her trips to London – 'reminding them I've got a place in their future.'

Their future. I didn't like the sound of that. It didn't seem *our* future so I didn't think about it.

She'd had a flat in a sidestreet off the Abingdon Road – just before Fat Phil's angling centre if you know it – but she abandoned that and moved into my non-des res. She came with her clothes, books and old CDs by Kodaly, Liszt, Bartok and Kalman. She had a green glazed pottery frog which she said brought her luck. She had no family photos. Her parents were divorced. Her mother had remarried and was living in New Zealand. Her father she had quarrelled with. She had a flat in London which she had rented out. She had friends in London too, a whole life before we married, but we had each other and my Oxford chums and that seemed enough. I never suggested we meet up with her old gang. For me London had shadows of Moira. My whole life was Eve, the here and now and forever. I thought that, I really did.

Six months on she said her time in Oxford was up. She had to return to work in London. She said it one evening as we were strolling back from a drink with Josh at the Temporary Sign, letting it drop quite casually as if she'd only just remembered.

She commuted from Oxford to London. The first week she took the Oxford Tube. She could pick it up near Magdalen Bridge – bit of a trek – and go the terminus in Victoria – definitely too far to walk to Whitehall.

Then she took the train, faster, though Oxford station was a way off and Paddington meant a longer journey through London at the other end. The travelling was wearing her down. She left before seven, got home well after eight. In October she announced that the daily commuting was hell so she intended to live the week in London. The tenants' lease was up and she had her flat back. She came to Oxford on Friday evening and returned to London early on Monday morning.

We had a weekend marriage.

We still had time together even when our careers separated us. We had a winter holiday in Luxor with a cruise up to Aswan and a couple of days in Cairo when Eve disappeared by herself to the embassy 'just to say hello to the boys and girls'. And I had nights in her London flat. And then…

February it was, two years ago, a Friday night. We had made love, a relief after the week's drought. It was no longer the 'going into outer space' of the first months – Eve's way of describing it. To me we were settling down. To her… You see, I was beginning to feel I was something of a stranger.

We were in bed, just the lamp on her side on, when she heaved herself up, sheet tucked under her chin, face shadowed so I couldn't be certain of her expression. 'Good news, bad news,' she said. I went cold. I felt she had issued a storm warning.

'What is it?' I asked.

'The good news is I've got promotion at last. The bad news… no, it's really good news when you look at it positively. I've got my first posting.'

I should have said congratulations. I know I should. But I was thunderstruck.

'What do you mean? Going abroad?'

'The Foreign Office doesn't have embassies in Britain, Baz. So yes, abroad.'

'Where?'

'Budapest, of course.' She sounded surprised. 'Why do you think I put in all this work with lectures, the Bodleian, Stumpf, films and the rest of it?'

'I thought the Foreign Office was hot on having generalists.' I began flailing around. 'Sort of a principle, I thought. Broaden their horizons. Soon as someone masters Japanese they get shipped off to Wagga Wagga land. You even picked up a bit of Arabic…I heard you in Egypt…good with languages.' I was floundering.

'I'm off to Hungary.' This is the woman who can halt Josh in mid flow. She taps my chest. 'Land of your fathers.'

She didn't suggest I accompany her. She could have said: Come with me and be the Budapest correspondent for the Beeb, you have the experience, you've got the language.

'Once I'm settled and found an apartment you'll come and visit. And I'll be back in England for consultations.'

'I don't want to be consulted.' The anger welled up in me. 'I'm your fucking husband.'

'There'll be lots of that when we meet.' There speaks the budding diplomat. 'And we'll have holidays together, Bazil.'

When was the last time she'd called me Bazil, not Baz or *kedves* or darling?

'So,' I say and pause. Rehashing this bit of my past has drained me. 'From a weekend marriage ours had slipped to a holiday fling.'

'I can see that,' Dexter says. 'And you did go to Budapest. You had a holiday there, right?'

I stare at him. It's as if I'd forgotten he was in the room. How much of my marital history have I dragged out in front of him? I can't decide.

'Yes. When she got a flat I went there. And I saw her when she came over here.'

I am picking among the pieces of a broken relationship. Dexter must feel something of this because he turns away. He fetches the bottle of Glenmorangie to refill our tumblers then excuses himself while he goes across the hall to the guests he left behind. The doors are open and it is the unmistakable tones of the university Chancellor I hear. 'No, really, I quite understand. You have a newspaper to run.'

Returning, Dexter carries on as if there had been no interruption. 'And you went to Budapest for the funeral.'

'The funeral. Jesus. The hassle. The red tape. You can have no idea.' Dexter gives a modest smile as if – to the contrary – he has to hack his way through thickets of the stuff every day but he's not going to boast about it.

'The ambassador couldn't attend,' I say. 'Holed up at their Foreign Ministry I was told.' West in particular I remember because he'd been Eve's immediate boss and the man I'd seen most of during those days. Do I tell Dexter about West? No. West means nothing to him. 'There were people from the embassy. Other embassies, too. Plus local friends. They were people I didn't know. They shook my hand and muttered the usual stuff.'

But there was a group of three men who didn't speak to me. Who were they? Gawpers, the curious, bystanders. Did they happen to be walking in the cemetery and say, Hang on, there's a burial we can watch? In my high emotional state I glared at them. What right did they have to feast their eyes on me? They weren't in mourning. Had they known Eve? When I asked West he told me to calm down. I was a mess, grieving and puzzled and angry. I even stooped down to pick up a clod of earth – to hurl in their faces? – but they moved off. I lobbed the clod into the open grave.

'Family come?' Dexter asks.

'What?' For a moment I have been lost in Kerepesi cemetery on that cold winter morning. 'No.'

'Her mother in New Zealand? Her father? Are they still alive?'

'I think so. Perhaps nobody let them know. Perhaps the Foreign Office doesn't have their addresses. I didn't.'

'She would have had to fill in a form when she joined the FO – before she met you – and put down her next of kin.'

'Her mother lives as far away as it is possible to be. And the quarrel with her father had been bitter.'

'Still, the death of an only child…' He pauses a beat. 'The alleged death.'

No, it was more than a quarrel, it was an armed stand-off. Her father had sexually abused her when – as she put it – she began busting out all over.

'That's how it was.' I shrug and take a deep breath. 'Funeral over, I locked up her flat and ran back here.'

Dexter is watching me, how I take my whisky in bird-like sips. I have given him the *Reader's Digest* condensed version of my marriage. Have I conveyed to him the intensity of the couple of years I knew Eve? Was our love a shooting star that burned out? Do I love her still? Is it her extraordinary disappearance that haunts me? I have thought a lot about this, a lot. I can't decide.

'Right, Baz,' Dexter says. He waits until I look at him. He has slipped a hand inside his shirt and is smoothing his chest. 'So what are you going to do about this story?'

There speaks an editor.

CHAPTER 5

I know what I'm going to do. So do you.

From the Temporary Sign to my non-des res it is a hundred and eighty paces, less if I am in a hurry. Hello, house, are you glad to see me? Have you been lonely during the day? Have your gutters wept, your sashes sagged? The heir to the throne can chat up trees so I can talk to my house. Am I demented? No. I'm angry at having a trick played on me. Also I may be nervy because they are many and I am one. So I salute my house as a friend.

It's time I ate something. I get a Thai chicken curry out of the freezer – hold on, let's be legal about this, an alleged Thai curry – and set it on the revolving platter in the microwave. While it hums and heats I have time to start getting ready for the flight tomorrow.

Where do you keep your passport? Mine is in the desk in the sitting room, bottom drawer, locked. Except the bottom drawer is not locked. My passport is not there. Of course it is, along with all the other documents to do with birth, copulation and death. I take the drawer out and dump everything on the desk. No passport. I hear a ping from the kitchen announcing dinner is served. Ignore it.

I lean back in the chair and close my eyes. Think, man. Where else could it be? Suitcase, shoulderbag, pocket, holiday book to mark the page, moneybelt? After the funeral visit to Budapest I threw all my clothes in the washing machine, my suit to the dry cleaners, my black shoes polished – a ritual cleansing. But the passport and Hungarian money, they went into the drawer. Check the forints. They're in an envelope, so I definitely used the drawer. Well, did I lock it? I was upset and confused. I might have forgotten. But no, I had the feeling I was locking away a bad memory. Another drawer? All the drawers are unlocked but that is normal – I only lock the bottom drawer. The middle one has packs of printer paper and ink cartridges. The top drawer has the usual jumble of pens, envelopes, paperclips, rubber bands. My passport has gone. Fact.

This is the point I admit to myself that something is seriously wrong.

I prowl the room, no longer searching for the passport but for any gaps where valuable items should be. I don't have many: a nine-teenth century carriage clock, a Georgian silver teapot, a painting by Gwen John, sister of the more famous Augustus. I stop in front of the painting. It's small, a portrait done in a Paris studio, a quiet slope-shouldered Madonna-like figure, unblinking eyes staring at me. She's telling me something. She's whispering. *It's not a burglar. Don't be a dimwit. It's you-know-who.*

I have a great need for comfort and support. Telephone Josh? He's away for the weekend. Two Boobs? Mary was leaving a message just as I was going out to the pub last night. I press the button on the answerphone to check what it was she said.

'Hiya, hunk, this is Mary. I've just had the most amazing news. Fancy a drink? I'm just off to the Glock. Ciao.'

A click, a pause, then a male mid-Atlantic voice drawls: 'Friday, 7.12 pm. No further messages.'

Hold on a minute. This is the thing. That wasn't left last night but tonight, yet the light wasn't blinking to show a new message was waiting. The intruder – whoever the bastard is - has already punched the replay button to listen to it. Someone is seeping into every crevice of my life.

It gives me the shivers. I need to speak to someone. Dexter is the one. I reach for the phone and stop. I don't trust it. Who'll be listening? We used to say this was good old Blighty and things like this didn't happen. But this is the twenty-first century and they do. There are no rules any more. Our masters lie and go blind and deaf when their minions break the law. We know that. An Englishman's home is no longer his castle. My house is less des than ever. It holds its breath and listens to me, I swear it. It hears me search for my passport, prowl as I do an inventory, listen to Mary's message. Have they found a way of reading my thoughts? They're working on it.

Who decided orange was the right colour for streetlights? Bloody sadist. I'm one step outside my front door. I don't move. I stand and stare. It could be a set for a horror film, houses, cars, everything bathed in orange. My non-des res is one of a terrace put up (an oval plaque tells us) in 1909 by Arnold Ritchie & Sons, Builders. Buildings to either side of mine are dark. But light shows above the curtains of the house directly opposite. Sam the Smuggler is home. We're not bosom pals but we have witty exchanges. Me: How was the land of the frog? Sam: Better than the land of the fog. All right, wit is stretching it. I cross over and press the bell. The door opens a crack.

'If that's the bloody Jehovah's Witnesses again, you can piss off.'

'Jehovah's Witnesses come in pairs. I'm on my tod.'

The gap widens enough for Sam to inspect me. His glance goes over my shoulder then back to my face.

'You,' Sam says, not much pleased. 'I don't deal from home. You should have rung me.'

'Sam, problem. Not sure the phone is all mine any more. I don't trust it. That's why I'm here.'

'The peekabo boys?' Sam gives this some thought. He unhooks the security chain but it is so he can come outside and stand on the doorstep. He looks down the road in the direction of the Temporary Sign, then the other way. 'You've got trouble. We'll talk inside.'

Sam's house is from the same mould as mine. On the ground floor two small rooms have been knocked into one with a kitchen beyond. Stairs lead up to, I suppose, two bedrooms and a poky bathroom. Sam is not married ('between wives, letting my bank account take a breather'), about the same age as me. I suspect he goes to a fitness club. There is a certain look to him - don't mess with me, pal. So he's tough but he doesn't look a thug. White shirt, dark blue tie with a cream diamond pattern, cardigan. He likes to look respectable when he goes to work. Seeing him behind the wheel of his ageing Volvo you would put him down as a solicitor who plays a lot of golf.

In the sitting room he says, 'Fancy one?' He pulls down the flap of a drink cabinet and it lights up like a Christmas tree. Bottles twinkle with reflected light.

'I've been on Glenmorangie,' I say.

'Nice,' Sam says. He wriggles a bottle out of the back of the cabinet. 'Care to sample the Laphroaig?'

This is the first time I have been further than Sam's hall. When I turn to look at the room I'm taken aback. Other folk have a bookcase against a wall. Not Sam. He has ranged a stack of cartons: Marlboro, Benson & Hedges, Silk Cut. It's like a second wall up to my waist. It stretches from the door to the back of a sofa.

'Close on eighty thou,' Sam says. 'Used to keep them in my lock-up until the mice got at them. Little buggers weren't interested in the baccy, they just chewed up the packaging.'

'The regulations are – correct me if I'm wrong – that you can bring them into the country for your own personal use.'

'True.'

'I can't see any ashtrays.'

He doesn't respond so I prod a bit.

'Do you smoke?'

'Never.' He hands me a glass. 'My personal use is making money.'

You have to admire his logic though I doubt Her Majesty's Customs & Excise would.

'In the normal run of things,' Sam says, 'I'm picky about who I invite inside. People talk. You won't talk, will you?' There's no threat in his voice. He's just stating a fact. 'You've got your own troubles. You've got to take care. Right?' He purses his lips and nods two or three times.

'Someone's been in my house,' I say.

'Yeah. Wasn't that long ago either. It was gloomy outside so I was drawing the curtains. Small car drove past. Ford Focus I believe. The driver... well, he was dawdling, leaning over to make out house numbers. Big bloke he was, almost filled the front of the car. Hello, I thought, what's he after? You might think I was being nosey since it was your house he wanted but it is my opinion that curiosity never killed the cat.'

'Police?'

Sam wags a finger – this is his story and he'll tell it how he wants.

'One man, that's good. If the rozzers wanted to see me there'd be a pair. He parked down there - end of the block - and walked back. He punched your bell and waited, turning his back on the door, casual like, just happening to look along the street both ways. By now I'm even more curious. There's a crack in the curtains – just there - so he never spotted me. He swung back to your door and fiddled round with something I couldn't make out, then Bob's your uncle. The door opened and he stepped inside smartish, door closed. No lights came on though I caught the odd flash of a torch. Maybe you wonder why I didn't ring the coppers but the police and me, well, you know how it is...' Delicately he waves the idea aside. 'I fetched that little stool and sat down to watch. He was inside fifteen minutes, maybe twenty, no more. It wasn't one of your normal burglaries, he didn't come staggering out with your telly in his arms. He knew what he was after, something small, got it and got out. There he was, walking down the street when he took a mobile out of his pocket. It was like he couldn't wait until he got back in the car to break the good news. You asked a question – police?' Sam extends his hand and teeters it side to side. 'If you press me I would say he was official but unofficial. That's the very worst because they deny it but mark you down as a troublemaker. Cheers,' he says and has a refreshing gulp from his tumbler. 'And he did get what he was looking for, I take it?'

'My passport.'

'Ouch. Put me out of business that would.'

That's their reasoning. Nip in before Potter gets back from London, grab his passport, stop him leaving the country. No court orders, no publicity. Simple. Low key. They pat themselves on the back for being clever. Too clever by half. They point a finger towards Budapest. They don't want me to go there.

'You want to make that phone call?' Sam asks.

Speak to Dexter? Have my hand held? My enthusiasm has faded and I shake my head.

'This spot of bother,' Sam says and picks his words with care. 'This isn't your line of business. Maybe I could help. Get a couple of lads round to have a word with him? Point out the error of his way. That's if you know who he is. I don't mean to pry.'

He's being dainty about it.

'It's to do with Eve.'

'Oh yes?'

'She was dead. Suddenly she isn't. But no one is supposed to know.'

'She worked for the government, right?' As if he is tired Sam closes his eyes and wipes the back of his hand over them. 'Yeah, I can see where getting mixed up in that might put you in a delicate position. You going walkabout?'

'I'm going to Budapest.'

'Without a passport?'

I tap my nose.

He gives a little frown. 'Bandit country from what I hear.'

'That's Bucharest.'

'Budapest, Bucharest…' He teeters his hand from side to side again as if there's little to choose between them. 'Well, it's your…' He hesitates a beat. Funeral? '…look-out.'

I'm in the doorway, thanking him for his whisky, when his eyes switch from my face. Turning I see a modest sized car crawling along the road. Sam lays a hand on my arm to draw me back inside. The car passes under a lamp which shows a man behind the wheel. He ducks his head down so he can inspect my windows. I had switched off the lights. I am not at home. Past my darkened house he accelerates away.

'Mate, you are in trouble.'

'Same man?' I ask.

Sam's eyes turn back to me. 'In this light I wouldn't recognise my own mother but he was the right size.'

'I don't understand.'

'Don't understand what?' Sam asks.

'They've stolen my passport. What more do they want?'

'At a guess,' Sam says, 'you.'

Back of the Oxford Playhouse theatre, in a gloomy Victorian hulk, are the editorial offices of the *Oxford Herald*. The Randolph hotel is also handy but the old boot in Accounts won't pay expenses for a Randolph bar bill. On a good day and with a following wind she'll nod through the Gloucester Arms.

I'm wary going past the Glock because it's closing time and you never know who you'll run into: could be luvvies, could be students, but it could be newshounds or Mary with her amazing news. I go direct to the Dickensian red brick sweatshop, open the street door with the key we all carry, climb the stairs, punch in the code and hear the lock click open to the suite of offices where we spend our days. Don't you just love 'suite'? Makes you think of Hollywood films and the kind of blonde behind the reception desk who makes you glad you're being kept waiting? It does? Then you've come to the wrong place.

The building started life as a wholesale warehouse so it had generous floorspace. When the *Old Hag* moved in partitions blocked off dark room, library, accounts, back numbers, advertising and circulation. The largest space (not *that* large) is the bearpit for us newshounds. Dexter has a partitioned-off corner. When he arrived he had the frosted glass taken out of his walls and clear glass put in so he could see us at our desks. It didn't take long before he appreciated that we could just as easily see him so he had venetian blinds hung. He wants to peek at us, he just fingers the slats apart.

Listen, I *love* this place. Go down Wapping way, Canary Wharf, wherever they fled when the papers left Fleet Street, and there's no soul. A newspaper office needs years of mistakes and rows and April Fool jokes and triumphs and graffiti and pinboards and a dartboard and coffee stains and mementoes and tearsheets and faxes and famous last words before it becomes human. There's a table against one wall which is our museum: an IBM golfball typewriter which replaced the solid Remington manual which replaced the fountain pen plus a goose quill as a joke. A shoebox marked Editor's Toys has a blue pencil, a spike and a green eyeshade (whoever wore a green eyeshade and shouted 'Hold the front page'?), a photo of Maxwell with a Magic Marker scrawl *Funny that Cap'n Bob's double was never seen again*. I like to look at the very naughty photo of – Hold on, who's this feller? Where did he spring from?

'What brings you here at this time of night?' he asks.

I've never seen him before. Mid-thirties, bomber jacket, blue shirt, tan trousers with a mobile phone and a black flashlight hooked to the belt. He has a meaningless smile as he strolls towards me. You can come a long way on a smile. On his chest is a badge that says PAX in a circle of oak leaves.

'Who are you?' I ask back at him.

'Security.'

The security man I've seen is an amiable black man from Antigua ('where Viv is from, or Sir Viv I should say').

'I don't know you.'

'Pax Security.' He taps his badge to prove it. 'Recently there was a break-in downstairs with sundry items stolen and there was a feeling that certain eyes may have been averted at the crucial moment – if you get my meaning.' Who wrote his lines, I wonder. Another performance and he might say them with more spontaneity. He hauls a laminated card from his breast pocket: a photo, a signature, PAX

SECURITY in bold black letters, other words rather more shy. 'So now Pax have got the contract,' he finishes with more conviction.

He's lying. Does he think a journalist wouldn't know of a break-in at his own building? That's not a crime, that's a story.

'Good for Pax,' I say. I want to escape from here, from him. 'Yes, very good. But you're not here on duty all the time.'

'Er no, I've got my round. I was checking doors and windows on the street when the lights came on here so I came up to look.'

Another lie. The door lock gives a clunk so I'd have heard him come in. He's been hanging around, peeping out through the venetian blind in Dexter's office.

'So you'll be on your way soon,' I say.

He ignores this. 'And you are…?'

'I work here.'

His eyes drop to the black shoulder bag I've rested on the floor.

'I see. Do you have some ID you could show me? Just so I can be easy in my own mind?'

'You think I've come to nick one of the computers?'

We have entered the new age of deference which is the reverse of the old age of deference. Under the old rules the security man would call you Sir; now you have to bow to him. In this brave new world it is forbidden to question anyone who thinks they have a smidgeon of power. He frowns at me.

'For God's sake,' I say, feeling the anger rising and making the most of it, 'I work for the *Old Hag*. Among other things I write Under the Carpet. Have you read it? The byline is Baz Faz.'

Old Hag? Under the Carpet? Baz Faz? There's no change in his expression.

'See that desk? Next one over? It's mine. The photo, my wife. My appointment diary.'

'May I?'

Whether he may or may not, he does. An elastic band holds the page open at today's date. With a stubby finger he points at an entry.

'Twelve noon,' he reads. 'Clip Joint.'

'That's to have my hair cut.'

There are ways of showing disbelief, a rising scale that goes roughly like this: the arched eyebrow, a pursing of the lips, a frown, a shake of the head, and most damning of all a belly laugh. The Paxman has none of these. He simply stares, head on one side. The smile he greeted me with has long gone.

'Let me tell you this,' he says. 'They didn't do a very good job. It's not cut so you'd notice.'

'I cancelled.'

'So we can't even check that they'll verify you.'

'Not at this time of night, no.'

'Yeah right. *Old Hag* you said you worked for? That's how you refer to your boss?'

'*Oxford Herald*. It's an office joke.' I sit in my chair, slide out a drawer and now we're coming to it. The drawer is a jumble just like my bottom drawer at home and I grope round, pull something out, no, drop it on my lap, pull out a file. 'Here. These are columns I've written.' I force the file into his hands. 'Go on, have a look. The strapline is Under the Carpet. Then there's the headline, whatever it is. Underneath is my byline. Even a little thumbnail mugshot of me. Go on, it won't bite.' He opens the file, his eyes drop down to the cuttings, and that's when I do it.

'By Baz Faz,' he reads. That seems to trouble him. 'Baz Faz is your name?'

'That's what I write under. I won't bore you with why so just accept it. My real name is Potter.'

'Mr Potter.' His eyes concentrate on mine. 'I'll just check with head office if you don't mind. Yes, I'll do that. We have lists of all employees.'

He is reaching for his mobile when I lurch to my feet.

'I fucking do mind. I mind about everything you do. I mind about your coming into my office in the middle of the night to question me. I mind about your ringing up God knows who and giving my name. Listen, you ring my boss, my editor, and check with him. Use the phone in his office because it's a direct line.'

I am physically pushing him. He's bigger than me but he is not too bright and he is confused and he retreats. I've got to keep talking. I've got to stop his brain working.

'What you do is punch in star-zero-one and it rings straight through to his study at home. You explain to him how you questioned me when I came in to get a story ready for Monday's edition and then you apologise to me. Understand? Do you?'

We've moved inside Dexter's office.

'There's his desk. Use the green phone. There it is. Go on, just press star-zero-one.'

He doesn't want to speak to Dexter. Of course he doesn't. Under this torrent of words he hasn't worked that out. In about two seconds he will. He half turns towards Dexter's desk. I pull the key out of the door, push it into the outer side, and I slam the door and lock him in.

I grab my shoulder bag and at the door on my way out I catch a glimpse of his face at a gap he has fingered in the venetian blind. He is talking into his mobile phone.

I've never done anything like that. I'm not a man of action – I'm just like you – but I did it. My heart is pumping. I feel the adrenaline. I'm scared and I'm thrilled. I'm a movie star. I want to hug someone. My hands are shaking. My chest feels clammy. I have an urgent desire to pee.

There is a bus for Heathrow at 2 am. Why? Airport workers, I guess. At the airport I can kill time until a flight to Budapest. Sitting in the bus I want to hide my face behind a newspaper but I haven't got one. Instead I hunch down into my coat and crook an arm over my face. Sweet dreams.

Of course I don't sleep, I run it all through my mind. The TV news item that has been wiped off the tape, the con with the programming schedule, my passport being stolen, my answerphone being listened to, the car idling past to check my house, the bogus security guard in the office – that is a lot in twenty-four hours.

Why? To put a scare in me?

But they are such bumblers.

My squashy black shoulder bag rests on my lap. In it are the clothes and sponge bag I stuffed in at my non-des res in five minutes flat. In my breast pocket, nestling against my credit card wallet, is my passport.

My other passport.

A couple of years ago I had a brainwave: Eve would be even more immersed in Magyar culture if she was married to a Hungarian. At least I think that was my reasoning. I engaged the bureaucracy at the Hungarian embassy in Eaton Place in hand-to-hand combat, and bloody and bruised I triumphed. I spoke to them only in the Magyar language which was an essential start. My parents, though dead, had both been Hungarian. I was born in Britain but that was the fault of the communist system and the bloodbath of 1956 which forced them to flee the country. I dwelt on my parents' heroic resistance as the Red Army tanks rolled onto the streets of Budapest. My uncle has a place of honour in Kerepesi cemetery and I think it was that which finally won it for me. I got my Hungarian passport.

Why do I keep it in my desk at the office? In a word: bloody laziness. OK, I know, that's two words. Some while ago during the run-up to the European Cup, Hungary was drawn to play against England. The *Old Hag* was going to run a feature and somebody came up with the idea of a shot of passports leaning against a football. My Hungarian passport volunteered. It is the usual burgundy red job with ÚTLEVÉL in very big letters in case anyone thought it might be your shopping list. Mary took the shot but somehow I never got round to taking my passport back home. So when Paxman was glowering at me I slipped it out of the desk drawer onto my lap and when he was distracted with the file it made its way into my pocket.

Today I am discovering skills I never knew I had.

What name is it in? Bazil Fazekas, though it was another nightmare getting the bureaucrats to accept that and not the name on my birth certificate. The computers at Heathrow will never make the Fazekas-Potter link.

CHAPTER 6

'Bazil, it is time we had a talk, you know, father to son.'

'Yes, papa?'

'I mean, the facts of life.'

In one hand he held a cigarette, in the other a can of Guinness. Like everyone who lived in the old Soviet bloc he smoked. And he drank Guinness because he said that in communist Hungary there was nothing like it. Yet at home we ate *gombaleves* and *retes*, and on the table beside the salt and pepper was a shaker of paprika. In the old days, during the accursed forty years, every restaurant table had a shaker of paprika, a symbol of national consciousness. Sprinkle it on your food and you held Magyar culture in your mouth. My father rejected his inheritance at the same time as he cherished it.

'Not facts of life like sex,' he went on after he had refreshed himself with a swallow of Guinness. 'You know about *fucking* because kids talk about it when their balls drop and they notice that girls have an interesting shape.'

It was a Saturday afternoon, my mother was out shopping. My father had already sunk a couple of the black stuff at the pub. They were making him philosophical. As always at home we were speaking Hungarian except he used the English word *fucking* as if such a subject did not reflect the true Magyar spirit.

'Living in a dangerous world, that's what I want to instruct you in.' He leaned forward for emphasis. 'That Brezhnev – I don't trust him. What's he hiding behind those eyebrows? He will – all right, only maybe but we must be prepared – Brezhnev will maybe fool the Americans into going back home, NATO is finished, and the Red Army strolls west through Europe. Who's going to stop them? Germany? Listen, that long retreat from Stalingrad still haunts them, even the ones who weren't born then. France and Italy – they're full of communists who take their orders from Moscow. They'll hang out their red flags to welcome their socialist brothers. Belgium? Excuse me, I can never find Belgium on the map. Maybe the Ivans reach the Channel and decide to invade England so we must be prepared. Facts of life, I said. So today, my only son, I instruct you how to make a Molotov cocktail.'

Is this a normal conversation between father and son? Not in England. Definitely not. It took place in 1976, that really hot summer, just after the *Guardian* ran an article on the coming ice age. The doors and windows were open for any breeze going. I could hear neighbours' voices, boys kicking a football, a barking dog joining in the fun, the Grateful Dead on somebody's radio, and my father is telling me how to make a Molotov cocktail.

He refreshed himself from the can, a good long swallow. Talking makes you thirsty which is why when friends gather together to talk, they drink. That is what my father said. Even as a boy I thought he got it the wrong way round.

'Right, first you buy a bottle of vodka. Stolichnaya is good because it is Russian, just like Molotov was, and you are going to give it back to them. Next – most important – you drink the vodka, you and two friends. Three people is right for one bottle. If you try to drink it all by yourself, bye-bye, you fall down drunk. But three people will find themselves filled with courage, you know.' His eyes sparkled with the same bravado that had strengthened him in Budapest. 'Then you pour paraffin into the bottle until it is almost up to the neck. Everybody says petrol but in my opinion that could be asking for trouble. You must plug a piece of rag into the bottle so about a hand's length hangs out. When you put a match to that, if it is petrol you must be careful it doesn't blow up in your face. With paraffin, no problem. Others may disagree but this is my opinion. You put your hand behind you and hurl it over-arm so the bottle lands on the tank and shatters. The flames cover the tank and are drawn in through the ventilation system and the Ivans come out screaming.'

Picture it yourself, the gestures, lifting the imaginary vodka bottle to his lips, transferring paraffin, jamming in the rag to plug the bottle, the match striking. My father loved his bits of theatrical business just like I do. It's in the Fazekas genes, I expect. Finally he hurled the Guinness can over arm against the sitting room wall. Luckily, for the sake of marital peace, it was empty. No, I do him a disservice, luck played no part. What Hungarian would wantonly throw away a drink?

'This is what I learnt in 1956, beginning of November. Krushchev ordered the tanks back into Budapest.' He pointed at the open window. 'Imagine. We look out there now and see tanks coming down the street, past number 28, good day to you Mrs Chauncy.' He shakes his head.' And I was so young, not long married, with a kid on the way.' He blinked. 'We lost it.'

He stopped. The past could silence him.

And the past floods back to me. I have memories of something I never saw. Tell me how that can be.

I have made my escape from Oxford and I'm in Budapest. The past I didn't experience is vivid in my head. Down Ulloi ut was the Killian barracks where the army, loyal to the people, tried to fight the Red Army. 1956 I'm talking about, before I was born but I see it. To one side, out of sight in a maze of little alleys, is the Corvin cinema. The approaches are too narrow for tanks; so none of my father's Molotov cocktails. The Corvin building is defended by teenagers, schoolchildren. There's a statue of one; a boy, about fourteen, rifle in his hands, beret on his head. When I saw the statue last December someone had laid a wreath over the boy's shoulders. I'll find time to bow my head in front of it, but not now.

It's late afternoon when I come up the steps from the metro at

Ferenc körút. I push back the memories of things I never saw to orient myself. An old man carrying a pot of cyclamen is walking towards me. I ask him where the Ibis Styles is. He doesn't answer, just points to my right, towards the river. I don't think he likes my accent.

I had the shiver at Ferihegy airport. I have it again, going not through my body but my inner self. It is speaking and hearing the language again. 'It's like adjusting to a new lover,' Eve once said, with her smile that invited you to share her secret but not probe deeper.

In the end I didn't fly direct to Budapest. That's what they (whoever they are) would expect. I went first to Paris on the earliest BA flight and changed planes there. While I was kicking my heels at CDG I went to the hotel booking desk. Can I reserve a room at Ibis in Paris? *Bien sûr, monsieur.* I don't want to stay in Paris but kindly get Ibis to book me a room in Budapest, the Ibis Styles. My name is Fazekas. I got a very French sigh from the woman at the desk, but I waited while she did it

There's more than one Ibis hotel in Budapest. I choose the Styles because it is close to the river. Petőfi Bridge is a stroll away. It is not a flash district. The suburban railway terminus is not an architectural gem. No one will look for me here.

I'm learning.

Sunday morning.

I have relatives here. Let's see: an uncle, aunts, cousins, even an aged great aunt in Debrecen. In particular, there is my cousin Jozsef. He's useful, very. But he's married to the flamboyant Adel for whom no day is complete without a drama, raised voices, tears, reconciliation. Besides, to get involved with Jozsef on a Sunday is to lose momentum. It is the big meal, roast pork Gypsy style, another bottle of Villány, have you heard the latest about Zsuzsa, you're never going to believe what she's got herself into, we could do with Maggie here to sort out the railway workers, who finished that bottle, so on.

I put Jozsef to one side. Tomorrow maybe. Not now.

I ring West at his home number, wherever his home may be. He never invited me there.

'Hello,' a woman answers, a firm daughter-of-the-raj voice, then more uncertainly as if her lessons in the native dialect are proving the most frightful bore, *'Jo napot.'*

'Is he there? Can I speak to him?'

'Who shall I say is calling?'

'Tell him an old chum.'

'An old chum.' It seems this is the right thing to say as if West has many people claiming they are old chums and needing to speak to him. 'Oh, right then.'

Another pause.

'West speaking.'

'Hello, it's Baz. You know, Bazil Potter.'

Yet another pause while I could be pondering on a dozen things but mainly I am thinking this is a dialogue written by Harold Pinter... all these pauses... did you know that Pinter is a Hungarian name? Does that explain him? The pause lengthens into a silence, not one of my father's end-of-the-conversation silences but long enough to have significance if I could work out what it was.

'You still there? Magyar Telekom hasn't cut us off?'

I have a memory he is called Peter but I hold back from calling him that. He's Foreign Office, don't you know.

'I'm here. And you, Potter, where are you? Are you calling from Oxford? Is everything all right?'

'I'm in Budapest. It's why I'm ringing you.'

'What a surprise. Where are you staying?'

'I've only just arrived.' Caution makes the lie come easily. 'I'd like to meet you. There are things I want to talk about which I'd prefer not to discuss over the phone.'

'Oh, quite.' Now there is a diplomatic word, meaning anything you like, meaning nothing. He goes on, 'Just a minute. Darling!' The phone goes dead as a hand is clamped over the receiver. I'm adrift in one of those silences again. Peter West was the man I saw most when I came over to arrange Eve's interment (his word), my conduit to British bureaucracy and a hand with its Hungarian counterpart, helping the two to mesh together. I expected the bureaucracies to clash – each lot jealous of their territory – and there was deadlock over the acceptance of a hand instead of a whole body as evidence of death. On my fourth day in Budapest, West and I were summoned to the Interior Ministry and the official we saw was all smiles and everything was agreed. 'Why the change in the weather?' I asked West, 'why is it all sunny now? Did you send him a crate of Scotch? What did you do?' 'Just my job,' he said. I was blunt. 'What actually is your job?' He raised his eyebrows as if I wasn't showing good form. 'Oh, we're a bit like an extended family, d'you see, so I'm sort of First Secretary twice removed.'

Reminiscing over.

'Sorry to keep you, Potter. I've talked to Kitty and she's given me day release so why don't we meet for a spot of lunch. You're familiar with the Mercure Hotel, I take it.'

The pause is on my side this time. Did he really say First Secretary twice removed?

'Oh sorry,' he says. 'I don't mean to confuse you because Mercure hotels keep popping up all over town. I mean the one on Kalvin Square.'

'I'll find it,' I say.

'Not the hotel itself. There's a pub-cum-restaurant in the street next to the hotel. I've been racking my brains but the name eludes me. Doesn't matter, you can't mistake it. Look through the plate glass window and you'll see a bicycle suspended over the bar.'

'A bicycle,' I say. 'Got it.'

'Twelve thirtyish.'

'I'll be there.'

West is the kind of man who says 'Righty-o' at the end of a conversation, but I hear a click. That's it. He's gone. I stand in the kiosk in the plaza under the Petőfi Bridge, rocking back and forth on my heels. I had it wrong. What West said was: 'I'm sort of a Second Secretary, once removed.'

Does that make sense? Me neither. But I think about it.

I don't have long before my lunch with West, just time for a little wander, checking behind me. I remember something Eve said, that I had inherited a sceptical Hungarian gene. Sceptical? When someone has stolen my passport to stop me coming? And why did West ask where I was staying?

Once we had an argument and Eve went further: 'You Hungarians have a reputation for being cynical and devious and I can see why.'

'And you British are known for being perfidious and hypocrit-ical,' I retorted.

Just a lovers' tiff. We kissed and made up.

You Hungarians, she said, but I'm not. I am my own country. For a time she was part of it.

I'm early in Kalvin square. I loiter, adjusting to the city and its people. It's not a leafy London square. It's traffic hell with one side a jungle of scaffolding while a bit more of old Budapest is destroyed in the name of concrete. I pick my way through this building site. I have to adjust to the people too. A group of teenage girls are giving me the eye. Why? I greet an old woman - mauve coat, bonnet, a Pekinese on a lead. Why is there suspicion in her frown? My accent, I suppose. I pause by a shop with a display of men's ties in the window. I linger to admire them. In the plate glass is the reflection of the entrance to the Mercure Korona. A taxi draws up. Out steps Peter West, Second Secretary, once removed. And why not? A cabbie would know the Mercure better than a restaurant with a bicycle above the bar.

I watch West, still his reflection. He disappears into the hotel. Why? Not to have a quick one before our rendezvous because we are meeting in a bar. For a pee? Same reasoning. I stand and stare. Reminds me of the times I did this along with Fleet Street's finest. Waiting for the latest disgraced politician to emerge muttering sour nothings. Five minutes pass. West emerges and goes down the little side street. I don't move. All right, West is a diplomat and he has other concerns apart from me. Maybe. I let a few minutes pass and follow him.

Only a blind person could miss the restaurant. A bicycle is indeed riding through the air above the bar. That's not all. There's a stuffed parrot in a glass case, a ship's bell marked RMS Titanic, a wagon wheel, other jokey stuff. On the walls are posters of Elvis Presley, a Harley-Davidson and Santa Claus ho-ho-hoing over a bottle of Coke. The restaurant is half full so why has West chosen a table at the back near the service door? He feels happiest in shadows, I decide. He holds a menu in his hand, frowning. Seeing me, he half rises.

'Hello old chap, good to see you. You had no trouble finding the place?'

He drops the menu to shake hands.

'Hello, West.'

'The waiter's gone to find an English menu. He brought me a German one. Why do I so dislike being taken for German?'

Don't mention the war, I think. Hungary joined Germany in invading the Soviet Union. When the Red Army in its turn invaded Hungary and finally besieged Budapest, were they liberators or conquerors, did they free the Hungarians or punish them? Whatever, the Russians didn't move on so many people blame the Germans for bringing about the accursed forty years of communism.

'Thank you,' West says to the waiter who brings the English menu. He runs a finger down it like someone choosing a horse on a race card. 'Got fixed up with your hotel yet?'

'I'll do it this afternoon.'

'No suitcase with you?'

'I put it in Left Luggage.' I don't say where.

'What do you suppose Farmer's Breakfast is?'

'Pig,' I tell him.

'Well basically,' he says, looking up from the menu, 'in Hungary one either eats pig or one eats pig, so on balance I think I'll eat pig. What brings you to Budapest, dropping in without warning?'

'Do I have to warn you?'

West smiles and doesn't answer. He asked me in the same tone of voice as he gave his menu choice to the waiter, matter of fact, though to me there are undertones. You see, I no longer find anything matter of fact. Rather like one of those films I watched at the Phoenix, the sentences may be straightforward but the universe they describe is strange. He wasn't expecting me, he hadn't been warned I was coming, so did he telephone someone in London and they were baffled? Potter has no passport, he can't board a plane at Heathrow for Budapest. Is that what has happened? I decide to be open about why I have come.

'On Thursday evening I saw Eve on the television news. She was here in Budapest but I don't know what the news story was. Do you know?'

'You saw Eve?'

'Yes.'

'Baz.' It is the first time he's used my first name. Is that significant? He takes it slowly. 'Really, you know, er, I don't think that is possible. She died months ago, well, disappeared. I know no body has been found except…' He stops, looks at the hand he was gesturing with and seems embarrassed. 'Sorry.'

'So when I saw her on television on Thursday…'

'It could be some old story being rehashed…' he begins brightly. Then, 'I don't know,' he says, seeming to lose his way, giving a baffled shake of his head.

'If it was an old story, why has it come alive again? Perhaps it was something she was working on when there was the accident.'

'Well, I can't possibly say.'

'*Can't*? You mean it was secret and you're not allowed to?'

'No. No, not that at all. I mean I simply do not have any facts that will help.'

'What *was* she working on?'

'Normal embassy jobs.'

'I'm a stranger in the diplomatic world. Like what?'

'She was a generalist. Bit of everything.'

I wait. Treat it as an interview, I tell myself. The interviewee gets uneasy as the silence prolongs itself and in the end talks.

'Well, mostly taking an interest in the economic side, development, currency fluctuations, joint ventures, that sort of thing.'

'That sort of thing,' I echo.

'Yes, you know.'

I don't know. That sort of thing wouldn't interest my Eve. She needed more stimulus to make her spark and her choice of the Foreign Office had always seemed odd.

'What was she *really* doing?'

'Really doing? Surely you're not expecting reality in a diplomat?' He gives a disarming little smile.

'I'm hoping to learn the truth.'

'The truth is what you've got. She had a broad brief: the economy, trade relations, business opportunities, the personalities involved, cultivating links. That was her job and jolly good at it she was. Amen.'

This is not how my lunch with West is meant to be. I am supposed to be digging out the buried part of Eve's life. West is brushing over the traces.

'I've been a reporter a long time,' I say. Any subtlety I possess is slipping away from me. I know it is. It's that smooth face of his, the twitch of his lips, his superior air. 'I have interviewed a lot of politicians. A lot. I can pick up weasel words and meaningless guff and spin. That's what I'm getting. There is some secret that is being hidden from me.'

Perhaps it's as well I can't go any further. The waiter is a distraction, putting the Farmer's Breakfast in front of West, and for me the pork fillet with mushroom sauce and yesterday's noodles. There is a sort of truce while we each chew a couple of forkfuls before I return to the TV news.

'Believe me, it wasn't some old film I saw, it was recent. Eve had changed her hairstyle and lost weight.'

'Different hair, different looks. You're making,' he gives a wry smile, 'an amazingly poor case for it being Eve.'

'I saw her. It was Eve.'

'Is there a sister? I haven't studied her personnel file. Does she have a younger sister? Or older come to that?'

'When you live with someone, sleep with someone, you *know* that person. In any case she has no sister.'

'Or a cousin?' He gives me a sympathetic glance. 'They can look, you know, the same only different.'

'It was Eve.' Did I shout? West looks startled. 'And the BBC was ordered to destroy the footage. Why was that?'

'Really, that's a question for the BBC. You can't come to Budapest and ask me.' His eyes slip away towards a TV set in the corner where a kung fu movie is in full swing. Chinese actors kick each other in the face and swear in Hungarian. It seems to trouble West. 'Wretched thing. Why can't they let us eat in peace?'

For a few moments we do eat in silence except for the cries and thuds of kung fu. We have a drink of our beers, chew some more. As the silence continues I realise West has forced a sort of *omerta* on himself, concentrating on his salami and ham and blood sausage, cutting them into very small pieces before putting them in his mouth, and saying nothing. I will get nowhere asking what Eve and the unknown man were doing that was newsworthy. The waiter, observing this pool of silence, limps over to our table. With my eyes down all I see is his dark trousers and black shoes, cracked leather, toes almost peeping through. Those feet look as if they have tramped on dirt tracks from Pecs, round Lake Balaton, all the way to the big city in search of work.

'*Alles ist gut?*' he asks.

'We're English,' West says.

It was a mistake meeting West. He won't help me because he's been told I have the evil eye.

'What are you doing?'

I am standing up, dropping some notes on the table. Two thousand forints should cover it.

'I'm leaving.'

'Where are you going?'

'Out.'

'Just a minute, I'm talking to you. You can't just – '

'Yes, I can.'

It's not the first time I've stormed out of a meeting. I did it with Lovegrove. Hm, there's a thought.

'I had a posting in La Paz once.' This is how I remember West, a breezy whimsical side to him, not the buttoned-up diplomat he was today. 'Here's a Trivial Pursuit question. What do Bolivia and Hungary have in common? Give up? They both lost their coastlines. Bolivia was celebrating carnival while Peru and Chile did a pincer movement on their Pacific coast. And Hungary lost its Adriatic coast in the Treaty of Trianon.'

West made light of it, but I remember my father still felt cheated seventy years later.

'So we lost our coast,' my father said. 'That was bad enough. It was the loss of the navy that was the real tragedy. What does an admiral do without ships to play with?'

When I told West this he grinned.

'There is the South American solution – he becomes president.'

I cannot imagine my father and West in the same room together.

'Bloody Admiral Horthy,' my father said, 'became pals with Hitler, lost our brave soldiers at Stalingrad. So the Russians marched in to punish us.'

Don't mention the war. Hungary always does badly out of wars.

Outside in the street I glance back through the window and see West, phone in hand, beckoning the waiter, just a glimpse before I stride away. I reach Kalvin Square, go down the metro steps to the booking hall, then straight on down the escalator towards the platforms and walk into a reception committee.

'Jegy, kerem.'

There are two of them in uniform, a man and a woman both thick around the waist in middle age, ticket inspectors. I bought a weekly pass this morning and dig it out of my pocket. There's a train approaching and they are being mean and suspicious as if they think the pass is a forgery. The pass is handed back, I grab it and run. Behind me I hear voices raised. *'Jegy…egy pilanat.'* Another man is being embraced by the female ticket inspector, straining to break free of her beefy arms. Resistance is useless. As the train doors close I see his eyes locked on me. Bully has had me followed.

My wife is not dead.

Lovegrove lied, the BBC tape was wiped, my passport was stolen, my office was under surveillance, the embassy Second Secretary clammed up.

I am not a cop or a private eye or a spy or James Bloody Bond. I am a newspaperman. I'll find out what is going on.

CHAPTER 7

Did you ever see Richard Nixon's signature? Compared it when he was a run of the mill tricky politician with the end when he was a foul-mouthed, vindictive, conspiring liar? In the post-Watergate days, with the vultures circling lower, his signature degenerated until it was no more than a wavy line with a single angry slash to make the X.

The cash machine outside the bank is broken so I have gone inside to get money. The girl looks at the signature in my passport and compares it with the signature I have scrawled on the receipt. Fazekas has deteriorated to a squiggle with a furious Nazi Z in the middle. She looks at the photo then at my face and sees the anger and decides she will simply count out the notes and get me out of the door.

I've abandoned my mobile phone because it's a spy. Don't tell me I'm crazy. If they can steal my passport they can find out where I am from that mobile phone. Whoever they are. From a kiosk within sight of the parliament building I ring Mike, my old chum at the *Mirror*. It's Sunday lunchtime so he'll be at home. To my relief it's not Gloria who answers because she thinks I lead Mike astray.

'The Simmons residence.'

It's his Jeeves voice. The truth is nobody leads Mike astray, he's way out in front, carving the air with his sabre, urging us laggards to catch up. In the background I hear voices and snatches of music. I went to a number of Mike's Sunday lunch parties, though in recollection they become one long hazy afternoon.

71

'Greetings, *tovarich*, Baz here.'

'Baz old mate, so what's with the *tovarich*? Where are you holed up – Moscow?'

'Not quite.'

'Hold on a sec.' Voices and music fade as a door is closed. 'OK.'

'Are you?' I ask. 'OK I mean? No repercussions from asking questions at the Beeb?'

Bit of a pause but I'm used to them.

'Strange you mention that. I had to go into the office yesterday afternoon and I got a look from the boss. Nothing too heavy but it was there. A little later I was at my desk hammering out a piece for Monday's edition when he wandered over and stood behind me. A hand squeezed my collar and he bent down as if reading my copy over my shoulder. It wasn't that. He breathed in my ear: "Word to the wise: no BBC specials. News clips that have gone walkabout are *verboten*. Got that?"' There is something of a break here while I ponder what to say until Mike bounces back in cheerful mode. 'Hey, I've got a rather jolly New Zealand sauvignon blanc in my hand, cheeky but slips down a treat. Cheers.'

'Cheers,' I echo but I'm thinking someone has been leaning on his editor, one of the people Dexter warns about, the spin doctors, the string pullers, the awkward squad, the deniables out to suppress real news. 'Mike, I've got another small favour to ask.'

'Jesus,' he whispers.

'The exclusive will be yours, I promise.'

The noise I hear is a strangled grunt as if I have caught him drinking.

'Who does the rag use in Budapest these days? A name is all I want. You don't have to do anything.'

My pal, my old mate, my companion of a thousand glasses actually has to consider before agreeing. 'Hang on. I'll dig out the bible.'

It's the directory of names, email addresses and telephone numbers of staff in London and Manchester, freelances, correspondents abroad, photographers, line services, so on.

'Right,' he says. 'Hungary. It's no big deal. Let's see. We have a stringer in Budapest, another in – '

'Just Budapest.'

'Name of Harry Bath.'

'English?'

'Harry? From dandruff to Hush Puppies.' I hear the sigh. 'I ran into him when he did the rounds in London, and I mean rounds. I only just got out alive. Reprobate from old Fleet Street, his own monogrammed corkscrew in El Vino.'

Of course. Harry Bath, I remember now. Ripples of his reputation even reached the *Old Hag*. The Dylan Thomas of Fleet Street without the poetry, Josh called him. 'I've heard the stories.'

'Only the half of them, believe me, only the half. Got pen and paper? I'll give you his mobile.'

And he does. Plus a run down on the more lurid of Harry's antics.

Harry Bath – does that name ring a bell with you? When Clinton was President, he stopped off in Budapest on a swing through Europe. Harry filed a light-hearted piece along these lines: 'Bill came alone – no First Lady, no First Daughter, no First Dog, no First Bimbo or indeed Twentieth Bimbo. Bill came with his roving eye and, according to certain disreputable sources, his roving hand.' What is known as a diplomatic incident followed, the special relationship went into spasm and the British government came out with its usual grovel. Now does the name Harry Bath come to mind? A faint tinkle surely?

'What was all the fuss about?' Harry seems genuinely perplexed when I meet him and remind him of this episode. 'What I wrote was like pissing in the sea: it makes you feel better but you don't raise the water level. Clinton came unhindered by wife or baggage, that's God's truth, so why the fuss? The Yanks are such sensitive violets.'

He takes a drink but not like other people do. When Harry raises the glass it is to drain it. He learnt the knack in the old days when Fleet Street was Fleet Street, when journos had their very own barmaid at the Wig and Pen, when the empty champagne bottles used to be lined up on the bar at El Vino. But he's from the old school that never lets a good lunch get in the way of writing their six hundred words on the latest scandal.

'Mike sends his love, by the way.'

'Mike?' For a moment he looks lost.

'Mike Simmons. Remember? I said he'd given me your number.'

'Of course I remember. Good chap, Mike.'

'A prince,' I agree.

'I had a quick one with him when I was last over there. He had to duck out, go and interview some snotty pop singer.'

'It's what he does, showbiz.'

'Shame really. Here's to Mike.'

We drink.

We are in a bar on the Buda side of the river, near Deli station, almost in the shadow of Castle Hill. The bar is a basic sort of place where locals come to drink. The drinkers grip their glasses as if wary they might be snatched away. We are at a table by the window with a bottle of *Tokaj Furmint* between us, dry with a grapey flavour. Harry called it a 'shy little afternoon tipple'.

We gossip about mutual acquaintances, how was Rosie managing, was Ian Hislop ever mistaken for William Hague, what was life like out in the wilds? I'm closer to London than you are, I remind him. I tell him about the *Old Hag* and Dexter, how for him it is a stepping-stone to London. So what's your editor doing packing you off to Budapest?

Ah, here we are, quite naturally, at the point where I want us to be. In days gone by there was a tradition in Fleet Street that dog don't eat dog, and Harry Bath is old Fleet Street. I trust him not to file about me and my reason for coming. The story of Eve's car in the Danube and only her hand being recovered never saw the light of day – West saw to it – so I tell Harry about that and then about Eve being on the news and the BBC wiping the tape. That's enough to get Harry's eyes focusing.

'Do you believe in resurrection?' he asks.

'No.'

'So she was never dead. Why did the BBC wipe the tape?'

'Orders.'

'Who from?'

I shrug. 'The spies, the pols, the faceless men. No one is meant to know she's alive. It's a secret. So I want to talk to whoever shot that news item. That's my starting point.'

Harry tells me Magyar TV is the outfit that supplies news clips to the BBC. He gives me a name: Pal Pokorni.

'I call him Pee Pee. Get it?'

'I can get my brain round that, yes.'

'He doesn't seem to find that funny. No sense of humour, that's the trouble with Hungarians.'

There's a suggestion that we telephone Pee Pee right now, invite him over for a drink, get the inside stuff from him. I wean Harry away from this, insisting it's not work but personal.

'It's about my *wife*,' I tell him.

When I leave, after copious thanks, a puzzled look has clouded his face. Wife? At the door I look over and raise a hand in farewell. Wife? He still looks baffled.

It's Sunday. Pal Pokorni is not at work today. Magyar TV will not give his home number, not even when I lie and say I am from the BBC. It's urgent, I tell the woman. I hear a rustling over the phone, the rearrangement of an armour-plated corset. No, she says, and cuts the connection. I know the type. She is not a relic from the communist empire but from the much older Habsburg empire. Picture to yourself a stern governess in Victorian England.

Pokorni is not listed in the telephone directory.

Sunday, bloody Sunday.

'Hello Dexter, your roving correspondent calling from abroad. Recognise the voice?'

There is a short silence. 'You're being cautious.'

'With reason.'

'Do you want to tell me?'

'Tell you and who else?' I say.

'We live in a democracy, you know.'

'So I've been told.'

Silence again.

'Well, if you're going to spill your problems, go ahead,' he says.

'Dexter, my problems are your problems. Some thug came to check on me at the *OH* and I had to lock him in your office. He may have had a tantrum and broken his way out.'

'Indeed so,' Dexter says. His voice is distant, like an echo. 'We'll talk about that when you get back.'

'There's more,' I battle on. 'My passport was stolen. Also I had lunch with an embassy man today and he was putting up a smokescreen.'

'Interesting.'

Interesting? Is that all he has to say?

'You mean like the old Chinese curse: May you live in interesting times.'

'All right, my turn.' Ah, now we're getting to it. Call me mystic but to my ears Dexter's voice changes, tightens, provides no chink where a dissenting word might slip in. 'Some toad in London telephoned this morning. Sunday, mark you, since when did toads work on Sundays? He propositioned me. Not, Come to bed darling, not quite. It wasn't exactly laid out as a proposition but that is what it was. The department was setting up a working party to advise on how the regional press could be used more effectively to promote official policies. I didn't quite catch which department this was. Apparently it was held – who was doing the holding also a mystery – that one possibility for explaining policy initiatives more fully would be to have informal seminars in places away from the pressures of daily life. Naturally there would be varied facilities for relaxation. My imagination may have gone into overdrive but I believe the varied facilities were blonde, red head or Afro according to taste. This was really exciting, the toad informed me, because it meant I was becoming known in official circles and other committees would follow. Also, he could tell me in strictest confidence, a significant change in official policy was being mooted – lovely word – to bring youth to the fore in such bodies as the Press Council and the Arts Council. Suddenly I am a youth.'

'What did you say?'

'I would have to think very carefully about what he proposed. So I thought carefully for two seconds and interrupted his flow about the duty we owed our country and I said No. He broke off. What did you say? I said No, you can't bribe me to keep quiet.'

'That was well said.' I feel warmly towards Dexter, which is stupid of me.

'Are you making progress?' he asks.

'Tomorrow.'

'Keep me informed. I'll need to contact you so where are you staying?'

I tell him the hotel. I still have a warm feeling towards Dexter and I even tell him I am registered under the name Fazekas.

We all make mistakes.

A dubious meal, a restless night, a bright morning that promises spring is waking up. Daffodils are coming into bloom. In Oxford they've been out for a month.

'You know the Korzo?' Pal Pokorni says.

'Where the whores walk up and down?'

'So you know them? Not during the day. Be there about ten.'

'What's the name of the café?'

'No café,' he says. 'I'll be outside.'

'Mingling with the whores?'

'Yeah, right.'

'How do I recognise you?' I ask.

But I've had my fifteen seconds of his time and he's hung up. I should have realised our meeting was going to be a scene written by an absurdist playwright.

When I arrive I find the ladies of the night have risen early. Look at their footwear first. Some wear high leather boots, others sport stiletto heels and straps crisscrossing up their calves, one has a pair of pink rubber wellies. Now raise your eyes. When did you last see skirts so short? One has those tight slacks that end just below the knee and were known as pedal pushers when they were first in fashion. There is a gaggle of the girls sharing cigarettes with three of Budapest's finest in uniform. Out in the river a launch idles with its nose pointing upstream. On its side and roof is painted Rendőrség. Haven't I told you already that Hungarian is a crazy language? Would you know that means Police?

There is a group of the curious, passers-by, shoppers, mothers with push-chairs, boys with skinhead haircuts who should be at school, men with red-veined noses and white stubble on their cheeks, one distinguished old gentleman in a well-pressed suit, white shirt, tie with a gold tie-pin – and brown felt slippers. It's all very Budapest. The cops and the girls and the TV camera have drawn them. Pal Pokorni is talking to one of the whores – I know it is him. His head turns in my direction and he knows it is me. In Hungary there is an aura about me which I cannot see but others can, that says I may have Hungarian roots and speak the language but I am not one of them because I have not lived through what they have.

He comes over and shakes my hand.

'Pokorni,' he says.

'Fazekas,' I say, and add, 'Bazil.'

'Pal,' he says.

We shake hands a second time. Even the informality is formal. I guess he is in his late forties but they look as if they've been hard years: his eyes have seen too much, his nose has dipped into too many rotten secrets, his ears have heard too many whispered betrayals. Could it be me if my parents hadn't escaped the accursed forty years?

'What's this about?' I ask in Hungarian.

'Watch. You're just in time.' He makes a point of replying in English, putting me in my place as a foreigner.

Pal – think Paul – walks back to the camera operator as there is a ripple in the little crowd and arms lift to point. What I see is quite extraordinary. Across the Danube, up on top of the hill by the old Royal Palace, there is a flutter like washing blowing in the wind. Something is moving, coming this way. It shows in the sky above the National Gallery but I can't make it out. Is it a giant bat? No. A kite? No. The perspective changes as it drops lower and I make out a figure, a hang glider, aiming towards us. The hang glider clears the river, the police launch, the embankment, the tram lines and makes a running landing on the Korzo to some scattered applause. It is a woman who struggles out of the harness. She is dressed in a shimmering silver catsuit and has long blonde tresses. Yes, tresses. Maybe the word sounds over the top but there is a theatrical glitz to that hair. The camera focuses on her while Pal steps forward for the interview. I can't hear what he asks or what she replies because the ladies of the night have set up a chant.

'Hungarian girls for Hungarian men! Hungarian girls for Hungarian men!'

The police look bemused but not unhappy as the whores link arms with them.

'Hungarian girls for Hungarian men!'

Then, in the way of media events, the chanting comes to an abrupt halt, the girls drop their arms from the police and Pal, after a word with the cameraman, bustles over to me. I raise an eyebrow.

'Just a stunt, good for the early news,' he says. I look at the silver-suited blonde, at the retreating whores, at the police getting in their car, and he takes my silence as a rebuke. 'OK, so it's not your great Jeremy Paxman. We're a small-time outfit and everybody has to piss in the pot.' The launch has turned and is powering away downstream. 'The floozies wanted Bertalan – that's the silver bird – to come down right in front of parliament so they could lobby some of their best customers but that was vetoed. He'd have got shot as a security threat. Here is close enough.'

'Bertalan?' I turn to look at the silvery figure. With the blonde wig taken off, seductive female features have turned into a man with wolfish eyes and a dangerous edge to his grin.

'Bertalan's a real pro.'

'What's it about?'

'A protest against foreign prostitutes. Whores from Russia and Romania are undercutting our girls.'

'I thought you said the whores weren't here during the day.'

'I lied.' He has his own wolfish look about him. 'I wanted to surprise you. I wanted you to experience in one beautiful image just where our country is now. For forty years we had pricks who fucked us up. Now the cunts say it is their turn. So welcome to Hungary. Have a nice day. Then go home.'

The Korzo has gone back to its daytime parade of men with mobile phones and women with shopping bags. Look at the lamps, trees and café tables through half-closed eyes and it is elegant enough. Bertalan in his catsuit and the chanting whores were just a mirage.

'You're not from the BBC,' Pal says. 'That's what you told the office.'

'I lied,' I say. 'I wanted to surprise you.'

I am watching his reaction and for a second I see a different Pal Pokorni, not the TV journalist but the self that gets hidden away. He is not angry at my little duplicity. On the contrary it confirms his deepest feelings – that the outside world will always deceive a Hungarian, cheat him out of his birthright. He was doing exactly the same to me? Bah, that doesn't count. As a Hungarian he had to trick me just to keep even. The look was no more than a flash in his eyes and a lip twitching. Then he nods. I thought I might get a smile out of him but you can twiddle your thumbs for a week in Budapest and not see a smile.

'So what are you?'

'Press,' I tell him.

'What's the story?'

'I'm not here for a story. I'm trying to find my wife.'

'She ran away from you?'

'I…' Well, I stop. When Dexter said a couple of nights ago that I didn't know Eve it wounded me. Now the idea that she ran away from me causes another stab of pain.

'Look,' Pal says, 'I'm not the missing persons bureau. I'm a TV reporter.'

'That's why I want to talk to you.'

From my wallet I dig out the photo of Eve I always carry. It's not a studio portrait but one I took one sunny Sunday afternoon last August when we went punting on the Cherwell. She was doing all the work while I crouched in front of her with the camera. She is not smiling but her face is full of life and beauty and strength. I love her for that. I love looking at the photo though recently, I mean in the last forty-eight hours, I have studied it and found no serenity in her features nor, I confess to myself, any real happiness. The effort she put into punting left no room for happiness to show, it must be that. We tied up the punt and went into a meadow for a picnic. Ants carried off our crumbs as if they had been waiting all their lives for this moment. Pigeons billed and cooed in the trees and butterflies did a swooping mating dance. Encouraged by nature we made love. She took the lead, with a hand under my T-shirt, and then unbuckling my belt. Afterwards we lay back, sheltered by the weeping willows, and listened to the sounds of the river. Another punt passed slowly upstream, an ancient wind-up gramophone with a horn speaker playing *La Donna è mobile*, a man wearing a boater punting, his lady in a frilly frock trailing her fingers in the water, a bottle of champagne in an ice bucket just visible. Who were they? It was the long vacation so undergraduates seemed unlikely. 'Posers,' Eve murmured. 'Aren't we all?' I said, don't ask me why. Eve turned her head to study me but didn't reply.

Pal holds the photo for a few seconds before shaking his head. 'I don't know her.' He studies her again. 'But I'd like to.'

'You filmed her.'

'I don't remember.'

'It was on the BBC news last Thursday evening. Just over there.' I point across the river to a spot near the Chain Bridge, at the bottom of the Castle Hill cliff from where the hang glider launched himself. 'You were trying to interview a man and – '

Pal is suddenly on his feet and making swift horizontal sweeps with both hands, the film world's sign to cut. At a café thirty metres away I spot the TV cameraman. I hadn't noticed we were being recorded, too bound up with Pal and the photo of Eve and memories.

Pal has never handed the photo back. He studies it closely before giving it to me. 'I still don't know her but the news story, that is something else.' He takes out his cigarettes and lights one. 'My life was threatened after that story. I got a recorded message on my answerphone at home. It was: If you do that again…' He raises his hand to make a pistol and points two fingers at his temple. 'Bang! They actually fired off a pistol to make it more realistic. I didn't know why you asked to see me so I wanted a record of this meeting. Then, when you said what it was about, I didn't want a record.'

He wears a blouson. Clipped to the zippered edge is the green and white lapel pin of FTC, the football club. He snatches the lapel pin off. The tricks of another person's trade are fascinating: with wiring leading to a battery this is a miniaturised radio mike which he stuffs into a pocket.

'What's her name?' he asks.

'Eve.'

'Eva,' he says, instantly turning her Hungarian. 'Do you believe that old Biblical story of Eva giving Adam the apple? Eva the seductress? Innocence lost?'

It's a myth, everybody knows that. It was made up by frightened men, devastated by their sexual needs and the hold women had over them. Look here, God, they pleaded, don't go blaming us for our sins, it's all the fault of woman the temptress. Pal and I could have a glass or two one evening discussing that, but not now. I shrug.

82

'Don't be offended,' Pal says, 'but you do have to wonder about the nature of the relationship your Eva has with this guy.'

I make a pause while Pal inspects the tip of his cigarette rather than me. This is it, the first real step towards tracking down my wife. A frown draws Pal's brows together. I hesitate, I confess I do, before asking for the truth.

'Who is he?'

Pal draws on his cigarette then flicks it away, half-smoked. 'Goenz, Gyula Goenz.'

Goenz. Well, have you heard of him? The name means nothing to me.

Pal lifts his eyes to my face. 'Mafia,' he says, and watches for my reaction.

'Mafia? *Mafia?*'

Everyone knows about the Mafia. Its birthplace is Sicily, in Naples it's called the Camorra, further south it's the Ndrangheta. We've read about the five Mafia families who carved up New York. They're more than slum gangs, they are organised. They have a *capo* and soldiers and rules and punishments. They are all over mainland Europe, separate until the bosses get together to agree a share-out of the rackets – drugs, arms, blackmail, protection, usury, corruption, smuggling, prostitution. We all know this up here, in our heads. But I know down here in my guts that Eve is not part of the Mafia. Can't be. It's not in her DNA. End of story. I am shaking my head in rejection.

'Well, she's your wife,' Pal says, 'but you asked the question.'

'What was the story?' I ask. 'What were you trying to interview Goenz about?'

Pal lights another cigarette, taking his time over it, frowning, tapping off non-existent ash, casting a long look round the Korzo.

'There has been friction in Budapest between Goenz and Arpad Hamori, leaders of two rival clans, you understand, with their families reaching out into the provinces. Last year the rivalry became murderous. Three bombs were planted in restaurants. People said it was because the restaurants weren't paying protection to the right mob. Then in November there was a fourth bomb, in a bar where a government minister was relaxing. There are bars and bars, you know, and this was definitely one of the more interesting ones. Then a thousand theories bloomed. Hungarians are world champions at theories. No doubt about it.' He pokes his cigarette at me. 'For instance, the minister was bringing a message from the government, or the minister being inside the bar was pure coincidence, or the minister was having a bit of fun, or the minister was gathering evidence of racketeering, or the minister was there for his own pay-off. Me, my theory is that the minister was in the pay of Goenz's outfit and that Hamori wanted him dead. See? Corruption at the heart of the government. Things have been quiet all winter, no more theories, just a rumour that the two Mafia families had decided to work together.'

'What's the difference between a theory and a rumour?'

'A theory is what intellectuals have and it vanishes like smoke.'

Pal waves his cigarette in the air and brushes away the smoke in case I haven't got it.

'And a rumour?'

'A rumour is a theory with balls. So what is there to back up this rumour? What is big enough to bring these two families together and share the spoils? Last week, by chance, I came across Goenz over there,' he nods over the river, 'so I asked him straight out. Simple as that. I never took in the woman standing at his shoulder. I was concentrating on Goenz, what he would say. I never got an answer, or rather I got the answer later to shut my mouth or have it shut for me. I was told there would be no second warning.'

Again he raises his hand as a pistol but this time the fingers point straight between my eyes.

'I've no idea what your Eva was doing there, what her part is. Now if you will excuse me,' he says with that abrupt Hungarian politeness that means too bad if you don't, 'I must go and edit that very important piece about Hungarian tarts for Hungarian men.'

'Wait.' A dozen questions need answering.

No use. There is an urgency about the way he hustles off. Could be it's not just work that beckons but a need to get away from me. A few paces off he does turn back as if to say something. No. He raises his hand like a pistol and points it at my face again.

'Bang,' he mouths.

CHAPTER 8

Down by the Chain Bridge you'll find a statue called Kilometre Zero. Miklós Borsos got the commission for the job. He was a sculptor. He must have scratched his head while he searched for inspiration. Nothing. He must have scratched his head again. Still nothing. Then inspiration struck. It's Nothing. So there it is. The statue is three metres high. It shows a mighty '0'. It rests on a cube marked KM. That's it. Well done, Miklos. I wonder how much his cheque was. All distances in Hungary are measured from this point.

I have a contrary thought. You take the road to Budapest, in through the suburbs, right to the centre of the city. You arrive at this spot and what do you find? A big nothing at the heart of the country. That's symbolism for you, a very Hungarian way of viewing life today.

I do what a reporter does at the scene of an incident. Eyes first. Then brain. Best of all imagination. I work out what happened. Skirting the shrubs I walk a few paces towards the Danube, looking at the lay-out of the bridge and the roads. In my head I have the framing of the shot that Pal took. Here – to catch the car driving off to cross the Chain Bridge. Upstream is the Parliament Building. Goenz and Eve were standing where? Just there. The car was waiting to pick them up, causing a hell of a nuisance to the traffic, but Goenz wouldn't give a damn. So where had Eve and Goenz come from? Not along the road beside the river or the car would have gone to meet them.

I turn slowly, my back to the river. Now I face Castle Hill. My eyes go up and up. Tiny figures at the top are leaning over the wall.

My eyes come down again and stop at the entrance to the *Siklo*, the funicular. Castle Hill has a vast palace, museums, churches, a Hilton Hotel, restaurants, cafés, shops. It also has a number of houses, grand ones. Makes you think, doesn't it.

Goenz and Eve could have come down in the funicular to where the car and driver were waiting and been spotted by Pal who just happened to be passing. Snatched moments with a camera are every TV reporter's dream.

Spring sun is fickle. Sudden heavy showers drive me back to my hotel to collect my stubby umbrella and I am standing by the window – is that patch of blue sky headed this way? – when the telephone rings. I stare at it. No one knows I am staying at the Ibis Styles. Correction: I told Dexter. So when I answer I am taken aback when it is the clipped tones of West in my ear.

'Ah Potter, splendid. Glad I caught you at home, as it were.'

'How did you know where I was staying?'

'What?' He sounds perplexed. 'You must have told me, I suppose.'

'You suppose? I hadn't got a hotel when we met.' At least not one I told him about.

'Hang on, you're right. To be honest, old chap, I have no idea. I just asked Susan to get you on the phone. Tremendously efficient, Susan, and resourceful. That's what I ask in a Girl Friday. I wouldn't be surprised if she rang round the hotels until one said: Hold on, we're putting you through.'

'She started with the Gellert, then the Kempinski, the Grand – '

'That sort of thing. And here you are. Well done.'

A slightly superior tone of voice. Well done me for being here. Well done Susan for tracking me down. He's lying.

'I wonder if you could pop round to the shop,' West says.

'Pop round?'

'Yes. Why not come round now and we could have a spot of… no, hang on, there's some wretched trade thing I have to attend, warm Riesling and salmonella tart. After lunch then. That do you?'

'Is this to do with Eve?'

He pauses a beat. 'Matters appertaining. Three-ish shall we say?'

Have you looked at your passport recently? The opening page declares, 'Her Britannic Majesty's Secretary of State Requests and Requires…' Her Britannic Majesty's representative on earth has just required. When West hangs up I discover I am standing to attention.

A memory hits me, of going to Gerbaud with Eve. 'It's a setting for an opera,' I said, looking round, 'gilt and chandeliers and a chorus of waitresses.'

'And my jealous husband is hiding behind the velvet drapes,' she said.

'But I'm your husband,' I said.

Her attention had switched to the menu, running a finger down the list of pastries. 'I'll have *dobos torta* and *zserbo*.' She looked at me, raising an eyebrow. 'One is never enough.'

Was she talking about pastries?

A cream puff's throw away from Gerbaud is Her Britannic Majesty's embassy. Metal hurdles have turned the street into a cul-de-sac. The building is the colour of mayonnaise, four storeys high, empire style though not the British empire. Two windows on the third floor are boarded up. That must be where they keep the secrets. I am collected at Reception and escorted by a pleasant woman in a floral frock and a diamanté brooch.

'Are you Susan?' I ask.

She considers the question for security implications. 'Yes.' Her voice keeps its distance.

'I like the flowers on your dress. Very spring-like. What are they?'

She lifts one plump sleeve to study it. 'Daisies,' she decides. 'Bachelor's Buttons. Daddy used to grow them.' She gives me a motherly smile.

I do not think West is bedding her.

'How did you – '

Too late. I was just moving on to how she tracked me down to the Ibis Styles where I'm registered under the name Fazekas when she ushers me through a secretarial office straight into the presence. West rises in his chair to greet me.

'Well done,' he says. And to Susan, 'Do you think you could rustle up some tea for us? Thank you.' He gives me a vague smile. I get it. He doesn't want to talk about Eve in front of the servants. 'Do you know that *tea* is the only English word in the Hungarian food and drink vocabulary? Oh, I suppose you do.'

I say nothing and West ploughs on.

'It is extraordinary what one nation borrows linguistically from another. I was in Warsaw under the old regime and went to a Solidarity rally. The speaker used the English word *strike* half a dozen times. It was as if the Polish word didn't have the proper impact.'

I glance round the office. It's anonymous, two metal filing cabinets, Constable prints behind glass, a desk that is bare except for a couple of telephones. Oh, and a framed photo of a woman in pearls and twinset. Must be his wife, off to meet the Queen.

'It was as if the Poles had never had a real strike. It needed English workers to teach them.'

He smiles again, hoping I will join him. Susan brings in two cups of tea. West sips his. It's too hot. Now there is nothing more to delay him so he must start.

'When we met yesterday you stood up abruptly and left the restaurant which was…' He hesitates. Rude? But West is a diplomat. '…a sign of how upset you were. You felt you had not been dealt with in an open and straightforward manner.'

'Yes.' I meant to say nothing but the word slips out.

'I was in two minds whether to tell you this yesterday, what I am going to tell you now.'

This inelegant syntax brings a frown to West's face. He pauses. How can he go on? He regroups his thoughts. Strange – it suddenly hits me – neither a smile nor a frown seems to come naturally. His face is a blank.

'If I didn't tell you yesterday it was solely out of concern for you. You were troubled, disturbed. You still are today, and angry with me. If I don't tell you, you will stay troubled and upset. But if I do tell you, you will be hurt, terribly hurt. See my dilemma?'

After this confused ramble he looks at me hopefully. I say nothing. What's he talking about?

He has a sip of tea, frowns and takes a breath. 'Some months ago Eve formed an attachment with a man here. This is one of the dangers when one spouse is *en poste* and the other spouse remains in the UK.'

'Just a minute.' I am having trouble with my hearing. What he said was *attaché*. Of course, that's it. She's become some sort of *attaché*. Or did he say attachment, something to be fastened? Meaning a bond. Such as fidelity. A bond of affection. Can infidelity be a bond? It takes a second for this nonsense to ricochet round my head. My world rocks and now it steadies. 'An attachment? You mean Eve had an affair?'

For once I get a plain reply. 'Yes.'

'She had a lover? My wife? Is that it?'

A rare expression flits across West's face, a grimace drawing his brows into a sort of knot. 'Sorry but there it is. There's never any way to break this kind of news gently.'

He stops. His gaze is fixed on me like an interrogator waiting for a scream for mercy. I have a mental block. Not Eve, no no no. Pal Pokorni raised it – that TV clip, the nature of the relationship, even hinted that Eve could have been the seductress. Never. I cannot accept it. The silence has gone on long enough in West's view.

'Most attachments – and I have seen a number in the cities I have been posted to – are to someone within the diplomatic community. These are the people one sees most often. They are intelligent. They come from one's own social *milieu*, it is an artificial life we lead anyway.'

Eve with a lover. West's voice is a drone and my imagination begins its subversive work. Eve kissing. Eve naked. Eve stretched out on a bed with another man touching her. I lean back and back, tilting my chair, staring above West's head. I see Eve astride the stranger. I see Eve panting with her mouth open. West's voice comes from a distance. He's talking about the six psychological stages. He's talking gibberish. Eve is not a psychological stage. Eve is my wife. Now it's emotional reversal… emotional reversal? What does that mean? His voice fades. Instead I hear Eve explain *We don't have to bother with the coffee*. I see Eve's face, my English Eve, full of life and beauty and strength as she punts, full of passion as we roll over on the grass under the weeping willow, full of love and intensity, full of me. Her face is not clear but misted, then it is red as if blood has washed over it, or blood has exploded inside my head.

'Potter? Are you all right?'

I am on all fours, head hanging low towards the carpet like a dog that has been beaten. I study the carpet. Best government-issue grey. I don't understand how I am here. Must have tipped over the chair. West puts his hands under my armpits to haul me up but I shrug his help away. His touch is repellent. He has brought terrible news. Bit by bit, using the chair and the desk as handholds, I clamber upright and sit down again.

'It's a mercy about the carpet.' His voice is soothing. 'You gave your head quite a nasty – '

'Who is he?'

West has gone back to his chair and is leaning over his desk to inspect me. 'He is not someone from the diplomatic world.'

'So who is he?'

'This is not a route we should go down.'

'His name. You can't go this far and just clam up.'

It is like drawing teeth. West does not want to go further.

'All right,' I say. 'I'll give you a name and you tell me – '

'*No*. Don't say any more. I am not denying or confirming anything.'

'What? I don't believe what I'm hearing. You have known or

suspected for months – so you say – and you've never said anything to me. Why wasn't I told? Why was I lied to? Why are you keeping me in the dark now?'

Anger has overwhelmed me. No, rage. I am on my feet. I have the urge to attack West but the way he scrambles up and slips a hand inside his jacket makes me pause. What is that hand reaching for? Can he have a gun in there? I can't believe he does. And yet… There is a calculating look that I haven't seen on his face before. His posting is diplomatic but what is his background?

'Why wasn't I told?' I am leaning over his desk to scream at him but it comes out as a whisper. I sound desperate.

There'd been a hint of war in the air but it passes. We both sit back in our chairs.

'Tell me,' I insist.

'I wish you had been told,' he says. Part of me wants to believe him and part of me says he is lying. 'Once one starts down the path of deception it's difficult to stop. I was Eve's boss and I told her the affair had to stop, he's a big time criminal, such conduct cannot be tolerated. You're in Her Majesty's diplomatic service. I was too pompous. She said, Don't give me that crap – '

'Just a minute.' I think of Pal Pokorni. I think of his arm raised towards me, two fingers pointing in my face like a gun. 'You mean he's a gangster, some Mafia *capo*?'

There's the suspicion of a nod, a sort of agreement. 'Eve called him a businessman who supplied what people wanted. I couldn't believe my ears, making him sound like a trader in Heinz baked beans. I actually said this and she laughed, as if I was making some sort of joke.' There is disapproval in his voice. 'I am your direct superior, I said, and I am warning you that you cannot keep your position in the diplomatic service if you continue with this liaison. And do you know what?'

This is my Eve he is talking about? And there is more? 'Go on, tell me.'

'She stormed out.'

He glances at the door, waiting to hear the bang as she slams it shut.

'Why wasn't I told about this?'

'You should have been. I sincerely believe that.' He leans towards me over the desk with his hands together. 'But then there was Eve's car found in the Danube, crashed through the barrier, and she was gone. Dead. Don't pile on the agony, I was advised, poor fellow's had enough of a shock. Don't break the news about the affair as well. It will do no good. It'll just sully the memory of his wife.'

'So you went along with this, keeping me in the dark until now.'

He purses his lips, pondering his response.

'Listen. In the Foreign Office there are orders and then there is how you actually do the job. People who sit behind desks in Whitehall don't know what's happening at the sharp end.'

The twists and turns of this conversation leave me baffled.

'You mean you used your own initiative.'

'Precisely.'

'So before you were obeying orders and now you are out in front on your own.'

'The know-alls in London were scared witless because you were a journalist. That strikes terror into their hearts. If they have them.'

'I'm a journalist… They thought I would file a story about my own wife having it off with some big hoodlum.'

He flips his hand over, a gesture of exasperation.

'All right,' I say. There is still the matter of his identity. Pal Pokorni had no doubt but I want it from West. 'Who is the Mafia boss? You know so give me his name.'

West shakes his head. 'I've gone as far as I can, further than I should have because I think you have a right to know.'

'But I won't know if you don't answer me. All right, I'll give you a name.'

'No.' He claps his hands over his ears. 'I'm not listening.'

He ducks his head down so he isn't even looking. After a long silence I slap the desk in front of him. Startled, he looks up.

'If any of this conversation finds its way into print,' he says, 'I'll be out on my ear and probably lose my pension. I can't give you a name because the London people are afraid of libel. Me, I'd be frightened for my life.'

'You talk of London people – Lovegrove you mean?'

'Apparently Lovegrove thought you were behaving like a reptile. That was his word.'

'What?'

'You wanted a bribe to keep quiet.'

Jesus Christ, I can take no more. I push out of my chair so abruptly it falls over.

'He doesn't have a high opinion of the media,' West says.

'Lovegrove lied and tried to trick me. What do you think my opinion is of him?'

'What are you doing?' West says. 'Look, go back home, pick up the pieces of your life. I can only apologise this matter was kept from you.'

'Apologise?' I start for the door then turn back. 'Eve is alive. I saw her on television.'

'Potter, her car – '

'Whose hand was found in the car?'

'Hers.'

'That's what I was meant to think. Right, we'll see.'

'What do you mean? What are you going to do? Baz, come back.'

He's used my first name. He must be desperate. I don't slam the door. I don't even close it.

I am passing Susan's desk. She looks up from the *Telegraph* cross-word but doesn't speak.

There's a telephone not far from the embassy. It is mounted on a wall with Perspex sides for privacy. I glance back. I am not being followed unless West has hired a gang of teenage girls. I can hear the faint ring of the phone in far away England. The ringing stops.

'What is it?' A snappy, out of sorts voice.

'Listen carefully,' I say. 'Are you speaking on a mobile?'

In the background in far away England I hear subdued male voices and the sound of hammering. Here the gaggle of schoolgirls has just bought ice creams and they're strolling towards me across Vörösmarty Square.

'What the hell are you – '

'Answer me,' I cut in. Remember Mr Manners. 'Please.'

There is a pause, not surely while Dexter checks his phone but while he considers whether to fire me now or when I return.

'I am holding the phone at the moment as far as the flex will stretch. That banging – hear it? A couple of Oxford's finest craftsmen were persuaded to put down their cans of lager and come to fix the door in my office. No, no, please, gentlemen,' his voice grows distant, speaking off the handset, 'you carry on, don't mind me.'

'But the phone on the desk back home in your study – that's cordless, right? You like to prowl round while you talk and I'm surprised you haven't got one at the office.'

'So am I. I'll order one. What is this?'

'People have listened in. Special Branch, security people, freelances, I don't know.'

'Phone tapping needs a minister's signature or a close approximation. Of course it can be done outside the law, we know that. What's going on?'

'With a mobile it may not be legal but it's easier. Think of hacking the phones of the politicians and celebs and all that mess.'

One of those fine Oxford craftsmen is whistling while he works. Dexter is considering what I've said.

'I bet there's a white van parked round the corner by your house, listening to every secret you spill. Has to be. I was contacted here by the embassy. It's possible they rang all the hotels until they reached mine – though that is stretching it – but they wouldn't know what name I was using. Someone overheard me tell you and passed it on. I've told no one else.'

'Welcome to 1984,' Dexter says. 'Orwell just got the date wrong.'

'Here's the news.' I'm no more than the newsreader, my voice disembodied, my words dead, reciting facts, leaving out adjectives. 'Man at the embassy called West was Eve's boss. He says Eve was having an affair with a Mafia chief. The Foreign Office is desperate to avoid scandal. They've kept me in the dark because I'm a journalist and they're scared I might make a splash in the *Herald*.'

'Hmm, well,' I can hear the lift in Dexter's voice 'it's starting to sound promising.'

'Jesus.'

I cut the connection. A couple of the schoolgirls glance over at me. One girl, swelling out of childhood, fixes her eyes on me. She gives her ice cream cone a slow lick.

The French have a phrase *chasse-cousin* for a wine of such mouth-puckering awfulness that a free-loading cousin who has been outstaying his welcome will take one sip and go upstairs to pack his bags. In Hungary cousins are made of sterner stuff, in particular my cousin Jozsef. He is my father's brother's son, so we are both Fazekas. He is six years older than me. You can see the family resemblance except his face is a little roughed up. The early years of his working life were spent on the street. He is a police inspector 'but I don't deal in parking tickets – my work is national stuff.' Make of that what you will. I met him when I came after Eve's accident and Jozsef arrived at my hotel at breakfast time. I was staying at the Astoria which is used to the ways of journalists and cops so his order of *szilvapalinka* at that hour raised no eyebrows. This is plum brandy - 'to give the coffee bite', he said.

Today we meet at the Kempinski, handy for the embassy and police quarters. Jozsef chooses a discreet table in the bar. For me a coffee, for Jozsef a beer. On the telephone I'd stressed it was important so social chit-chat is kept to a minimum. I've learnt that once you start on family gossip there is no stopping. But it is polite to enquire after his wife Adel (to which he growls, 'Don't ask') and his mother (his father was a hero of 1956 and in Hungary all heroes are dead). Then, with a signal to the barman for another beer, his eyes settle on my face.

'You appear in Budapest, you telephone that you have a problem, so I assume it is woman trouble. Or is it to do with the late Eva?'

'She's not dead,' I say. 'She never was.'

Jozsef sighs, and not with relief. It is the sigh of a man whose working life is spent dealing with criminals, liars, bureaucrats, politicians, con men and friends of the rich and powerful. And now me, family. I tell him the story, pared to highlights, from seeing Eve on the TV news to West saying this is impossible because she is dead, then changing this to saying she was having an affair with a criminal he won't name but a TV journalist says is Gyula Goenz.

So what effect does the name Goenz have on this police inspector?

Answer: his face is a mask of serenity.

Do you remember when you were at school and played that game of outstaring another kid? Jozsef and I are two kids, but never try to outstare a cop. Finally I look down into my cup though there is no coffee left.

He says, 'Goenz, eh?' He says it as if there is nothing more to say but of course there is. 'If your lady was going to choose a bastard she certainly picked the top one. Bazil, you should be proud of her. What do you know about Goenz?'

I feel a mix of emotions: protective of Eve but sick in my stomach if she is involved with Goenz. All I do is shrug.

'In England you have criminal gangs and fine upstanding fellows they are as one would expect of a country that used to be landlord of a quarter of the world. Tell me, what's your population? Sixty million? Sixty-five? Your gangs are outnumbered. Now Hungary is a small country so a criminal can exert much more leverage. There are fewer people you need to frighten, fewer to beat up, fewer to bribe. Also, when the old regime vanished this left something of a vacuum. You could no longer get a shitface in the Party to fix something for you – a licence, a business deal, a building project – so Goenz and his like stepped in. Give him the nod and he'll send a couple of his boys round to be persuasive. Or a couple of girls. The girls are the worst.'

I wait but Jozsef is quiet about the girls and what they do.

'When are you flying back to England?' he asks.

'I'm not. Or not yet.'

'How can I persuade you to? Goenz is bad news.'

'Eve is my wife.' Or she was but I keep that dark thought to myself.

'Try to understand, Bazil, that is not the perspective Goenz has. Goenz sees her as his woman, if what you say is true. That's assuming she's still alive. However if Goenz has killed her…' He makes a sour face.

'But I saw her on TV.'

'That was last week.' He tips his beer from side to side, watching the foam slide down the glass. Doubts niggle at me. Damn him, he knew I'd start to worry. He's using police tactics on me. Jozsef raises an eyebrow then goes on. 'Goenz has never been a problem I've had to deal with, nor his organisation. He has simply not been in my area of responsibility. For that I offer thanks. I drink a toast to whatever devil has me in his care.' He drains his glass. 'However, with a heavy heart I'll see what I can find out. I mean, why for God's sake should Eva fall for him? You're only my young cousin but you're not too bad.'

Is that praise?

I'll walk back to my hotel. It'll calm the dangerous chaos in my head. I hope. I keep replaying what Jozsef said. *If your lady was going to choose a bastard she certainly picked the top one.* How could she? My wife is not like that. *Goenz sees her as his woman.* Jozsef is more than a sceptic, he is a cynic. I had to pay for his beers too. He said an honest police inspector couldn't afford Kempinski prices.

I walk down the Korzo and cut in from the river to go down Vaci utca. In the accursed forty years this had been called the Bond Street of Budapest but the Hungarian sense of humour has always been a bit strange. I skirt the market, take an alley or two and eventually arrive at my hotel. I want to go up to my room, lie on the bed and think about what I have decided to do. In Váci utca, between displays of painted plastic eggs and T-shirts and peasant smocks only a matron from Milwaukee would wear, I found a shop that sold pot plants and cut flowers and garden tools and made my purchase. But I still need to spend some time planning.

I take the lift to the third floor, unlock the door and know even as I step into the tiny entrance hall that there's someone in the bedroom. I smell cigarette smoke. At this point a rational person would back out into the corridor and go for help but after the rollercoaster of the last four days I have taken leave of my senses. The door into the bedroom is ajar, allowing me a view of the end of the bed. I creep closer, peek round the doorframe and see a figure stretched out. Outside it is dusk, in here it is gloom but I can make out the shape, the hip, the contours of a woman. My heart jumps, a flash of light bursts in my head, I feel a surge of optimism. She's returned, it was all a misunderstanding, Eve has come back, she'll explain everything. I stumble over a pair of shoes, hurrying to sweep her up and embrace her, and come to an abrupt halt. For the second time this afternoon rage explodes in me.

'Out! Out! Get out!'

She scrambles off the bed in alarm. I have been shouting in Hungarian.

'Who let you in? Why are you following me? How did you know where to come? What do you want from me?'

Dear God.

CHAPTER 9

Her eyes are like a cat's, big and round, catching a glint from a street-lamp. One arm is raised across her breasts to fend off an attack. She takes a step back, fumbles with the bedside lamp and switches it on.

'Why are you here?'

'Why do you bloody think?' It is Mary Monroe recovered from her moment of panic.

'Tell me.'

'Dexter sent me. Sexy Dexy in one of his Napoleon-deploying-the-cavalry moods. Dexter says you need support. Dexter says this is going to be much more than your personal crusade and he wants pix. Dexter says he has a nose for this kind of thing and his nose is twitching.'

Dexter sees not just a national story but an international one. Dexter sees the big time like a glorious sunrise. Dexter Dexter Dexter, his name like a machine gun rattle.

'How did you get in my room?'

'Easy peasy. That dishy black guy in Reception – know who I mean? Turns out he's French, from sexy Martinique. Hey, I've been on holiday there, I said, so we had a friendly natter. I told him I was your fiancée and I wanted to surprise you so he gave me a key.'

'Just like that? Jesus, that's some security.'

'Well, thank you for your enthusiasm. Don't worry, I told him I was saving myself for our wedding night so I've got a room a couple of floors up. Fuck you, Potter, you know how to make a girl feel welcome.'

Mary – aka Two Boobs but not in her presence – glowers. She stomps off to the bathroom and I hear the sound of a running tap. Mary is a snapper and they are all foul-mouthed. They spend too much time on the street. When she comes back her face is damp from the water she has splashed on it but we are both calmer.

'Baz, you are so amazingly knotted up inside. You're going to give yourself an ulcer or explode or start molesting small boys. Come on, let's go out and get pissed. Charge it up to Dexter.'

Do you happen to own a vaulted cellar in Budapest? Then here's the thing to do: open a restaurant. The food is not memorable but the service is attentive. This is the effect that Mary has on waiters. We drink *olasz rizling* while I tell her what has happened. We sit facing each other across the table, a candle to one side with a flame that dances whenever the door to the street opens. Mary fidgets with the stem of her wine glass and when I reach the end of my saga she drains the glass and fills it up again.

'So Eve's been having a tumble with a crook. Why? For kicks?'

I have no answer.

'And your policeman cousin suspects he may have bumped her off,' she continues. 'Is that it?'

'It's not possible because I saw her on TV.'

'But how about since then?'

I frown.

'Anyway, wasn't her hand found in her car?'

Again when I don't reply her eyes drop to the chair beside me where I have put the carrier bag with my purchase. I haven't explained the bag.

'Baz, I think you still love her.'

Do I? Can I love someone and then feel revulsion half an hour later? And still love her? Do we ever make sense of emotions? No. Emotions are beyond rational explanation. Why am I treating this like a university tutorial while Mary is staring at me?

'She has hurt me,' I say. 'She has ignored me. She has tricked me.'

'But you still love her.'

I think of my furious reaction when I realised it was not Eve but Mary lying on my bed.

'Maybe. Maybe not. Or both.'

I am silent a long time.

'No telling. I need an explanation. I have to understand.' I gulp some wine. 'What Americans call closure?'

'Psychobabble.'

'What I do know is that I must have the truth,' I say more forcefully. 'And I am going to find it.'

I explain what we are going to do. She shakes her head in disbelief.

'Jesus,' she murmurs, all her breath coming out in a long sigh. 'You're fucking mad.'

In a competitive world you need a gimmick to prosper. The waiter brings the bill in a red leather wallet which he puts down beside me. In front of Mary he places three dice.

'Is custom of restaurant,' he explains. 'You play one time with dice. Is all the same number, mister no have to pay bill.'

Mary hunches forward to pick up the dice which is what the waiter has been hoping for. He swallows and bites his lip, his eyes on her breasts. She rolls and the dice tumble and stop with five, three and two pips showing.'

'Sorry, Baz, I fucked that up.'

She lifts her face up to the waiter and smiles, a thousand-watt beam. Transfixed he says, 'One more time.'

This time she rolls the dice one at a time. First a six. Then another six. Now the odds are only five to one. She cups the die in her hand then holds it out to me.

'Blow on it for luck.'

I take her wrist in one hand and with the other I unfold her fingers. Opening her fist, bending down over her palm, blowing on the ivory-coloured cube nestling there, seems like an act of possession.

Mary rolls the die across the table. It rattles against the empty wine bottle and is still. It is a third six.

'Three sixes,' she says, 'the devil's number.'

'Jesus wept,' Mary mutters. We come up from the metro into a world of drunks, beggars, hawkers, pickpockets, gypsy children, skinheads, hookers, homeless, touts, thugs, addicts, all the lost and lonely who make the space in front of Keleti station their playground at night. Orange lights bathe the scene in an end-of-the-world glow just like my non-des res in Oxford. This is the theatre of the crazies. The police look on in benign neglect; better to bunch them all together here than spread out through the city. Instead of benches there are concrete blocks. Two old men wrapped in overcoats have put out a chess set and are deep in intellectual war. Dead foot soldiers lie on their sides beside the board where they have been dropped.

From here it is a ten-minute walk down an avenue with bars, a pizza outlet and a Bulgarian kebab joint. Shops with darkened windows are jumbled with tiles, suitcases, light fittings, crockery, fishing tackle. This is not a district of thrusting businesses but dying ones. Trams, lorries and motorbikes pass us but not many cars. A wall that looks endless stretches ahead.

'What's the plan?' Mary wants to know. I've kept her in the dark because I don't know. 'Go to the gate? Ring the bell?'

There is no plan. There is only my bloody mindedness.

An alley leads off the avenue. The wall here is lower but we can't hop over. Barbed wire on top says no.

'Down here.'

You're about to do something idiotic so sound confident. Follow me, troops. Get away from passing traffic, that's common sense. We walk, we don't talk. Streetlights and traffic noises fade. On our left the buildings show knife blades of light from curtained windows. The wall on our right hides Kerepesi cemetery. It's not Budapest's biggest, that is out beyond a brewery in a dreadful suburb. I had refused with granite stubbornness to have Eve's hand buried there. Kerepesi is where the great and the good lie, sometimes under the ground, sometimes in vast mausoleums. The bad and the ugly have ended up here too. How come? It's logic of a Hungarian kind. They look at their country's troubled history and shrug. It's seldom final who is good and who is evil so come on, let's be pragmatic about this. Put them all in the ground or in those mini skyscrapers.

We don't speak. We edge our way down the alley. There's a noise just ahead and we stop.

'Baz, someone's waiting for us.' Mary whispers.

We don't move. Then we see the glint of a cat's eyes. The eyes vanish and we start moving again.

I'm not counting. Maybe we go forty steps, fifty steps. I stop. Mary has been close behind. Now she is closer still, a hand on my shoulder. I point up at the top of the wall where it cuts into the starry night sky.

'Someone has snipped the barbed wire and folded it back.'

'Who?'

'I don't know. Boys having a lark, thieves, homeless.'

'Why?'

To get in the cemetery. Obvious. How do they do it? Across the alley, jammed against a building with darkened windows, is a beer crate. Why would anyone bring a beer crate down the alley? Lay it against the cemetery wall and you realise why. Standing on it, with Mary pushing and me hauling myself up I gain the top of the wall where the barbed wire has been cleared. Leaning down I grab one hand and pull and then she gets a purchase on the top of the wall with her free hand. We sit there, breathless. Kerepesi is laid out in front of us. City of the dead.

'Great,' she says. 'And how do we get back out?'

No problem. The earth on the cemetery side runs like a ramp up the wall. Best guess is that soil dug from graves has been barrowed here and dumped. Our perch is a fine look-out post. Trees, shrubs, paths disappear into darkness. There are no lamps but the stars give a little light. Jumping down I stumble on the slope. Mary does the same, a soft lurch into me. We walk a few steps before she stops.

'Know what, Potter,' she says, 'I need a wee.'

'Know what, Monroe,' I say, 'so do I.'

What's this business with surnames? I wonder. Everybody uses first names now so using surnames makes it a bit special. Is that it?

'It's the wine,' she says.

'The wine,' I agree.

Neither of us mentions nerves. I use a tree trunk, she squats behind a bush.

'Have you pissed in a cemetery before?' she asks.

'I don't remember.'

'Don't *remember*? C'mon, that's not an everyday thing.'

'You?'

'In Malaysia one time. A Chinese cemetery. They're the best.'

'Why's that?'

'It's their final resting place so they want somewhere with a great view. I was there with a boy and went in on a dare. It was scary, know what I mean? Going on midnight, up on a hill, crashing sea down below, wild in places. The wind whipping the grass. Is that a robber creeping up? Boy who came with me thought it was a ghost.'

'It was the wind.'

'No. Turned out there was someone, an old woman. There was a sort of crumbling temple to one side where she lived. She just crept over to watch us have a widdle. She cackled and said something. Don't know what. Crazy round eyes probably.' Mary stands up, rearranging her clothes. 'This was in Melaka, down in the south.'

'Melaka, eh?'

She could be passing on a recommendation for a hidden gem I mustn't miss if I ever pass that way. No, it's not that. We are in this together and she's sharing her past. It makes what we are doing almost normal. She steps from behind the bush and comes to stand close.

'Baz?'

No surname now.

'What is it?'

'Are you feeling OK?'

'Considering.' Neither of us speaks. I almost reach out to touch her, another human being, just to show we are both alive. 'Come on.'

She turns away. 'Look at it - like a bloody housing estate.'

We walk between lines of graves, cement headstones straight off the production line, squat, low, all the same.

'War dead. The Red Army and the Nazis slugged it out in 1945.'

'No flowers,' she says. 'Not a bloody one.' She pauses and seems to gather strength. 'No one remembers. No one gives a fuck any more.'

I do. It's why we're here.

Broad paths lead through the cemetery. Large areas are unused, as if waiting for some catastrophe. Tall trees are still winter bare, yews offer glimpses of slabs of concrete. A double circle of stone tablets is where the communists buried the dead after the '56 uprising.

'AVO,' I tell her.

'What are AVO?'

'Secret police. If they were caught, they were lynched.'

Darkness makes me lose the way. We walk too far then have to backtrack past what look like decaying tenements where champions of the proletarian struggle are packed into drawers, one on top of the other, half a dozen high. Most of the dead are from the accursed forty years but some heroes go back to the 'red terror' after the First World War. I know because I inspected this crumbling city of the dead last December. Mary veers aside, drawn by giant statues black against distant streetlights. She raps her knuckles against one. The metal rings thin and hollow. From her shoulder bag she produces a little flashlight and runs it over the figures. In the centre is a romantic worker, deep chested, shirt slipping off one shoulder, hand in hand with a woman with triumphant breasts. With his other arm he supports a flagging comrade.

'Why's she got her arm raised in front of her face?'

'She's frightened of what lies ahead,' I say, 'or she should be if she had any sense.'

Mary considers the trio some more. 'No more ridiculous than all those generals sitting on horses going nowhere you see in London.'

'Turn off the torch,' I murmur.

A sliver of moon has appeared and my eyes are playing tricks, perspective seems lost, objects fuse and separate, distance is deceptive. I close my eyes and look again. Is it forty metres, fifty metres away? A lantern is moving down a path, bobbing to each stride, flickering between the branches of bushes, disappearing behind these proletarian sculptures, reappearing and moving away. In a wash of light we can make out two pairs of legs and the skirts of long coats flapping like nightgowns. They reach what must be a junction of paths, go sharply right, grow dimmer and dimmer and vanish. The curious thing is that they made no sound, or none that carried as far as us, no footfalls, no voices. Could have been ghosts.

'Who the fuck?' Mary has moved close to me.

'Nightwatchmen, police, gay lovers, murderers, Satanists, I don't know.'

'Baz, I didn't know it was going to be like this.'

You want to get out? The wall's over there. I almost say it.

'Come on. Not far.'

The first grave almost trips us up, a slab set in the grass but not quite flush. Mary's flashlight darts left and right.

'Jesus, what is it?'

'Fighters who were killed in '56 were reburied here.'

'How many?'

'Three hundred. Four hundred. I don't know.'

Not all of them, I know that.

Some slabs have a name and the date 1956. That's all. No need to say more. Then there are proper headstones, some ornate, some simple. Mary's flashlight dances around and she bends to peer closer.

'Lajos…'

'Say it Loyosh. It's Louis.'

'He was twenty-six. Something Janos… thirty-three. Molnar Katinka – Katinka's a girl, right? Shit, she was thirteen. Died 26

October 1956. God, look at this. Pityaka was twelve, her sister Marika was ten. You said it was fighters buried here. These kids weren't fighters, were they? What did they do wrong?'

What they did wrong was get in the way of a tank. Or a grenade was thrown through a window. Or a machine gun caught the family running down a street.

'They were Hungarian,' I tell her. 'That was their crime.'

I move away but I can still hear her exclaiming. In the centre of this area set aside for martyrs is a semi-circle of twelve stones, one for each day until the uprising was crushed. Just beyond is what I'm searching for and I call Mary over.

'Put the flashlight on that.'

The beam finds a name.

'Fazekas. That's the name you're booked in at the hotel.'

'Yes.'

'Atilla. Atilla? Like the Hun?'

'It's a name here.'

'This is your uncle?'

She reads the date: 1st November 1956. She wants to know how he died. I've already told her over dinner but she wants to hear it again. The headstone, the date, the name make it real to her now.

'A bullet in the back. He wasn't running away. Russian soldiers came round the corner of a building behind him, saw he carried a rifle and one of them shot him. Probably a conscript, scared like everybody else. Told he was going to fight German fascists and found he was taking on the Hungarian people.'

What happened to the conscript? He could be buried in another part of the cemetery. I've been carrying a green plastic bag all evening and now I bring out a pot of primroses. The yellow flowers are grey in the torchlight. At the florist I also bought a trowel. Do I plant the primroses? I decide against it. The pot makes it look like an offering. I kneel down to place it on my uncle's grave.

My uncle Attila was dragged from the street into a building. The Russian soldiers didn't follow inside. They were scared of the reception they'd get. The building was a block of flats. It was simply not possible to get Attila to a hospital. He was laid on a bed and in the chaos of that day, with tank tracks grinding along the street, shots, screams, people running, he bled to death. I don't know how long it took. Maybe no one noticed when my uncle stopped breathing.

You can understand why my cousin Jozsef drinks a little too much. You can understand why the whole nation does.

When I stand up Mary puts her arms round my chest to hug me. She's a colleague. No, tonight she's a comrade. Clumsy word. She feels for me. She shows she cares. Caring is important to her. I remember her outburst about the war graves.

I untie the arms from round me.

'Turn the torch off.'

We stand together, looking all round, seeing no light except for a glow from the street. If someone steps out from behind a tree - a guard, a night watchman, a cop - I have my story ready: I have come to pay my respects to my uncle, one of the martyrs of 1956. Why do you climb over the wall like a thief? Why don't you come in the morning? Because tomorrow I have a plane to catch. See the pot of flowers I put on my uncle's grave? The Russians shot him in the back. They were too scared to meet our brave lads face to face. Then we would have gone to a bar together to raise a glass to my uncle, a glass to the struggles against the Ivans, against the Turks, against the Germans and the Serbs and the Romanians, against the French. A lot of glasses. You can measure Hungary's history in glasses.

I see nothing amiss and there's work to do.

'Come on.'

Always I am urging her forward.

Paths criss-cross Kerepesi, some tarred like roads, but this one is gravel and we step over it, past a line of straggly bushes into a different burial plot. Here the graves are recent. This is where I wanted Eve's remains to be interred, in a box made of wild cherry for its beautiful grain. Not possible, I was told by the penpushers.

It is within sight of the heroes' graves, I said, where my uncle Attila has his final resting place. It is not possible, more senior penpushers said, most definitely it is against the rules they insisted, as though rules had ever counted for much in this city. Eva Fazekas was a good friend of the Magyar people I told the most senior penpusher of all, also a good friend of the prime minister. That was no gamble – he'd never dare check. When I met the most senior penpusher of all he inspected his fingernails, raised an eyebrow, then ducked his head to one side as if he'd spotted something on the corner of his desk. 'I think I've swung it for you, Baz,' said West, 'I've been pulling strings damn hard.' With West's pull and my push here I am, standing above the resting place of my wife. Or her hand. Or what?

The plot is enclosed by a thin hedge grown wild. It's about the size of a tennis court. When I came for the burial in December there were four graves in a line and the rest of the area lay vacant. Eve's made five. Now, judging by the scattered earth spilled around and bootmarks, she has a new neighbour. I am peering at the ground when the scene is lit by a flash. For an instant my eyes are blinded.

'I'm making a record.' Mary holds her camera. 'That's what you said.'

'I was just…' Just what? '…not prepared.'

'Excellent,' says the snapper who treasures unguarded moments. 'You carry on. Pay no attention to me.'

A clod of earth has stuck to the headstone. My fist rubs it away. A flash of light freezes my movement. *Potter Eva*, the chiselled inscription reads, because this is Hungary so of course first names are put last. I had insisted she be remembered as Eve but the Hungarian stone cutter had had another drink and followed his instinct and the whole affair had been too rushed to have it redone. There is no sentimental inscription, no: *Gone but not forgotten*, or *Not dead but with the angels*. I wanted just her name and dates.

I lay the green plastic bag on the ground to kneel on and get to work with the trowel. This is crazy, you object. Of course it is. This is Hungary. The alternative is crazier. The struggle with the bureaucrats to get her hand buried here would be a skirmish compared with the battle to get it exhumed. What do you mean it might not be her hand? What evidence do you have? It is in order to get the evidence that I must dig it up. You must go to the police, go to the Bureau of Missing Persons, go to the courts, go to the ministry, to lots of ministries, of Justice, of the Interior, of Foreign Affairs. And answers will always be delivered with a frown: *Nem*.

If it is Eve's hand, how could she be on television? If it is someone else's hand, who has been murdered? Eve is a mystery wrapped in an enigma. The hand and its DNA is a start, all I have to go on.

What makes me look up? It isn't a movement that has caught my eye but a stillness. Three men stand motionless on the path that divides the heroes' burial place from the crumbling pantheon of proletarian stalwarts. They wear hats and overcoats, all charcoal grey. *Who are they?* I ask, and no one replies. *West, do you know?* He seems not to. A flash from Mary's camera wipes them out and it is darkness again. They were never there. Or rather they were there at the funeral in December, three sombre figures who stared and turned and walked away. Now I have had a memory surge, a hallucination, a visual feedback of their silent menace.

Grave diggers use spades but they have to dig wide and long and deep. The hand was placed in a casket the size of a shoebox. Nor was it buried deep. The earth is softer than I feared, not packed down by weather or feet. No grass has grown over it during the winter. In three or four minutes the trowel strikes wood. I attack the earth with furious energy or anger, making piles to the sides of the hole. At last I can insert the trowel down one aide and under the casket and with loosening and levering I raise it up. I hold it in both hands in front of the headstone, making sure the name is not obscured. Dexter will love this.

Flash.

For the record.

'Are you going to…?' Mary asks, or half asks.

'No. We'll take it back to the hotel.'

'Great,' she says. You'd best describe her tone of voice as ironic.

I fill in the hole, top it up with earth taken from the new grave at its side. The casket I place in the green plastic bag along with the trowel. I brush my hands as clean as I can. I am ready. Mary isn't.

'One for my memoirs,' she says.

She balances the camera on a tombstone, sets the delayed action and stands beside me, a hand resting on my shoulder.

Flash.

We are in my room at the Ibis Styles, the green plastic bag resting on the desk. Why do I go to wash my hands? To get the dirt off. But they'll get soiled again when I handle the casket.

'I don't want to do this,' Mary says.

'Tell that to Dexter,' I say.

'Fuck Dexter.'

I look at her and see her eyes are closed to slits.

'I need the evidence of your camera. Come on, you're a pro.'

I ease the casket out of the plastic bag. I smooth the bag on the desk and lay the casket on top. I don't want to do this. I'm no different from Mary. Earth clings to the box except where the trowel has scraped it clean. There the wood shows its grain, dark brown, beige, the annual rings of growth.

Flash.

'Have you got your boy scout penknife,' Mary asks. 'How are you going to open it?'

I hold up the trowel.

Flash.

It only takes a little twisting to insert the trowel between the lid and the box.

Flash.

I press down on the handle of the trowel and it eases up. There is the squeak of nails on damp wood but little resistance.

'Baz, I swear, if there's a stink, I'm going to be…'

She doesn't finish. The lid pops free with something like a gasp. It slides off and I grab it before it hits the floor.

Flash.

Lid on the desk. Then finally… I stand staring into the casket.

Flash.

'Baz?'

I say nothing. I can't. Words have died in me. Mary steps up beside me, camera focusing on the inside of the casket. There's no flash. Her hands sink down to rest by her side.

'Oh God,' she whispers.

CHAPTER 10

I have a sense of things sliding forward with nothing to stop them, one event nudging the next. The mess we call life is a haphazard collection of flukes and throws of the dice yet when we look back it seems to have an inevitable logic. A glance, a laugh, a shudder, a touch, a word is enough to turn us down a new path. There are bumps and twists and turbulence ahead but we keep on rolling.

'Jesus,' she breathes. 'What does… I mean, what the fuck?'

'I don't know.' Things that are beyond rational explanation are chilling. This is frightening because it is evidence of guilt and a great secret to be hidden, of ruthlessness and power and cunning.

'Jesus,' she mutters again, awestruck. 'I need a drink.' The wine we drank at dinner has evaporated as if a furnace door has been opened. 'Several drinks,' she corrects.

So we leave my room, take the lift up two floors. Her room, my room, they are clones except that Mary's personality overflows everywhere: a gaping suitcase with muddled clothes, an ashtray with cigarettes half smoked and bent double, a *Daily Mail*, Jilly Cooper's *Score* and an alarm clock by the bed, knickers kicked off in a corner, a hairbrush on the dressing table and beside it the red and yellow plastic bag from the duty-free shop at Heathrow.

'For some reason there's only one glass,' she says, coming out of the bathroom. 'Actually the reason is because I broke the other one.'

'We can share.'

'Right.' She lifts a bottle of Absolut vodka from the plastic bag. 'You like vodka, comrade?'

'Does it have alcohol?'

She studies the label. 'Forty-five per cent.'

'I like vodka.'

'I hate it actually so what I do – see – is I put a smidgen of Colgate toothpaste in and shake like a barman. Voila, a mint cocktail. Sort of. No? OK, neat then.'

We take turns with the tumbler, she taking half of it in three gulps, me finishing it. I can feel the burn down my gullet as if it is angry and attacking me. The second tumbler numbs the nerves. With the third I feel dizzy.

'The casket,' she says. Vodka-bold we edge closer to the subject. 'What does it mean?'

'I don't know,' I say. 'It gives me the shivers.'

You see, the casket is empty. Well not quite. Together with the hand I had buried the green pottery frog which Eve said brought her luck. The hand has gone, just the frog remaining like a squat Buddha, an enigmatic smile stretched across its face. Certainly the hand *had* been there because the sky blue satin cushion which it sat on carries a stain shaped very like Australia. And a hint of rottenness had wafted out as the lid was lifted.

'I don't understand,' she says.

'Nor do I.'

She pours another vodka. The level in the bottle is mid-way down the label. I feel giddy and retreat to the bathroom to cup water in my hand to dilute the booze. Half a dozen handfuls make no difference so I return to the bedroom to get the tumbler. She has filled it with vodka again and won't let me pour it back in the bottle. I don't know why. Yes, I do: it is the stubbornness of a drunk. So we finish the tumbler and it tips us over the edge into the future.

'Bloody casket's given me the creeps,' she says.

'Casket stays where it is.' My voice is captain-of-industry bold, crisp and decisive.

'I can still smell it. It's got up my nose.'

'Think of something else.'

'OK. I am thinking of something else,' she says. 'I'm thinking of bluebells in May, a drive in a shiny Jaguar, g and t in a country pub, sandwiches with thick chunks of ham and English mustard that gets up your nose and then I think of that bloody wooden box and its smell getting up my nose and I think I don't want to be alone.'

'Right.'

'Do we see eye to eye on this? Baz? You know what I mean?'

We are staring at each other. I know what she means. We have stolen a casket from a cemetery and when we have opened it there is nothing there and it has scared us. The unknown threatens us and our instinct is to cling to another human for support. Alone we feel helpless against hidden forces. Together we have a chance.

'I know,' I say but she has forgotten her question.

It's the middle of the bloody night and we are drinking vodka the way Hungarians do, until the bottle is dry. Why are we doing this? For oblivion, to chase away the demons, to hide our superstitious fears, for bonding, because she says she is a Pisces and I am a Sagittarius, for any damn reason you care to think of. It is our own small world we have created. Tomorrow will be different but now, in the hours of darkness, we are two against the rest.

'It's just you and me, Baz. We're the only ones who know.'

'Except for whoever took it,' I say. 'And the frog. Never forget the frog.'

She's not listening to me. She's listening to whatever voices are speaking in her head.

'Obviously the hand didn't walk out on two fingers,' she says.

'Obviously.'

'And it was definitely buried?'

'Definitely.'

'You didn't leave the casket alone while you went off to speak to the other mourners?'

'The hand was right there when the casket was lowered.'

'So someone has taken it.'

Didn't I just say that? I don't begrudge her repeating the obvious. The facts are awkward and it's a struggle to get things straight.

'Move over,' she says.

She hands me the tumbler so she can stretch out on the bed. Then in a vodka-induced slippage of reality her mind starts down a different road. 'You know what they call me around the office?' she asks.

'Tell me.'

'Come on, don't pretend that when you and Josh go to the boozer – '

But I hand her the tumbler and after a swig she forgets to interrogate me. She lies back, arm cushioning her head, staring at the ceiling.

'I'm known as Two Boobs. I overheard Carrots and Dodo talking about me. Two Boobs. What do you say to that?'

'Well,' I say, not knowing how I should react.

'Go on, say it.'

I take my time. She turns over on the bed so she's facing me.

'Go on, Baz.'

I look from her face all down the length of her body right to her feet and I remember coming into my room and seeing her lying on the bed like this and thinking it was Eve.

'Is there anything left in the bottle?' I ask. But I see it on its side on the floor.

'I want to hear you say it, Baz. I really do.'

'Mary, I…'

But I don't say anything more. I find myself floating in an illusion and she's a long way off and she's inspecting me and she opens her mouth but I don't hear her say anything.

A knocking at the door wakes me up. No, it's a knocking inside my head. It is pounding and with each beat the room pulses. The lights are still on but grey daylight creeps in the window.

I feel a movement and turn and find a body next to me. How did she get there? Then I look round and see it is her bedroom not mine and the whole of last night floods back. Mary is under the covers so I don't know whether she is naked but I am fully clothed. So we have slept together without sleeping together. *You mean you were with Two Boobs all night and you did nothing?* I hear Josh's voice, scornful and disbelieving and stricken with such a wasted opportunity. How could this have happened? I frown at the empty vodka bottle on the floor.

The casket. It is suddenly in my mind. I don't want to see it ever again but I feel I must give it a proper inspection. I should lift up the little satin cushion because – are there hopeless hopes? – there might be a note tucked in there with a full explanation.

I look down at Mary, sheet rising and falling with each breath. Two Boobs. Let her sleep.

I walk down two flights of stairs and as I open the door to my room I hear the telephone ringing. Do I want to answer? It won't be good news. It goes on ringing. Why are we slaves to telephones?

'Hello?'

'Are you a heavy sleeper or were you having a crap?' My cousin Jozsef's voice is in my ear and it sounds rough as if his day has started badly. 'I have news for you.'

'What is it?'

'Don't be such an idiot.'

Of course he can't tell me, not on the phone.

The outer suburbs are not Budapest's glory. The road climbs up to a plateau, the houses thin out, the fields are stony. At a guess the wind comes from Siberia and it snaps at your ankles.

'You want me to wait,' the taxi driver says. It's a statement of the obvious more than a question. When I say no his face clouds in puzzlement. 'You won't get another taxi out here. This isn't the Opera, you understand. Taxis don't hang around waiting for rich folk.'

'Maybe I'll like it so much I'll buy a house and live here.'

The taxi driver stares at me. There are flaws in that plan but he decides against pointing them out. The taxi sends up a muddy spray from the empty carpark as it rejoins the main road.

Strangely there is a house I can buy. Some architect, inspired by the number 8 on the gate, has designed a curious building of two touching circles. The view would never have been breath-taking: across a patch of derelict land, the highway to Lake Balaton and a line of electricity pylons. Then Statue Park was created and a surreal vision was added to desolation. A solid wall was an attempt to block this grotesque view but still Statue Park invaded their privacy so the house has been abandoned and the garden has returned to a weed-infested state of nature. *Elado*, a sign announces. For sale.

Tyres crunching over grit announce the arrival of Jozsef. He's not in one of the blue and white Opels the police drive but an elderly pastel green Volkswagen Golf. It's pitted and dented like his own face. We shake hands, interrupted by a coughing fit that doubles him up like a punch in the solar plexus.

'Greetings,' he gasps. 'Good morning again. How are you? I have to say you don't look well.'

This comment comes from a man whose coughing fit has turned his face pink and white and purple.

'*Macskajaj.*' I tell him.

'Aha.' He takes several rasping gulps of air and wipes tears from his eyes to look at me again. I have a hangover, like cats mating in my head.

'There were reasons,' I say.

'Even no reason is a reason,' he says, and sighs. I feel he is trying to tell me something but my own problem is enough for now. 'What were you drinking?'

'Wine. Then vodka. The whole bottle. A litre.'

'Between how many?'

'Two of us.'

'Three is the correct number for a bottle of vodka. It has the effect you want without the after effect. Myself, I always forget this simple rule. Come, let us go in.'

Three to a bottle; it must be folk wisdom. I smile at the memory of my father saying it.

A Roman arch recently built of red bricks leads the way. Jozsef holds back to light a cigarette, allowing me to buy the tickets. Then we stroll in among the statues whose arms can be seen waving from the highway. Come, these arms beckon, forward to the future, down with class enemies and imperialists, long live the proletariat and our wise rulers. For this is the Disneyland of Communism.

'You've been here before?' Jozsef asks. This morning his voice has a rasping grainy quality as if he has slept too little.

'I've heard about it.'

'Hearing is not enough. You are about to witness a piece of magic by the Magyar people. What was useless is gathered together and bestows riches on its new owners. It is a source of sadness that this magic does not work on our current leaders who are gathered together in parliament and produce not wealth but taxes and silly laws that create criminals where none existed before.'

'You are philosophical this morning.'

'Philosophical? Me?' He takes a deep pull at his cigarette and coughs out the smoke. 'Let me tell you my philosophy.' He drops the cigarette and crushes it with a badly scuffed shoe. 'I believe a good fuck solves more problems than a bad law.' He sighs. It's not from boredom, nor the sigh of someone at the end of his tether, more like a man with a load of problems. 'Come, let me show you a few treasures. You don't know about these statues, do you?'

'Of course I do. Every country in the Soviet bloc had statues glorifying the revolution.'

'You don't feel it here.' I get a policeman's fist prodding me in the guts. 'During the accursed forty years while you cowered under the lash of capitalism we grew rich. Rich, you understand, not in Mercedes and sixty varieties of dog food and washing machines that didn't explode. We grew rich in slogans and dialectical materialism and fraternal visits and statues. The problem is that what was once white is now black and we were left with statues all over the city surplus to requirements. They were an eyesore. No more than that, they were an embarrassment. Something had to be done. Break them up, melt them down, stuff them into old mines. Bah, that lacks a creative spark. Ship them off to North Korea – I liked that one. But suppose they send us Kim Il Sung statues in return. Nightmare. The best suggestion was to gather them here. Our young people can come to be instructed in the folly of political systems. Our foreign guests can come so they can feel superior and buy those empty cans labelled "Last breath of socialism". There you are. Education plus entertainment equals profit.'

I cannot make my cousin out today. He is on edge and cynical and patronising in one cocktail. Also long winded.

'Are we not an inventive nation? Biro with his ball point pen, Rubik with his cube, Tsa Tsa Gabor with her tits and this…this…this cemetery of statues. Lenin, Marx and we mustn't forget Engels – of course they must be here like you couldn't have a church without the Blessed Virgin Mary holding the holy infant.'

'We know about Lenin and Marx in England.' I feel I should say something just to show I am paying attention.

'Of course. Marx lived in London, didn't he. That's where he wrote *Das Kapital* and also fornicated, so he didn't entirely waste his time. Come on, why are you holding back?'

He's a tour guide with a lecture to give. But there has to be more to it than that: a motive. He has another cigarette in his hand though it is unlit. He uses it as a baton, pointing at this and that statue, at plaques, at sculptures.

'Here is the Red Army soldier who used to guard the Liberation Monument on Gellert Hill. He was put up in 1947, knocked down in '56, put up again, finally brought here. There was a real model for the soldier called Gol-something. I forget what gallantry he performed. Next to him is the Hungarian-Soviet Friendship Memorial. The statue was also knocked down in '56 and put up again. Here is a whole parade of Soviet Heroic Memorials. Every district had to have one. Here, this one gushes: *A grateful nation's deepest thanks to the Soviet liberators for our freedom,* See how the graffiti has been lovingly preserved: *Now piss off home.* And here…' Jozsef, frowning, pauses before a smaller than life size bronze statue. 'I look at this whenever I come here.'

'You come often?'

His attention is far away from me. 'Dimitrov, bloody Bulgarian. He even got a square named after him, now renamed Fövam. Another statue that was brought down in '56.' At last he lights the cigarette, brooding over the flame. 'My father had a hand in that.'

'Jozsef, I've been to Kerepesi. I laid some flowers on your father's grave.'

'You'd have done better to pour a glass or two of your vodka on it. He hasn't had a drink for half a century. Shit, even longer.' He pauses. 'But thank you for the flowers. Now come.' He claps his hands. 'We go down this path.'

We head towards the highway but we are not leaving. We pause before a massive construction that must have been hell to move. A dozen soldiers are setting out to charge an unseen enemy. Behind them, from the safety of a balcony, a romantic figure with a moustache indicates with a sweep of his hat the direction they should go. Forward, boys, to glory or death.

'Bela Kun,' Jozsef says, 'pre-war revolutionary. Commissar in the Red Republic. When that fell to pieces he fled to the Soviet Union. Not a good idea because Stalin ordered him to be liquidated. Uncle Joe had his good points after all. Now we come to it. Has your hangover gone because I need your full attention. Just a few steps further, here is Ferenc Műnnich, cut off at the knees, bring him down to our level. Know him?'

'No.'

'Usual success story. Spent time in the Soviet Union in its early days. Fought on the Republican side in Spain. Officer in the Red Army in the Second World War. At Stalingrad with Krushchev – good career move that. After the war he was in Budapest as…'

Jozsef leans close to whisper a great secret '…Chief of Police, but before my time. God is merciful sometimes. Then he took the caviar route, various ambassador jobs. Back here he helped crush the '56 revolution which really won him claps on the back. Nasty piece of work. Got a face like a pig, though I've nothing against pigs. Now an interesting little fact for you. He had himself a late spring when he was in his early seventies. No one ever said he didn't have balls. A son was born on the wrong side of the blanket. Officially he couldn't be the offspring of his important dad so he was called after his mother. Goenz was her name. And the little boy clamped to her tit is in the records as Gyula. You see, I told you Gyula Goenz was a bastard.'

I remember his exact words. We were in the Kempinski bar and Jozsef stared at me across the table.

'If your lady was going to choose a bastard she certainly picked the top one.'

Jozsef must have known something of Goenz's reputation but not his lineage. Does Eve? How could she not?

'Münnich's statue was in Nephadsereg Square, now reborn as Honvéd Square,' Jozef says, knuckling his eyes in tiredness. 'It's a stroll away from parliament.' He lines his hands up as if aiming a rifle. 'Bang, bang, bang. There were AVO sharpshooters up on the roofs there. I'm talking about 1956.'

'I know.'

'You *know* but you don't *feel*. That first night, twenty-third of October, the AVO were shooting down from on top of the buildings. My dad was part of the crowd and witnessed it all. There was a big student rally and a march to parliament and he joined in. The AVO shot into the crowd to create panic, start a stampede.'

I know. I know but I say nothing because this is part of Jozsef, the legend of his father, the grit in his soul, and he needs to tell me and he needs to tell himself: father as hero. It must be a terrible burden to bear. He can never live up to the legend except by dying a heroic death himself. Not every generation can choose to be martyrs so he is driven to talk. Today he seems to change his mind, shaking his head with a sigh, not going to relive the myth.

Now we are sitting in his car, the beat-up green Golf, in the carpark outside the entrance to Statue Park. It is one of those days that keeps changing its mind about whether spring has come. Big gambolling sheep of clouds are up there but when the sun rides out into the blue it makes your skin tingle with its strength. Jozsef winds down his window to feel the sun, screws up his face and mutters, 'Bugger.'

'There are pessimists,' I say, 'and then there are Hungarian pessimists. You know the difference?'

'Already I feel laughter bubbling inside me. Go on.'

'A pessimist thinks he will die of pneumonia next winter. The Hungarian pessimist believes he will die of pneumonia next winter provided he hasn't died of skin cancer in the summer.'

He nods his head and keeps on nodding it. 'I'll do my best to remember that one. It could be handy next time I'm out having a drink with the boys and we're desperate for a laugh. You know what your problem is, Bazil? You've become western living in England, never mind your father and my father were brothers. Here in Hungary is where the east begins, isn't it.'

'Black hair and high cheekbones and – '

'No. Blood feuds and revenge and fatalism. We have the invading hordes from Asia to thank for that. My father was even named after a bloodthirsty conqueror. Could be there's a bit of the east in you still. Is it revenge you're after?'

'Revenge on who? Eve? Goenz?'

Jozsef looks away towards a group who have just come out through the mock Roman arch. Two women of a certain age walk in front, their husbands behind. Snatches of the women's talk reach our ears, American voices.

'Wasn't that the most fun? That T-shirt with Lenin as Ronald McDonald? Billy'll think it's neat.'

'You know those statues? Why weren't they smashed up a bit? I was hoping for bullet holes.'

It is Jozsef's habit to sigh, I decide. He winds his window up, turns the key in the ignition and eases the clutch out. 'Yankees,' he says.

'You understand?' I am surprised. 'You've never let on.'

'The language I understand, the people…' He takes a hand off the steering wheel and tilts it side to side. We turn onto the highway, heading towards the city. 'And that's my job, understanding people, which is why I ask if you're after revenge.'

'I want to *know*.' My voice must be a little loud because Jozsef glances over at me. 'I have a right to know.'

'So when you know, then what do you do?'

'Is this Jozsef my cousin asking or Fazekas the policeman?'

He takes a hand off the steering wheel and again tilts it side to side.

'Listen,' he says, 'a word of advice. Let us suppose Eva is alive and you find her. If you're thinking of giving her a little slap around the face there isn't a husband in Hungary who wouldn't cheer you on. But if you're thinking of trying to kill Goenz, I have to tell you that would be fatal.'

For a moment I can hear the blood pounding in my ears. Kill Goenz? Kill anyone? I'm Bazil, I'm a journalist, I'm not a member of the killing classes. I'm not the Yorkshire Ripper or a Yardie hoodlum or Al Capone.

'I mean fatal for you,' Jozsef says in case I haven't followed him.

'I don't want to murder anyone.'

'Then we have to ask ourselves what it is you do want.'

'To be face to face with my wife.'

'But for what purpose? To swear at her? To beat her up? To plead with her to come back?' I shake my head. 'Well, there's something here you've got to get straight because I have to say I think you are confused.'

'I want to know the facts. I've told you.'

'Because you're a journalist and it's a story?'

'No.' Though I think of Mary and getting her to make a photographic record.

'No?'

'To see her, to have a confrontation, to have it all out, to learn the truth.'

'You don't want her back, you don't want revenge, you just want to know. Knowledge without action – I've never had that luxury.'

'Listen, it was my marriage and it shouldn't just drift into nothing. There should be an end, if that's what it is, a conclusion. It's so I can close the book and put it away.'

'To learn the truth.' Jozsef goes back to something I said. 'Truth is a dangerous commodity. That's what my life has taught me.'

'Your life as a cop?'

'Cops are like cats. There are all kinds of cats. Some are black, some are Siamese, some don't have tails. But they all catch mice and they all scratch.'

The car stops at a red light which gives Jozsef the chance to get out another cigarette. He opens his window a crack to let out some of the smoke. I sit there mulling over his cops are cats remark.

'I've always thought of you as an ordinary kind of policeman,' I say, 'at a desk in the headquarters.'

He waves a hand to say no. The light changes to green and we move off.

'I work in the Office for the Constitution. It is an outfit so small and so secret we don't exist. My office is in a building across the road from the main building. I can access headquarters by a passageway...' He uses a hand to sketch a tunnel down and up again. 'It was built by the old regime. No police headquarters in the Soviet bloc was complete without a secret tunnel. No doors are locked to us. There are no files we cannot see. This is how I found out about Goenz being the bastard son of Műnnich. Agreed the old man died years ago but his son has been able to use all the old connections in the ministries. Wasn't all that swept away in '89, you object? All right, the leopard rubs off its spots but that doesn't turn it into a poodle.

Those people in the ministries and the police and the syndicates and monopolies just nipped out to the shops, bought new hats, puffed out their cheeks and strolled back to their desks.'

A car overtakes and cuts in and Jozsef brakes sharply. Anyone else would have given a long blast on his horn. Jozsef lets out one of his sighs: life is so tiresome.

'Bazil, you need to understand what my job is and isn't. I don't waste time on computer fraud or tax evasion or paedophiles or any of the other growth industries of our time. None of that. My sole interest is the constitution and keeping to it. There must be no plots, no army coups and no communist comeback. Forty accursed years was enough. Now Gyula Goenz – well, I think I'm going to have to sniff a bit closer to him. He is Mafia plus. He has bad connections.'

'Eve is a bad connection? Is that what you're saying?'

'It's a thought.'

I don't know what to say.

'Let's put Eva aside for the moment. Goenz is the route to go. Yesterday, after I met you, I went to the restricted archives at head-quarters, a section I had to show my Cosmic pass to enter. The guard at the door enters my pass details into the computer. When I get inside the archivist enters the file titles I've requested into his computer. Computers are the spies of the twenty-first century which may explain why last night, as I was going to bed, I got a telephone call and a voice said, "You were making enquires in the restricted archives today. Stop whatever it is you are doing."'

'A voice you recognised?'

'Just a male voice. The voice wasn't well brought up. It didn't introduce itself. It simply gave an order.'

'Shit.'

'Well said.'

We have passed through the inner suburbs, an area of low-income housing, workshops, warehouses, land waiting for something to happen. We cross railway lines and pull up next to a bus terminus.

'I've always thought of you as a policeman but now you say you work for the Office for the Constitution.'

'Never heard of it,' Jozsef says.

'Have you always been in this non-existent outfit?'

Jozsef opens the window a crack once more to flick away his cigarette. 'While you were safe and comfortable in England, I was a cop here. Out on the street, then in the headquarters posted to Fraud. In the old days what fraud was there? Think about it. It was a socialist centrally-controlled economy so it was state employees who committed fraud. Big fraud could only be committed by big people. Occasionally something so big happened I couldn't help stumbling over it and I would start to earn my salary, see people, ask questions, stick my nose in to test the smell. Take a holiday, I'd be ordered, go to Cuba, drink some rum, fuck some black girls. When I came back I'd find my case had been closed: no action. After '89 when the system changed I slipped into my current job because I knew the faces and knew the names and knew the deals but I wasn't tainted.'

'You didn't know Goenz,' I point out. 'You had to go to the files.'

'You think you can do my job better than me?' He gives me a hard stare. 'This is as far as we ride together.'

I nod.

'Walk across the bus loading area and on the far side you can catch a tram to the centre.'

I get out of the car and as I am about to close the door Jozsef leans across the seat to say goodbye. Except it isn't goodbye.

'That telephone caller last night,' he says, 'he told me to lose interest in Goenz. He also told me to be careful who I met. He said they'd be watching. So that car that cut in front of us, I hope he wasn't having a serious look at you.' He raises a hand in salute. '*Ciao*.'

CHAPTER 11

This is the end of the tram line and I run to hop on the one standing with its doors gaping. It could have been a private carriage waiting just for me. A buzzer sounds, the doors close and it sets off with a lurch.

'Excuse me,' I say.

'It happens.'

The man I bumped into has a passing resemblance to the pottery frog that Eve believed brought her luck. Except he has grey hairs that sprout from under his flat cap.

'Where does this tram go?'

'Why did you get on it if you don't know where it is going?'

He is a truculent frog and I have had a difficult morning and I snap back at him, 'Because I didn't want to spend the rest of the day in Kelenföld.'

This is my mistake. The wild eyed, the fantasists, the persecuted, the flat earthers, the Tourette's syndrome shouters, the Elvis Lives believers, the conspiracy theorists – every city has them. Budapest, I swear, is the most richly endowed in the world. My curse is to have bumped into a lapel grabber.

'What's wrong with Kelenföld?' he says. 'Me, I live in Csepel. In the morning I draw the curtains open, hope to look out at blue sky, maybe the last sun of my life and do you know what I see from my window? What's been waiting all night to hit me in the face? Do you know? Can you guess?'

'I suspect it's not something that makes your heart sing.'

He glowers at me. 'I see Csepel, always Csepel, the steel works. Forty-three years I worked there until I got this.' He gives an impressive cough. 'So I draw my pension now but listen. Three years ago my wife died and you are going to find it difficult to believe this but it is the truth. I swear on her grave it is. After her funeral we were having some drinks and her sister, who is a widow and two years *older* than my wife, leaned over and suggested she move in with me.' One hand already has a grip on my lapel but he puts out the other to steady me from the shock. 'That's right. My wife has that very afternoon been lowered into the ground and here her sister is, wanting to move into my apartment. Do you know how many bedrooms it has?'

'No, how many bedrooms?'

'One. Do you know how many beds?

'I'm guessing here – one?'

He tips his head so he can observe me with a discerning eye. 'If you're thinking what I think you're thinking, you're right. And this is straight after my wife's funeral and I've only had one glass of brandy.'

'So you said no.'

This is the wrong response. His eyes are fixed on me like the Ancient Mariner's. 'This is my sister-in-law, two years older than my wife. She said to me, "Andris…" My name is really Andras but she was edging closer and calling me Andris. "Andris, when we get to our age we can't waste time tiptoeing around, know what I mean." I was a fool. If I'd moved in with her then I could have moved out. But letting her move in - now I'm stuck with her. Let me tell you what it's like. For a start…'

He clutches me. I am a raft on the stormy seas of his life and I nod and shake my head and raise my eyebrows while I speculate about my cousin. Jozsef is not the police inspector I imagined. He is a political sort of fellow and I can't square this with the man I know who enjoys a drink and goes to football matches and looks aside when someone brings up the subject of his wife

Adel and tends the monument that is his father. Today I learn he is a different sort of cat – his term. He still scratches and catches mice but he does it in his own way. Does he tap phones? Hide behind the arras?

'So you'll come over and see her?' the old man says, his frog eyes fixed on me.

'What?' What have I nodded agreement to?

'You're younger. You've got more strength. She's wearing me out.'

The tram grinds to a halt.

'Here we are,' he says.

'Where?'

'Where do you think? The end of the line. Moricz Zsigimond Square.'

We get down and I spot just beyond the tram stop a battered green Volkswagen Golf very like Jozsef's.

'Today she's gone to have lunch with her daughter but tomorrow would be good.'

It is Jozsef's car because Jozsef has got out and is walking towards us.

'We could go and have a beer now. In my opinion the first beer of the day is the best.'

'Then why don't you stop at one,' Jozsef growls, standing at the man's shoulder, 'if it's all downhill after that?'

'What?' The man blinks.

Jozsef opens his wallet to flash a card at him then grabs my arm. 'Come with me.'

Is my cousin arresting me? We go to his car and sit in the front seats. In the mirror I see the frogman staring our way.

'Who was your friend?' Jozsef asks.

'I have no idea but he is very generous. He just offered me his sister-in-law.'

Jozsef turns his head to give me a hard stare but doesn't speak.

'You followed me,' I say. 'You wanted to see if I was going to meet someone. You really want to know about that old man.'

'You're paranoid,' Joseph says. He sighs. 'It runs in the family. I got to thinking about how you put flowers on my father's grave. I saw you late yesterday afternoon and rang you early this morning. My brain did a little hop, skip and jump - how could you do this when the cemetery gates are closed?'

'I climbed over the wall.'

'You?'

I have never seen Jozsef dumbfounded before. I nod.

'I put flowers on his grave but there was another reason for going: I dug up the casket with Eve's hand.'

'Just a minute.' Jozsef makes scooping motions with a hand. 'You dug it up? Why?'

'To have it tested for DNA. If Eve is alive it's not her hand.'

'If it's not her hand, whose is it?'

'Good question. Well, you're the police cat.'

Jozsef stares at me. I've never known him at a loss for words. Since he can't seem to think of anything to say I leave him.

Hell hath no fury etcetera etcetera. I have come back to the Ibis Styles and I'm standing in my room – just standing and staring, but with good reason – when there is a tat-tat at the door. By the time I reach it those lady-like knuckles have changed to a fist. Mary brushes past me.

'So where the fuck have you been?'

'Out.'

'What kind of answer is that? Of course you've been out. What have you been doing?'

'Seeing someone.'

'I woke up and thought I'd be seeing you and when I turned over I found you'd sneaked out without saying a word.'

Is there what psychologists and sociologists and deconstructionists and other crazy thinkers of our times call a sub-text here? She wakes up in bed and expects to find me beside her so what does her frustration mean? I have no time to ponder this.

'Did you come downstairs to see if I was here?'

'Yes I did and for all I know you were in here hiding from me because there was no answer when I knocked.'

'You didn't come in?'

'How could I? The door was locked.'

'You have a key.'

'It didn't work.'

The dishy receptionist gave Mary a key because she told him she was my fiancée. It was a card-key you swipe, so maybe it was only valid for twenty-four hours. There's a joke hidden in there about how modern engagements don't last long these days. In better times at the *Old Hag* I might have risked it but not now.

'So,' I say and take a breath, 'it wasn't you who took the casket.'

She looks beyond me to the desk where last night we abandoned the casket. It's no longer there. First the hand was taken. Now even the casket and the cushion with the stain have gone. Even the smell has vanished. Was it Eve's hand that was buried or someone else's? I have no DNA, no evidence.

'Perhaps,' Mary says, 'the maid cleared it away.'

Perhaps.

In the high days of the Raj before an important sahib arrived at the Maharajah's summer palace he would summon his main man. Action! Go into the jungle, select the best spot, clear the field of fire, construct the hide in a tree, kill the goat, put it where the sahib can see it. The Maharajah and the sahib would clamber up into the hide and wait for the goat-smell to attract the tiger. That is my position exactly. No, not the sahib, the bloody goat.

I finally get through on the telephone.

'Yes, what is it?' That's the brusque greeting of a newsman with an eye on the clock, feeling the pressure.

'Pal?' I say. 'Pal Pokorni?'

'What damn fool is calling? Is that you Istvan?'

'It's Bazil. We talked on the bench after that tarts' stunt.'

'Wait.'

He presses the mute button while he orders someone out of earshot or he switches off the recorder that monitors calls or he switches it on, who knows.

'I thought you'd flown home.'

'Not yet.'

'Why not?'

So I outline my idea and he listens without interrupting. I tell him what help I'm looking for and he says, 'You're insane.'

'That's an opinion.'

'Don't expect me to do it.'

'I understand.'

'Do you? My life has been threatened already. What do you think they'll do to you? Why do you want to do it?'

To find out the truth? Because Eve is or was my wife? Because I resent being pushed around and threatened? Because I smell a rat? Because it's a story and I'm a professional? All of that or none of that. To be a hero? No, definitely not that. Sometimes it's for the stupidest reason of all.

'Because it's there.'

'What? What are you talking about?'

'Someone asked Hillary, the first man to climb Everest, why he did it and he answered "Because it's there."'

'The English are crazy. It's a well-known fact.'

'Hillary wasn't English.'

Pal pays no attention to this detail. 'Do not expect me to join you in your public suicide. I am a married man. Or close enough.'

'You can get someone else to do it. It could be an off-screen interviewer.'

'And you? Off-screen too? Otherwise every Mafia hoodlum in town will know your face.'

'I could do it back to camera.'

'You'll be following in the great tradition of Kadar. They used to say our illustrious leader spoke out of his arse.'

134

The phone goes dead, leaving me frowning, until I realise that in his own way Pal Pokorni has agreed.

Mary has been leaning close hoping to share in this telephone call but my side is all she's heard.

'What was that crap about Hillary climbing Everest because it was there? What's that got to do with this?'

Everybody probes for my motive as if knowing that will make the situation go away. To rescue Eve, to find out the truth, to follow a good story, to feel as if I am in control – does my motive shift?

'Sometimes you do something just because it's there to be done. Does that make sense?'

Mary stares at me. She says nothing. I remember Jozsef saying I was confused.

We are at the Magyar TV studios. Forget the programmes. They want to prove they are world leaders in bureaucracy. The grey men take over. Even the women are grey men. The news editor spares me a smidgeon of time, the line manager keeps looking over my shoulder, a grey man (female version) with a clipboard wants my date of birth and my next of kin. I sign papers that I am responsible for the content of the interview and Magyar TV will not be liable in any legal proceedings thereafter brought by any parties of the third part and my life will be in hock heretofore (perhaps I exaggerate), agreeing I shall be Fazekas not Potter, deciding I shan't turn my back to camera but will be shot unlit against a bright white background so my head will be in silhouette, my features blacked out like some criminal fingering a rival gang member. Then I am sent to make-up. Make-up? But my face will be blacked out, I tell the make-up girl. It's for your hair, *edesem*.

'I must have one of this,' Mary says.

Press cameras used to be cumbersome. Now they are tiny. But the flash is startling.

'What's that?' Pal Pokorni has appeared. 'Who is she? What's she doing? Who let her in?'

All this is in Hungarian which Mary doesn't understand. But Pal is facing her and has his arm out pointing at her and this she understands.

'Press,' she says because she's learnt that this excuses any intrusion, any rudeness, any excess. Pal is not impressed.

'No photos,' Pal tells her in English. 'This is a TV studio and we're working. This is not some refugee camp or a whorehouse… Jesus, stop that. Stop that now.'

Mary has raised her camera and is focusing on his angry face and pointing finger.

'She works with me,' I say.

'She's not working in here. I'm not having my face in the papers for Goenz and his mob to see. Get out. Where's the security guy?'

The security guard has a word with Mary. She has several words back. Do they have a common language? Unwisely he puts a hand on her shoulder and she slaps his face. Eventually she is escorted out. Finally I get to go before the camera where some youngster fresh out of training lobs me a few prompts. There is a glass panel to the control room and I am aware of Pal standing behind the engineer and producer and glaring at me. We do the recording in one take and I look at the producer and he turns to the engineer and he nods and everyone is happy with the exception of Pal. He runs a hand across his throat. Thanks for the encouragement, Pal.

Why do I think of Dexter? What did he say? Television is a substitute for sex. You have two hours of seduction, two minutes to do it, then afterwards you wonder if all the effort was worthwhile.

It seems Mary has been escorted not just out of the studio but right out of the Magyar TV building. She's standing on the pavement, camera dangling round her neck, hands on her hips. It's a fishwife stance. The air round her has a blue tinge. It's her fishwife language.

It's 5.45, fifteen minutes to the news programme. We are in Mary's room on the fifth floor because she says she needs to take a shower. I open a window even though it's a cold spring evening. Hotels like the Ibis Styles make me do that because they lack character so I like to let in the outside world which is messy, noisy, chaotic, dangerous. It's human, it's life. It's real, which reminds me of Dexter.

Ten minutes to the news.

I leave the window and step over to the bedside table where the phone is. I try the *Old Hag* office first and have a little chat with Liz who handles the switchboard and reception. She's a healthy girl and big with it, as Josh says, and I suspect Josh knows.

'How're you doing?' Liz wants to know.

'I'm hanging in there.'

'You've got company now,' she says. 'Everything nice and cosy?'

'I'm enjoying the sights.' What kind of silence is this? A smirky silence? A spill the beans silence? So I ask, 'Is the big white chief in?'

'No,' Liz tells me, 'he left early.'

'What's he doing, seeing his popsy?'

'How do you know I'm not his popsy?' she says and rings off.

Five minutes.

I try Dexter's home number but he hasn't gone home. I don't even get a giggle from one of his Thai girls, just the answerphone.

'This is Baz checking in. I'll speak to you later. I'm making progress but it may be backwards.'

Let Dexter worry about that.

Two minutes. I switch on the TV and give Mary a shout. I am sitting on the bed and staring at the opening shots of the news when Mary comes out of the bathroom. She wears a shower cap and has a towel wrapped round her body.

'That's me,' I say.

I'm silhouetted against a curving white board, head and shoulders, features blacked out except for a flare from the bridge of my nose when I nod and it catches the light.

'Your voice sounds funny.'

There is an edginess to the way I talk, too quick, too high pitched. Hearing a recording of your own voice is always a shock but this is more. I am being questioned and my replies sound as if I am pleading.

'Who's doing the interview?'

'Some girl, a trainee or something because Pal wouldn't do it himself. He's had death threats.'

'What are you saying?'

'Last year my wife died in a car accident. Her body was lost in the Danube, just her hand was recovered. Her hand was buried in Kerepesi near where the heroes of 1956 rest, including my uncle. But I have been tricked. My wife is not dead because I saw her on television last week.'

'What's the girl asking you?'

'She wants to know how I can be so sure I saw my wife on TV? And I say what I've said all along: a man knows his wife. There are things I must find out. I sound a bit desperate here. Where is my wife? It wasn't my wife's hand that was found so whose hand was it? Viewers can help me. If they know of a woman who lost a hand last December or they see my wife, please get in touch. Just leave a message with the police. Please. This is what my wife looks like though she may have changed her hair style.'

Pal wouldn't give me a still from last week's TV news so I used an old photo of Eve.

The programme moves to the next item so I switch off the TV. We stare at each other, saying nothing. The longer the silence lasts the more I am aware of the towel she has wrapped round herself and the damp patches where it clings to her body.

Have I said already that Mary has blonde hair? It used to be shoulder length and she'd tie it in a pony tail. Then she must have thought this wasn't the right image for a press photographer and she had it cut so it frames her face. She takes off the shower cap and runs her fingers through her hair. Is this to show there are no dark roots and she is a natural blonde? She lays her head on the pillow with her hair spread out like the golden halo round the Virgin Mary in some mediaeval stained-glass window. Some Virgin Mary.

'What are you going to do now, Baz?'

CHAPTER 12

Eve loved me. A year ago I knew that like I knew fire was hot and ice belonged in drinks. Now?

We cannot see the future. Even the past is not certain.

First the hand vanished, then the casket. I am left with nothing except the memory of a lingering smell. Mary is stretched out on the bed, a frown gathering on her face as she looks at me.

'I'm going out,' I say. 'There's something I've got to do.'

'I'll come,' she says. 'Give me a moment to get dressed.'

'It's something I have to do on my own.'

Is her frown baffled or angry or sceptical? Maybe jealous? I'd been prepared for an outburst but she doesn't say anything, just closes her eyes and dismisses me with a flick of her hand: get the hell out then, leave me alone.

How do you go back to a place where you once lived with someone before the dream shattered? Do you stand on the other side of the road and shake your head, puzzled? There? With her? Maybe you cross the road for a closer look, peering through the window, holding your breath. Maybe you pick up a stone and hurl it at the glass.

Eve had been offered an elegant apartment a stroll away from the City Park but she'd turned it down on the arbitrary grounds that her bedroom window would have faced the French embassy. Another was found half a dozen blocks further in towards the centre and she was enchanted until she discovered it backed onto what had been the headquarters of the Gestapo and afterwards during the accursed forty years of the AVO. She said she would hear screams at night. How about across the river on the lower slopes of the hills? Substantial houses are dotted among pine trees. Here is one like a Loire château… no, no, no. I heard this after the funeral from Harrach, the man who had to deal with the relocation demands of the embassy staff. He was a local. He was like an old butler who kept his head bowed but saw and heard a lot.

In the end Eve found a place herself. No one will track me down here, she told me after signing the lease. But who are you hiding from? I asked. Or maybe I only thought I asked. She could be sharp I was discovering.

The place she chose is in Obuda. This translates as Old Buda. It does have some Roman ruins but don't get excited. Go a little north of what remains of the amphitheatre – a couple more stops on a Number 17 tram – then go down a side street towards the river. On the right is a rustic style restaurant where I ate with Eve. I eat there again this evening. Picture plain wooden tables and chairs, dark wooden beams, a large pendulum clock, family photos of weddings and country excursions. One photo shows a fisherman standing with a rod in his left hand and a champion specimen in his right. I recognise him as the man who serves me.

'What is that fish?' I ask.

'*Fogas,*' he replies. Pike-perch.

'How much did it weigh?'

He lays his head to one side as he considers the photo on the wall. 'It weighed three bottles of *barackpalinka*. That was the first prize.'

I am given two fatty pork chops which are dipped in batter and deep fried then covered in a blanket of grated cheese for extra cholesterol. My mother used to cook them that way. I drink red wine from the barrel served in hero-sized tumblers. It is thin and harsh, a wine so terrible you know it will protect the restaurant from being on the tourist circuit.

Eve's flat is in the next block.

I say flat. Apartment is estate agent fol-de-rol for more expensive.

The building is early twentieth century, sort of art nouveau, a free-flowing style I called *Jugendstil*.

'Darling, it's not German.' She tapped me on the cheek. 'Think Austria, the *Secessionsgebäude* in Vienna.'

That stuns me. I am put in my place.

I have the keys. I climb up to the second floor and unlock the door to her flat. She'd renewed the lease and it ran to September so I told Harrach I would keep it on, please pay any bills. During the summer I'd visit and pack up her belongings. All I'd done after the funeral was chuck out the perishables.

Now when I open her front door I stop dead. What am I listening for? Why am I holding my breath? I have to order my feet to march. I go through the flat, switching on lights. The rooms are elegant with high ceilings but not many of them: a large sitting room, her bedroom, a poky room that might do for a small and tidy child but which she used as a study, a bathroom and a kitchen.

I return to the sitting room and look around. Eve bought all the furniture so it is her taste. It is certainly not like the jumble in my non-des res. There is a pair of long black leather sofas 'because leather is classless'. A huge Japanese lampshade of jade green and ultramarine blue silk hangs from a tall, curving stainless steel stem. It casts a drowsy intimate glow. A clear Perspex dining table is pushed against one wall with four chairs tucked into it. Her notion was to create a cool modern atmosphere inside the art nouveau shell. To be honest it looks like an art director's vision for a colour supplement of a decade or so ago. Pictures on the walls are blobs of bright colours: a bunch of huge red oriental poppies lying on a table, an overturned bottle spreading a tide of blue ink, a pair of green wellies one of which lies on its side, a lemon sliced open with a kitchen knife beside the two halves. I had always seen them as bold statements of colour to offset the furniture. Now, as I try to reassess Eve, it strikes me that all the paintings show things disturbed by humans but the humans have disappeared.

Unhappy at this thought I go to a table with a brass tray on which stand her bottles of booze. I choose *barackpalinka* which the waiter in the restaurant had won for catching the champion pike-perch. It is a colourless brandy distilled from apricots, dry, a suggestion of fruit which goes up your nostrils, strong, sometimes very strong.

With the glass to my lips I pass through into the bedroom and there it is: The Bed. It's more than double, it's king size. 'No, Baz, it's emperor size for when you visit, for your conjugal rights.' When I looked at her I saw a grin stretching her mouth wide like a little girl suggesting naughty things. The grin stayed and stayed and her eyes were a little too bright so that a procession of thoughts flashed through my mind: she's not a little girl at all but a woman with grown-up secrets, she's hinting at something, she's daring me to challenge her about the bed, she's proclaiming her independence, she wants me to fuck the smile off her face, no she doesn't because she doesn't give a damn. Or maybe it was no more than a tease. I couldn't take that grin any longer because of the uncertainty of what it meant and I turned aside.

I didn't know then and I don't know now. I rock on my feet, weakened by the memory of that occasion. Another thing comes back to me: she was wearing perfume. I never gave her any and I didn't know she even had any. Yet when we made love the perfume transferred itself from her body to mine, marking me as her possession. When I look round now there is no scent bottle on the dressing table.

I sip the *palinka* and move to the study and survey the desk and the filing cabinet. There are papers here to trawl through which is why I have come without Mary. There may be clues to what Eve has been doing but there'll also be the flotsam of our relationship. I pull out the chair, position myself at the desk and draw a breath. I don't want to do this and I hesitate. I feel I am a grave robber and the grave is our marriage. What will I find? First I move everything on top of the desk to one side so I can rearrange it in neat lines: the stapler, the destapler, the tangle of elastic bands in a tiny cardboard box of Harrods green, the ashtray pinched from the Hilton in Cairo filled with paperclips ('Isn't it marvellous the French call them *trombones*,' she said), a silver toast rack with envelopes, two Bic pens, a pencil sharpener, a glass paperweight with a portrait of Thomas à Becket looking stubborn, a *risqué* French postcard circa 1900 of a woman in a black corset sitting on a chair with her legs crossed, Sellotape, a special offer subscription form for the *Economist*, a small brass bell (to summon what servant?), an address book, a pottery mug with three pheasant feathers, a street atlas of Budapest, a landline telephone, a lamp. Everything is in military order awaiting inspection. I fiddle with the pottery mug, straightening its position. This is what psychologists call displacement activity.

I hesitate to open the desk drawers or the filing cabinet. Something is not right. I patrol the neat lines I have made. I rearrange them as if touching them will jog my memory. It does. Where's her engagement diary?

Think. Had a diary been on the desk when I was last here? Surely. Or maybe not. Why can't I remember what her diary looked like? When I came to the flat last December the reminders of her daily life knocked me out of kilter. Still do. I can't remember whether her diary was on top of the desk but she had one. She had to. A diplomat can't survive without an agenda. So what has happened to it? Did I put it away?

I pull up sharply. I have that eerie sensation of being watched but there is nobody here. A camera then? It could be concealed, just a little lens peeping out. I look at the pictures in turn, reproductions of glowing sunflowers by Guy Weir and Van Gogh. Nothing out of place.

I drop a hand to the desk drawer but decide I need fortifying first. I fetch the bottle of *palinka*, pour another tot and slide the top drawer open. Stationery, some of it with the embassy address and crest, 'lion and unicorn enjoying foreplay,' she called it. Other writing paper has the address of this flat in Föld utca. Ruler, more ball-points, stamps. Scissors are jammed at the side.

The middle drawer has pads of paper and stuffed at the back is a bundle of letters held together by a thick elastic band. I hold the pile in my hands, judging the weight of the letters, feeling them with both thumbs as if I could test them for explosive content. I turn into a spy, sliding a letter out from the rubber band, and see on the first page, *My sweet Peach Bum, You are so delicious I could eat you again like I did this morning...* The heat is in my cheeks, my heart thumps. Love letters, not in my writing. Peach Bum – I never called her that. It is embarrassing, sickening, maddening. Then I notice the date is late 2007. Turning over the page I see he signs off *Your bad Penny*. Eve had an old lover called Penfold. She made no secret of her previous affairs but I didn't know she treasured his letters. I scrabble round in the drawer. No letters of mine.

The bottom drawer is a jumble of printed material to do with travel. I flip through leaflets, booklets, timetables, maps, city plans of Buenos Aires, San Francisco, Riga, Prague, little pamphlets about a bamboo garden in the Cevennes, steamer trips on Lake Maggiore, helicopter rides over the Grand Canyon. I don't know what else. It slips through my fingers, then I stuff it all back. 'I want it all while it's still there, Baz.' She was hungry for experiences. She had dreams. Was I one of them? I think about this. I don't know.

On to the filing cabinet. It's locked but the master thief has spotted a likely key nestling among the paperclips. Two drawers. As good burglars should, I start with the bottom one. Not much. Files to do with the flat, electricity, telephone, insurance, bank and credit card statements up to last November. Harrach said he would come once a week to pick up any mail. She sponsors a boy in Uganda and a folder holds letters reputedly from him. What did she write back? I have deceived my husband today, I'm stepping out with a Mafia boss? Top drawer even thinner pickings. This was the work drawer with files giving addresses of embassy staff, communications from the Foreign Office on pension rights, salary review, daily allowances while travelling on official business. The only document to do with her job is a report of a working party on eliminating non-tariff trade barriers in the single market. I can imagine Eve stuffing it out of sight in this drawer and saying *bor-ing* in a ding-dong voice.

I sit back with another snifter to clear my brain. I think: where's her laptop? It could have been in the car when it plunged in the Danube. It would have been ruined so it might have been chucked but still… And there is no engagement diary, no letters or papers on outside interests apart from travel, no clues linking her in any way with Goenz. His name doesn't appear in the address book. I have drawn blank.

It is as if someone has come in and stolen her life.

There's an answerphone but the light is not flashing. On the off-chance I press the Message button and it rewinds to the messages that have not been wiped. I am rewarded with this. There is a pause with the vaguest hints of life at the other end of the line, then a male clearing of the throat. 'I've told him what you said. All right, he will see you at eleven. He's got important business afterwards so don't be late.' End of message. It was in Hungarian. No names used. Then, *'Hetfö, háromnegyed kilenc.'* Click. That is Monday 8.45 a.m., the time of the last recorded message. The Monday just past? Or Monday 3rd January? No clue. But the message has been played or the light would have been flashing.

It has drained me, this search for my unknown wife. Lines pulsate at the edge of vision and I close my eyes. How long have I been in the flat – an hour, longer, two hours because it takes a long time to bury a marriage – and I have found no hint of any other life for Eve. That's not right. OK she was a diplomat, trained to be secure. But if she was involved with Goenz then she was stepping out of her usual role. There should be some little thing she overlooked.

I open my eyes. I study the room, really look this time, at the bookshelf with dictionaries and reference books and weighty tomes of history and biographies and large volumes of reproductions of artists. Van Gogh was a favourite which is why there is the repro-duction of one of his Sunflower pictures on the wall and I stare at it and hear her voice: 'It's the one in the museum in Munich. Such vibrancy, bursting with life. Can't you feel the intensity, Baz?' The painting I recognise but the frame… I swear it is different, a chunky wooden job. So I go to the wall and see that at one side there is a slit and when I press the backing away I can just slide my index finger in and feel a sheet of paper hidden by the Sunflowers reproduction and I wiggle the paper out.

It is in her writing, no doubt of that. I stand with the paper tilted to a lamp while I study it.

	SRB	*ROM*
17 Dec	*BG187-FV*	*7*
7 Jan	*TM09RTS*	*11*
21 Jan	*B798LTV*	*2*
14 Feb	*PE445-LT*	*8*
2 Mar	*B475TLS*	*18!!*
18 Mar	*BG984-ST*	*4*
2 Apr	*AR77FDE*	*6*

The final date is last Friday, if the dates are this year's. And if the dates are this year's then Eve (presumably) has been coming back to her flat to make a record on the hidden piece of paper.

I can scarcely breathe. Eve has come alive. The glimpse of her on TV has been replaced by physical evidence in her flat. I look at my glass. The *palinka* is finished and in any case my mouth is dry and I want a glass of water. I go to the kitchen and fill a glass from the tap and stand staring at the sheet of paper. Why has she written these columns of letters and figures and what do they mean? Why on 2nd March does the number 18 have two screamers?

Maybe the alcohol is pushing me down a wrong road but I feel I must have answers so I stuff the paper in my pocket and return to the desk. I smooth a sheet of paper with the Föld utca address on the desk and come to a sudden halt with a pen in my hand. How do I start off? *Dear Eve?* In my confused state that seems too formal. *Darling?* No, I don't think she is my darling any more, nor I hers.

Dear E

What a mess. Before I do anything further we must talk. You were

on BBC news last Thursday standing behind GG and there was a great
scramble to cover it up. I've seen Lovegrove and he tried to bribe me.
I've met West a couple of times and he is flailing around. My cousin
Jozsef – a secret policeman of a very special kind – tells me…

I stop. The noise from the street outside makes me drop the pen
and hustle back to the kitchen window. A car door slams and there
are voices. Looking down I see a man ducking his head as he locks
the driver's door. My eyes switch to the figure crossing the road,
a woman taking long dipping strides. It is her. My God, it's Eve.
The man says something and she stops a moment and turns back
towards him, laughing at what he said.

There is a pain in my guts and a tight band round my forehead
and I cannot breathe. I have come all this way. I have been searching
for her. I have been battling with the bureaucrats and all the secret
apparatus of the state to get to this point where I can hear her story. I
have just written *We must talk*. Now, the idea of her coming upstairs
with whoever he is, confronting her, not knowing what emotion
I'll see in her face, greetings, explanations, sifting truth from lies,
consequences – I can't do it. I revolt against the idea. I must get
out. I just have time to turn off the lights in the kitchen and study,
put back the bottle, rinse the glass and then I dash into the sitting
room. I switch the last light off. I am out of the door and easing it
closed until I hear the click of the lock.

There are footsteps on the staircase. They have reached the landing
on the floor below so I turn and climb up to the turn of the stairs
to the floor above. I flatten myself against the wall, feeling the beat
of my heart, breathing as gently as I can through an open mouth.
There's a man's voice but it seems to bounce off the walls. I can't
make out what he says.

'That's because I'm younger.' It is her voice, Eve's. She is ahead
of him. Six or seven seconds of silence. 'Where's the key? Bugger
bugger bugger. I didn't give it to you, did I? Oh no, found it.'
Another pause and I close my eyes for no rational reason. I see
nothing therefore the world doesn't exist.

'Made it. Bloody stairs. All right, so you're younger. Don't grin at me. Who was it who said: Youth is wasted on the young?'

My eyes fly open. I cannot believe this. My brain refuses to take it in. First Eve. Now West.

Only afterwards did I realise that what I had just done changed everything. I left my coat in the flat. I took one step outside the building and the cold night air hit me and I knew what I had done. I was in too much of a hurry, getting out before they reached the second floor and I overlooked the coat. Mistake, simple. West has seen me in it but he might not remember it. Eve will know it is mine. Why have they gone to her flat? Why has West lied and lied again? Maybe they are having an affair and it is nothing to do with Goenz.

I peer up at the flat. The sitting room window is ablaze and then I see a light go on in the kitchen. It will be the study next and I panic. The letter, half finished. I left that too in my scramble.

They could come down. West could come after me in his car. I set off in a run up the street, aiming for the main road ahead. Another thought hits me: the card-key is in my coat pocket. West knows I am staying at the Ibis Styles because he telephoned me there. They'll know my room number now and have the key to get in. Then behind me I hear a car door slam. An engine starts and there is the sound of a car doing a three-point turn, abrupt gear changes. I am by the restaurant where I had dinner. It is closed but there are tubs of shrubs by the door which hide me.

The car passes. Eve is driving, West peering up the road ahead. His arm is across his body as if he's prodding Eve's ribs. I watch the red tail-lights dwindle and at the top the car swings left towards the city centre. I wait in the shadows and try to think it through. They got out fast therefore they know it was me in the flat. Did they think I had got out just ahead of them? Were they searching for me? When they don't find me will they return? Maybe try the other direction on the main road? I simply don't know. I don't know why West was prodding Eve in the ribs. I remember the confrontation in

West's office, how his hand slipped inside his jacket as if he had an undiplomatic pistol hidden there. He is no limp wristed diplomat and I wonder what Eve has got herself into.

Föld utca is quiet. No car comes down, no eyes probe the shadows After five minutes I leave my shelter and go up to the main road and turn left, as they did. I came by tram but the service must have stopped and I start to walk. It's a long way and three of four times I pull back into shadows as a car's headlights approach until at last I see the sign on a taxi. I don't mess about flapping an arm at it but stand right in the middle of the road, arms wide like a man crucified. Its lights grow bigger, I don't move, it slams on its brakes. In the headlights I hold up a five thousand forint note and wave it about. The driver winds down his window.

'You want to take some care. Are you tired of life?'

'Here, take it.' I thrust the note at him.

'Where do you want to go? The hospital? The cemetery?'

'The Korzo.'

'Korzo? Bloody Korzo did you say?'

For a moment he lifts his eyes heavenwards as if I had asked to go to some far-off planet. He relents enough to switch on the courtesy light and examine the note. Are the colours true? Is the watermark there? I climb in the back. The front passenger seat is occupied by a dog, a mongrelly variation of a terrier that gives a ritual growl and bares its teeth.

'Don't try to pet him. He bites.'

'What's his name?'

'Dog.'

The taxi gets going. In the mirror I see his face switching on and off with the passing streetlamps. I glance to the side as a car over-takes us and it's not West. They would have seen the coat straight away. I imagine West turning out the pockets. Did they find the half-written letter on the desk?

'I asked why you want to go to the Korzo this time of night. No cause to be bashful. You want a girl? You got the urge?' He glances in the mirror to frown at me. 'Listen, you don't need to go that far. I know a girl up the road in Kiscelli who'll do anything for two thousand five. A straight fuck is only two. She's a Chink, see, maybe Vietnamish, one of those, but don't worry, she's very clean.' After a pause to let me consider this offer he says, 'Bloody middle of the night, why were you walking down the road?'

'Trouble with my wife.'

'Listen, a wife is like a coffin: there's a body in there but you don't want to spend the rest of your life in it. Say the word and I'll turn round and drive you to Kiscelli.'

I don't answer because my mind is racing. Eve as coffin is a difficult concept. Then the image of the casket with the hand in it flashes into my head. And its disappearance. How does Eve fit into that? What is she doing? Why is West going to her flat? Sex, is that it? If not, what?

'You don't say much.'

'No.'

'Listen, you want my advice, you're better off without her. I should know, I used to be married but I got out. I want a fuck, there's the girl in Kiscelli. Two thousand forints and I'm ahead of the game 'cos it's cheaper than new clothes for the wife and going to the hairdresser and chocolates and new bloody curtains. My wife, she had a thing about curtains, you know, a feckish. She kept thinking the neighbours could see through them, see her undressing. Listen, I said, you think people are actually queuing up to get an eyeful of you? I laughed until she got mad. You want to know what I've learned? Without a wife you can go and get rat-arsed whenever you like. You don't have to be polite to her mother. You can smoke in bed, pick your nose without her nagging. Believe me, *pajtás*, you could be looking at a brighter future.'

'Thank you.'

The philosopher glares at me in the mirror some more. 'One day, if you follow my advice, you will thank me.'

'Thank you,' I say again and we continue in silence. I told him to go to the Korzo because I don't want to arrive at the Ibis Styles in a blaze of headlights. I want to take it slowly, see if anyone is waiting in a doorway. He stops at the edge of the Korzo and I get out.

'Just a minute,' he says. He's not expecting a tip is he? 'Listen, I've been watching you in the mirror and I think you're a puritan, that's why you won't speak about it. You come here but all you'll do is look at the girls and then you'll go back home and taunt your wife about the good time you've had. Stop pretending. Listen, do it instead of just looking and you'll get double the satisfaction.'

Why does he keep saying *Listen*? Is it because nobody ever does listen to him? Another crazy. Two in one day is about par for Budapest.

I stand under one of the white globes of the streetlamps, watching him drive away, then start to walk.

'*Szia, drágám, saját?*' This is no girl but someone older with too much make-up. I imagine she's a desperate mother with two kids whose husband has followed the taxi driver's advice.

'Hello my friend. There's a dark room very close where we could get to know each other better.' It's a man in a leather jacket who steps in front of me then has to step back.

'Buy me a drink, mister.' Now who? One of those Russian blondes Pal Pokorni says are undercutting local talent.

I smile and walk on, refusing all offers because I am a puritan.

I'm on the fourth floor of the hotel, hesitating for just a moment outside her door. My room is no longer safe so why didn't I check into another hotel? It never crossed my mind. I was drawn back to the Ibis Styles because here is someone I know and trust.

I knock and wait and knock again.

'Who is it?'

'Baz.'

'What do you want?'

'To get in.'

'Why?'

'Just open the bloody door.' Remember Mr Manners. No, sod it. There is silence and I wait then get impatient. 'Mary?'

Finally the door opens. I suppose Mary was in bed naked and has been to fetch the bath towel she was wearing when I went out. It is tucked under her armpits and reaches half way between her hips and her knees. She has seen my eyes travel down her body and back up to her face.

'Well?' she says. She is stony faced as she stares at the man who walked out and left her to an evening of soggy pizza and TV.

'Are you going to invite me in?'

CHAPTER 13

'Shit.'

Morning has come – does Mary always greet dawn this way? A sharp elbow in the ribs jolts me awake.

'What bastard is this?' she mutters.

Has she forgotten who she's in bed with? I'm the waif who came in from the cold and she decided to warm up. How it played last night comes vividly back to me. Mary was perched on the edge of the bed with her knees and thighs catching the soft light from the bedside lamp while I told her what had happened at Eve's flat.

'So West is bedding your wife – is that what you think?' Mary asked.

'Yes… No… How can I tell?'

'You're an idiot if you think that way,' she said. 'Maybe they're in bed together, maybe they're not, but that is not what this is about. You don't fake your own suicide and disappear for four months because you want to shag your boss.'

It had been a long day with a lot happening and my brain couldn't cope any more. 'So what is happening?'

'Jesus, Potter, isn't that what you're here to find out? And why Dexter sent me to take photos? But…' She leant forward. 'I'll give it to you straight. She is no longer behaving like a wife. Whatever she's involved in, she has cut you out.'

Then she leaned back to watch me. I turned over what she said and yes, it is true: Eve has dropped me, abandoned me, left me. I nodded.

'Close your eyes,' she said. 'No peeping. Put your hands over them.'

I heard her stand up from the bed.

'All right, you can look now.'

Oh.

I'm hung over, I'm scared, I'm confused. Sometimes I hate Eve for what she's done, sometimes I hate myself for hating her – that is true confusion. A taxi driver said I was better off without her because I could pick my nose when I wanted to. He had a dog called Dog. Crossing the Korzo a leather boy invited me to go in a dark room with him. A tart wanted to know if I was all on my own. No longer. Mary was standing there with the towel on the carpet by her feet, one hand resting on a hip, lamp light shadowing the valley between her breasts. I gazed until she cocked an eyebrow.

'Does sir approve?'

There is no defence against such beauty. I got to my feet and she put her arms round my neck and stood on tiptoe to kiss me. She pulled back to look in my eyes. Did I want her? She kissed me again to make me want her more.

'Yes,' she said, 'oh yes.' We went to bed and the bleakness and loneliness inside me disappeared with the feel of her. 'Kiss me,' she said. 'Oh yes.' I was more desperate than passionate. That's the truth. We slept and loved and slept some more.

It comes again, the knock at the door when all I want is to doze and everything to be made better.

'You going to see who it is?' Mary asks. 'I'm naked.'

So am I but I pick up her towel from the floor to tie round my waist. The third knock is more fist than knuckles.

'Who is it?'

'Father Christmas.'

My hand hovers over the handle a moment. The voice I recognise but how do I know he doesn't have someone jabbing a pistol in his back?

'Open the goddam door or do I break it down?'

So I ease the door open a crack, have it shoved in my face and a hand spread on my chest pushes me back. It is my cousin Jozsef acting the bad cop while I continue my retreat into the bedroom. The bedside lamp casts shadows into the little nicks and scars on his face.

'How did you…?' I begin.

There is a lot of anger in Jozsef and he cuts in. 'Find you? I went to your room and knocked on the door and gave it the same treatment as here. I heard someone putting the security chain on and the door opened. A man's head was in the gap, hair the fashionable prison cut, nose that had met a fist, piggy eyes. "What do you want?" A couple of steps behind him was another toughie and it wasn't you. "I'm looking for Zoltan," I said, "so who are you?" He was the strong silent type and he just stared at me. "This is room 331, isn't it?" I said. He could speak after all. "Wrong floor." He jabbed a finger up. I went to the lift and the heavy mob was still watching so I took the lift up a floor in case he checked and then went down to the ground floor.'

'How did he…?' I begin, but remember that West must have my key.

'At reception I said that Mr Fazekas did not seem to be in his room. Has he checked out? No, but try his fiancée's room. So you're his fiancée?' He swivels to point at Mary.

'What's he saying?' Mary asks because Jozsef has let loose a fusillade of Hungarian.

'I am saying hello,' Jozsef tells her in English.

'Who are you?'

'I am Bazil's cousin. My name is Jozsef and I am a policeman. At this moment I am a very unhappy man who is about to do something he will live to regret. That happens often in my life. And you are his fiancée?'

'We're just good friends,' she says.

The little world which was our own has been invaded. Men are from Mars, women are from Venus, Jozsef is from a different solar system, an alien with unfathomable ways of behaviour. Mary is sitting up in bed with the sheet tucked under her chin. With every breath the sheet moulds itself to her breasts.

'Some good friends are better than others,' Jozsef says.

'All right,' Mary says, 'I'm getting up to shower and put some clothes on so turn round to the wall.'

'How can you be sure I won't take a peek?'

'Why? Haven't you seen a woman's tits before?'

Jozsef considers this. 'OK.' He turns to face the wall. When he hears the bathroom door close he says to me, 'Good looker, most definitely, good spirit too. You didn't introduce your good friend. What's her name?'

'Mary.'

'Mary. Like the Virgin. Now Eva is also a good looker. It beats me how you attract them.'

'It's known as charm, Jozsef. Politeness plus a sense of humour.'

'That explains why I am doing so badly.'

There is something of a pause which Jozsef doesn't fill while I think about this remark. So I have to ask the obvious.

'How's Adel?'

Adel is Jozsef's wife of long standing, mother of two rebellious teenagers. She works at the Opera House in Andrassy Street, just down the road from the old secret police headquarters. She doesn't sing arias or saw a violin or carry a spear. She works in the box office but some of the glamour of the place has rubbed off on her. Also, no disputing, some of the artistic spirit. She can throw a fit or a coffee cup. Passion runs deep in her and, in the artistic way, runs free.

'Adel is well,' Jozsef says with some care, 'or so I am told.'

'You've left her?'

'Other way round. She is with some warbler in the chorus, ten years her junior. Why couldn't she have an affair like a normal person and shut up about it? Why did she leave?'

'Did she leave long ago?'

'Four days.'

For a moment I screw up my eyes. I am in the front line, bearing the brunt of Jozsef's anger.

'I'm sorry.'

'You're sorry. It happened to you, didn't it? Now your second wife's gone. Charm doesn't seem to last long. I thought you were meant to be the big expert on women.'

'The only thing I'm an expert on is confusion.'

'Confusion is right. You didn't warn me you were going on TV last night making a big appeal. This morning I got a phone call from my boss. I could hear the thunder rumbling in his voice. I'm due to see him in an hour.' He looks at his watch. 'Less.'

I think of saying I'm sorry again but I'm not, so I wait for Jozsef to go on.

'The only good news is I have tracked down the address of Goenz's house in Budapest. It's on Castle Hill so I thought we'd pay a call after I've seen my boss. Eleven o'clock by the Military History Museum.'

'What...'

'No questions, Bazil. I don't have time to hold your hand. Say goodbye to your very good friend for me.'

Mary reminded me we are here for work so I check in with our editor.

'Hello, Dexter, it's your roving reporter.'

But in Dexter's world Hello is a relative term. 'Just a minute,' he says.

In the background there is a hubbub of voices, none I can pick out individually. The *Oxford Herald* has gone into First Edition panic mode and these are the sounds of subs and reporters and what Josh is pleased to call 'the fancy goods' cursing the approaching deadline. Josh despises PC, bless him. A door is shut, the noise cut off.

'What the hell is going on?' Dexter says. 'Why haven't you filed a story? Are you there on holiday?'

This is Dexter in Lord Copper mode. I take the telephone away from my ear and wrinkle my nose at it. Dexter is my boss and entitled to a stretch of despotic ranting. Good luck to him. Doesn't mean I have to listen. I close my eyes, more than a little weary. A series of squawks like a yard full of chickens prompts me to put the receiver to my ear again.

'Do you understand? Hello? Have you been cut off? Did you hear what I was saying?'

'Up to a point.'

There is a pause.

'Oh, forget it – provided you've got something for me.'

'Last night I went out to Eve's flat armed with my fine-tooth comb. I turned up a document she'd hidden that showed she has been coming there regularly since her quote accident unquote and disappearance. The paper is a list of dates and letters and numbers.'

'Meaning what?'

'I'm looking into that.' Damn, why didn't I show it to Jozsef? 'I had to leave in a hurry when Eve returned.'

'Why didn't you confront her?'

'Her boss was with her. He's the man who's lied to me and I don't want a confrontation until I know what it's about.'

'So you haven't got a story.'

'Ah, wait. I'm going out now to the house of the gang boss that Eve is possibly having an affair with. He is also the illegitimate son of a former communist minister so he's got some chums still round in high places.'

'There could be an angle there.'

'They stick together, help each other out. Bit like the Masons.'

Dexter doesn't react. Perhaps he's a Mason.

'Right, I've got to leave now.'

'Is Two Boobs with you?'

'She is.'

'Tell her I want photos.'

'I will.'

I think he missed that because he hung up.

Mary is stretched out on the bed. 'What was he saying about me?'

'He said to tell you he loves you.'

* * *

We are on the early side of eleven o'clock. Mary has wandered off with her camera. I lean against the parapet outside the Military History Museum. I love the feel of spring sun on my face. In the distance are the Buda hills, wooded and dotted with country mansions. Eve took against living there for no rational reason.

The hills are hazed, hiding their secrets. I should go there, stroll among the pine trees, cast an eye over the *dachas* of the great and the good, the sly and the evil, old money, new money, dirty money. The higher the fences, the lower the morals. Listen to the dogs as I pass: are you a pet or a hunting companion or a throat ripper? This is where the old guard retreated after the accursed forty years, glowering at the city that no longer jumped to their commands.

Somewhere a clock is striking eleven. I turn and see Jozsef. The look of thunder on his face earlier this morning hasn't cleared. He puts an arm round my shoulder to nudge me close to the parapet.

'Tempted to commit suicide, are you, cousin?'

'What's happened?'

'Inside the museum,' he tips his head to the right, 'they've got a video of the Thirteen Days back in '56. You can ease back on a creaky plastic chair and watch newsreel footage, home movies, stills all spliced together. I have seen it and picked out my father but it is something I find infinitely painful. A grainy black and white photo shows him holding a rifle and pressed into a doorway while a Soviet tank rumbles past. It's part of our nation's history, part of my family's history, but not any more. Yesterday a colleague was here with a foreign visitor. They watched the video and those six or seven seconds of the shot of my father have been edited out. Vanished. Never was. Understand?'

He squeezes my shoulder. I have been staring at the Buda hills and when I turn to look at him there is a heat in his face that warns me to keep quiet.

'Cast your mind back to the old days when the Party ruled. When someone high-up fell out of favour he was airbrushed out of photographs. That is what has happened to my father – yes, even in this brave new democracy of ours. The reason why my dad was cut out of the film is because I am suspect. Yes me, Jozsef Fazekas. You are probably wanting to know why.'

He waits. Jozsef is full of rage. Like a prairie fire it spreads in all directions, takes me unaware.

'What are you suspected of?'

'Knowing you.'

There is a squeeze of my shoulder again, rather harder.

'I don't know what you're talking about.'

'I have a boss. Let me tell you in one sentence what kind of man he is: he does his best work at the lunch table and often doesn't return in the afternoon. This morning he sent for me. My boss is called A because he thinks that a very secret policeman should keep his name secret. He has seen too many James Bond movies. There is no visitor's chair in front of A's desk so I slouch to attention while he clears his throat and issues his commands. I, Jozsef, am to keep my nose out of matters that do not concern me, I am to have nothing more to do with you, I am not to pursue Goenz, I am not to interest myself in your lovely wife – not that I have been interesting myself in *that* way. It is an ultra-secret matter, I was told, so lay off. Just like the old days. I am surprised I wasn't advised to go to Cuba to drink rum and screw some black girls. I must be naive to have thought everything had changed. All right, I want to know if you have any secrets.'

'Secrets? What secrets?'

'Things you are hiding from me that I should know.' He leans close to whisper in my ear. 'Secrets like who's going to win the next election, what Einstein's Theory of Relativity means, what the hell your wife is up to with Goenz. That kind of secret.'

'You know why I came. That's not a secret. And I'd never heard of Goenz.'

'Funny in a way,' Jozsef says but doesn't look amused, 'until you came and stirred things up – or stirred me up – I knew nothing about Goenz except he was a big-time crook. I didn't know about his web of connections that seems to stretch to my boss.'

'And we're here now because you've found out where Goenz lives.'

'Once again you're wrong. I know he owns the house. Does he live here? That's something we are about to find out. We're here because I don't like sitting behind a desk and twiddling my thumbs. Because I don't take orders from a crooked boss. Because I am contrary. Because I am Hungarian.' He takes his arm off my shoulder to make a grand sweep towards the Buda hills. 'Maybe because…' He gives a baffled shrug. 'Adel's come back.'

I search Jozsef's face for a clue to his feelings. It was only earlier this morning he told me Adel had left and he was angry. His wife has returned and his face is set in stone.

'Is this…a matter for congratulation?' My words are clumsy and I stumble over them.

'You congratulate a person for achieving something. What have I achieved? Nothing. I called back home to pick something up,' he pats the side of his chest, 'and there she was, unpacking her suitcase. I didn't have time to sort anything out.' Jozsef pauses a beat. 'The man she fancied wasn't some great *basso profundo*, I was told, just someone in the chorus. Maybe it turned out he was only a light tenor in the bed department.'

Jozsef makes a joke because he doesn't want to talk of it any more.

'Women,' I say, for male solidarity.

'What are you complaining about? You come here looking for your wife and forty-eight hours later you've found a good friend. Where is she?'

'She wandered off.'

'Well, I am not hanging around. We're going to have a look at Goenz's house.'

'Just a minute. I was in Eve's flat last night and I found this sheet of paper she'd hidden.'

Jozsef takes it from me and runs his finger down the column of dates.

'Every two or three weeks.' He peers at the paper and waggles his head from side to side. 'You found nothing that would explain the other columns?'

'No.'

'I'll look into it.' He stuffs it in his pocket. 'Come on. There's no point waiting…'

He breaks off. His eyes are gazing beyond me and he draws a breath.

'No, *no*,' he shouts in English. 'Stop it. No.' He switches back to Hungarian. 'You tell your friend to stop at once. There must be no record of the two of us together.'

'Hi, fellas.'

Mary, camera raised, is leaning against a statue.

'Put your arm round Baz and whisper in his ear like you did before. The secret policeman telling secrets. I love it.'

From which it is obvious she has been behind the statue for some time.

'So there it is, Goenz's house.' Jozsef doesn't point, just nods his head.

We are in Uri utca, and our excuse is that we are examining the ruins of a church destroyed in the battle for the city at the end of the war. There is not much left except a bell tower. A pillar gives us some shelter but Jozsef was still careful when he ducked his head towards the house across the road. It has a pair of solid wooden gates wide enough to drive a coach and horses through. If you've left the cavalry behind there is a human-sized door inset into the gates. Look up and you'll see shutters closed over the upper windows. Windows on the ground floor have grilles, not the vertical bars of prisons but in a diamond pattern. Between the two storeys is a ledge, very narrow, looking like a rope tying the house together. It is just wide enough for pigeons to strut and do their courting.

'There's no guard, no one sitting in a car reading a newspaper. Half an hour ago I rang from my phone and nobody answered. Is this our lucky day? All right, we want to get inside to have a look round but first we'll just check that nobody is at home. Your good friend and I will play tourists and she must photograph the very interesting ruins of Mary Magdalene church. You go and ring the bell. Think you can do that? Not beyond you?'

I'm a pro. I've rung the doorbells of people who've lost their family in a disaster or won the lottery or whose husbands have turned into what the tabloids call love rats. I've stuck my foot in the door and done the job. That was as a reporter. Suppose we're out of luck and someone does answer the door. I'll ask if Mr Hadik is home and then say I must have got the address wrong. Jozsef could do this but he is angry because I have got him into this and his boss is breathing down his neck and Adel has left him and come back. Yes, I can do this. But suppose, just suppose, it is Goenz I am faced with. And suppose Eve has shown him a photo of me. I'll get a warm welcome. The wrong kind of warm.

'And if it is Goenz?'

'Goenz isn't in the doorbell answering classes. Now tell her what's going on.'

I explain to Mary in English.

'All right, now do it.'

I float across the road. That's what it seems like. My face is a good liar: serene, confident. But inside… A fresh worry grips me, not that Goenz will open the door but Eve herself will. Last night I couldn't face her so how do I feel now? Life, I tell myself, is full of what-ifs and who-the-hell-knows. The door inset into the gates has a knocker in the shape of a Venetian hand so I try that first. I'm so cool I turn my back on the door while I wait and see Jozsef with a hand resting on Mary's shoulder while she photographs the bell tower then turns and takes one of this historic mansion which just happens to include me. No answer to the knocker. Fixed to the wall at the side is a public letter box, which is odd. I don't puzzle about it for long because beside it is a bell-push. I press it, noticing as I do a bullet hole half concealed by the box. Nothing to do with Goenz, I decide. It is too weathered, a relic from the WW2 battle.

'The dogs must be out scavenging. Good.'

Jozsef is at my side. Reaching inside his coat he draws out a pistol.

'This is your cousin?' Mary says. There are two ways to take this: she is impressed by the cop's derring-do, or she sniffs at my Caspar Milquetoast feebleness in contrast to his macho action.

'Yes, I am his cousin. I go after his wife with a gun. Maybe one day he does the same for me. I don't usually go round carrying artillery. I had to go home to fetch it.'

Where he encountered Adel which has soured the day for him.

With a brief glance both ways down the deserted street he places the muzzle against the wood by the lock and fires. It's the loudest gunshot ever. It scares the pigeons. There are answering explosions as they lift from the ledge, their wings clapping in alarm. Jozsef squeezes the trigger again. He puts his shoulder to the door and shoves it open with a splintering of wood.

'Get in, be quick,' he orders. 'One bang is OK, maybe car back-fires. Two bangs…'

It's a different age we step into: a cobbled courtyard, stable doors at the south end, stone walls to either side, casement windows, benches tucked under a wooden table, grape vines trained on wires, a wine cask sawn in half and filled with earth but no plants, a few of last autumn's leaves blown in one corner, a choice of three doors to enter the house. There is an air of emptiness and neglect except for the car that's jammed against the stable doors. It's a Skoda, gleaming, not one of the old jokes but an Octavia with the German engineering. Jozsef prowls the yard, pistol in hand, casually laying a hand on the bonnet of the car, while Mary snaps everything in sight and I stare at the windows. No faces peer at us. Jozsef's tour takes him past the doors which are half glazed. He places his cheek against the glass to peer down and at the third he makes a gesture at us to keep back. I am a couple of paces behind Jozsef. I always will be: it's the years he has on me and the life he's led. With the butt of his pistol he smashes the pane, reaches inside and turns a key.

I am crossing another frontier. A step inside and this is

breaking-and-entering. Even the phone hackers of Fleet Street draw back from that. My cousin follows Hungarian logic: if the most effective way of defending the constitution is by breaking the law, then go for it. He jerks his head: come on, be quick.

No alarm sounds and we pass into a kitchen. Jozsef holds up his hand and we listen to silence. No, not quite silence. There are no voices or creaks or footsteps, just a faint hum. Electronic security wizardry? None that we can see. No serious cooking is done here, I would guess. The flimsy appliances could be relics from the socialist era except for a huge fridge with a Westinghouse logo, source of the hum. It's tall enough to hold a corpse. Mary edges up to it and opens the door. The internal light shines on cartons of milk, bottles of beer, mineral water, bread, butter, pickles, salami, a hunk of trappista cheese.

Jozsef's pistol leads the way. We follow into a dining room with a stuffed boar's head snarling above the fireplace, into a reception room with dark baronial furniture, then it has to be upstairs to the first floor and it is here I falter. I have done this, searching for my wife in her flat last night. Searching for my wife in another man's house seems different. My wife? After what she has done? After last night with Mary? Why do I think of her like that? There's no logic to human feelings?

Mary gives me a push and we climb the stairs. The windows are shuttered and Jozsef switches on lights. We pass the master bedroom plus three other bedrooms and two bathrooms. A narrow staircase leads up to where servants used to huddle under the roof. We take the more generous stairs back down to the far side of the courtyard, a store room, a play room for the staff with an English dartboard, a TV, another more modest fridge and a card table. Beyond that is a study. Jozsef shrugs.

'You've found nothing.'

Mary is pointing out the obvious but Jozsef will have none of it.

'On the contrary we have learnt much. We know that Goenz is not here and nor is anybody else so it is not his headquarters. To take the optimistic view we only have the rest of the country to find him in. He is somewhere out there.'

He swings his arm wide then lets it fall.

He shakes his head and slips into Hungarian. 'I must find Goenz because I was told not to. That is clear. Normally my boss's face is like a mask, smooth, not troubled, as if God had performed a skilled surgical operation and removed his intelligence. This morning his face showed some emotion though I can't decide what. At one time I thought he was embarrassed but he doesn't have the imagination to be embarrassed. Pity? Resigned? To what? Some thunderclap from the gods that cannot be avoided?'

'Care to share that with me?' Mary says. 'It sounded like the confession of some sin.'

'You must forgive me for speaking my own language. I am just hoping that lunch will restore my boss to his normal state of a sleeping brain. Now to work.'

I try to think generously of Eve, the woman who swept into my life and took it over and brought her own brilliance to light it up. Inevitably my thoughts turn to the darkness that followed her disappearance. I leave Jozsef and Mary and make for the stairs.

The door to the master bedroom creaks as I push it wider. It's like the lid of a trunk full of secrets. Stupid thought. Right, here we have it: a bed so big you could hold a party in it and perhaps Goenz has. He favours the left-hand side. The night table has a lamp and a telephone and an ashtray with half a dozen stubs. On the lower shelf is a Hungarian edition of *Playboy*. Under that is a book. Curiosity about the man makes me pull it out. I'm expecting – what – a sex manual? It's a translation of a Jeffrey Archer novel. I'd say Goenz does sleep here but not regularly.

The far side of the bed is for Goenz's partner. For Eve? I have to check. My feet slip one after the other. I distract myself opening a wardrobe: his jackets, a row of half a dozen. I have never thought jackets could look dead without a live body until now. There are his trousers, a leather blouson for when he wants to play street tough, shoes lined up for inspection, ties hanging from a rack. *I'm borrowing that blue one with the yellow fleur-de-lys*, I remember her saying. *I need a bit of male power to face them down at the Office.* Her voice gave a capital O to Office, shorthand for Foreign Office. A shelf has shirts. Another shelf has socks and underwear, all male. I make another eight steps. A man measuring the condemned cell does this. I reach the far side of the bed where the night table has a lamp. The drawer contains a packet of tissues, nothing more.

I rock on my feet with my eyes closed, picturing life with Eve. She would have had a pile of books, a pad and pen for those brilliant thoughts that come to the sleepless, an alarm clock, a discarded necklace. Oh, and if he was in favour the green pottery frog last seen in the burial casket after the hand had been stolen. I lift the pillow. Nothing, no *galibeyeh*. In a final act of violation I dip my face to smell the pillow. Again, nothing.

'Last week I was doing that.'

Jozsef is standing in the doorway. Recently he has been – how can I put it? – all scowl and growl but his voice is surprisingly delicate.

'Then she came back,' he says and shrugs.

His eyes have squeezed to slits as if he is driving into the setting sun. What's he thinking? Impossible to know. Adel has left before and come back. Jozsef too has left and come back. It's like watching a tennis match - him, her, him, her – with their marriage as the ball. He walks round the bed and drapes an arm round my shoulders. 'I'd say Eva has a bedroom of her own.'

'She has a whole life of her own.'

Jozsef nods. 'In the study I found these. Recognise them?'

There is an address book and a red leather engagement diary published by the *Economist*. I open the diary at random. *K & H bank – 14.30. GG Bucharest 14.30 Tarom.* The entries are in Eve's handwriting. It is what I was searching for last night.

'Her diary,' I say.

'Top drawer of the desk in the study. There's also a brute of a safe, big free-standing one, made by the same company that supplied

Fort Knox. In films there's always someone with sensitive fingers who can feel when the tumblers in the lock fall into place.' He looks at a calloused hand and shrugs. 'Movies are all crap.'

Flash.

To Jozsef's fury Mary captures the moment.

'Let's get our sweet little bodies the hell out of here.' His growl is back. 'Women, do they listen?'

We go Indian file, me in the lead, Mary, and Jozsef switching off lights, out of the master bedroom, down the stairs, through the reception room, the dining room, the kitchen and out into the courtyard where I pull up short, Mary knocks into me and Jozsef holds back. Two men are bending over the door set into the wooden gates to the street, one of them fingering the splintered wood round the lock. These are Goenz's boys: chipped faces, eyes as dead as statues. Jozsef drifts round to my side, his hand scratching his ribs near the holster where he stuffed his pistol. His hand freezes as the two men in a single movement produce their guns. Behind me I feel Mary gripping my belt.

'Hey,' one of the boys says, 'who are you?'

'What the fuck are you doing here?' His colleague is not so well brought up. 'You're in shit street – you understand what I mean? – and you're the shit.'

CHAPTER 14

There are voices inside Jozsef's head only he can hear. The voices mock him about Adel's infidelity, unpacking her bag as if she'd just been out to the supermarket. The voices whisper about his heroic father being cut from the video of the Uprising. They berate him for the risk he runs by helping his cousin from England. They fuel his anger.

'Do not turn round,' Jozsef says in English. 'Do not look to your back. Got it?'

Mary grips her jacket tight across her chest. There is heat in her face and a fire flickering at the back of her eyes. She has carried her camera to the worst disasters and those eyes have stayed cool and professional. But not now.

'Do not speak. Do not say anything. They watch or they hear. We don't know.'

I Bazil Potter, aka Bazil Fazekas, aka Baz Faz, am the reason we are walking along Uri utca, not looking back, keeping our thoughts and emotions bolted down. We could be observed. Goenz's boys could be loping behind us on wolf's paws, waiting to strike down the intruders in their boss's hide-out. Except it isn't his hide-out. He's gone to earth somewhere else. I may be the reason we are padding down this street in silence but Eve is the root cause of it: her disappearance, her reappearance, her liaison, her criminality.

We are confronted by a group of tourists. They are Austrians according to the little flag the leader carries, reliving the glories of the Austro-Hungarian empire. We are forced off the pavement. Stepping into the road I sneak a look behind: the thugs are not on

169

our heels. We are free, but it was close. Thinking back it is already unbelievable, the stuff of legends. Jozsef is a magician and the constitution is safe in his hands. He divines other people's weaknesses, conjures a fantasy world out of his own devious mind using whatever props are to hand – viz Two Boobs. I use the nickname in a proper sense of reverence.

'Who are you?' one of the boys had asked. 'You're in shit street,' the other said, 'and you're the shit.'

This is when Jozsef created the myth. His chin went up and his shoulders went back and his scowl turned to thunder. He stepped forward until the nearest bully boy's pistol was jammed in his chest.

'Does she look like shit?' he demanded. 'Don't look at me, look at her. Go on, *look*.'

He didn't raise his voice but he spoke with enough authority so that both the toughs switched their gaze beyond his shoulders. Mary had moved beside me and I could feel her shiver as dark eyes roamed over her body.

'You know who she is? The Virgin Mary.'

Jozsef waited until they looked back at him.

'Find me a virgin who scores one hundred round the chest – those were Gyula's exact words – and I'll give you fifty times a hundred. Dollars I'm talking about, five thousand for a certified virgin, one hundred centimetres in the upper storey, willing and able. That's Mary, attested *virgo intacta* by a doctor.'

Jozsef took swift steps to Mary, pulled her jacket aside, put his hands under her breasts and lifted them higher.

'One hundred centimetres round her tits.'

She had no warning. She didn't understand what Jozsef was saying. She screamed 'Fuck off' and squirmed to get away. Something in Jozsef's eyes stilled her.

The tougher boy, the one who called us shits, walked up and put out the hand that didn't hold the pistol. Jozsef batted it away.

'Are you as stupid as you look? She's for Gyula. You can read the recipe but you can't taste the dish.'

'Why didn't the boss tell us you were coming?'

'How would I know? Doesn't he have secrets he keeps from you? Ask him yourself. He said he would meet us here so where is he?'

'Who's he?' the boy pointed at me.

'He's nobody,' Jozsef said. 'Just her "friend". But she's still a virgin, mind. Attested by a doctor in Belvaros. Imagine how much that cost me. So I want my five thousand.'

'Why did you break down the door?'

'Know what – you're crazy.' Jozsef's voice had turned from anger to scorn. 'When we got here the door was wide open. What kind of security is that? It was me who closed it though I don't know what difference that made as the lock is smashed. So we came in, looking for Gyula and he's not here. What time is he coming back?'

'He didn't say.'

'Has he gone out to the country?'

They didn't answer.

'Bloody hell.' Jozsef ducked his head down as if he was considering his options. He grunted. He shook his head. He grunted again. 'I'm not happy about this. You understand? Is there some problem? A crisis?'

The boys looked at each other: the boss didn't tell them things like that.

'This is a stinking box of fish dumped on me. Do you hear me? Stinking. Putrid. I'm not leaving her with you two hungry boys. No chance. She comes with me and I'll telephone this evening. Tell your boss – when he comes back – tell Gyula that I kept my part of the deal. I brought the Virgin Mary. I expect him to honour his part. Cash-cash.' He rubbed his thumb and index finger together. 'Five thousand US. Come on, I'm not wasting any more time here.' He gave us a nod.

'Who are you? Who do we say came round?'

Jozsef paused, the door in his hand, then came back a couple of steps.

'Christ almighty, don't you recognise me?'

Shake of the head.

'Janos, but I'm known as Don Juan. Back a while I was with Arpad Hamori until we had a difference of opinion. I am what you could call freelance now. I specialise in girls, all tastes catered for. Don Juan, remember that.'

He gestured to Mary and me to go out first because he had a parting shot. 'Get that lock fixed before Gyula comes back or you'll be the ones in shit street.'

Don't look back. Don't look back. Don't look back. We walked down Uri utca with his orders ringing in our ears.

Now, as we march into the square in front of Matyas church, the small bus that will deliver us from Castle Hill draws into sight. Jozsef sets off in a lumbering trot to the bus stop and we wait for its doors to open.

'Just a minute.' Mary prods a sharp finger in his side. Jozsef swings round and she lands a stinging slap on his face. The blood rises to Jozsef's face, both cheeks not just the one that was smacked. He is shocked, at a loss what to say. She has hit him hard and looks as if she might do it again. 'I don't know what you were telling those fuckwits but don't grope me again, not ever.'

'Ha!' Jozsef lets out a bellow of fury or it could be a shout of laughter.

We come down from Castle Hill to the maelstrom of buses, trams and cars that is Moskva ter. Jozsef has parked his Golf in a side street and announces he needs a drink but not in any of the dingy rat-holes here. We drive west, climb a hill, and as the city drops below the houses grow grander and their gardens larger and their walls higher until we breast the top of the hill and come out into unexpected country. Jozsef stops at something not much more than a hut in a clearing of woodland. The hut has a hatch with a bunch of withered vine shoots over it and sells sausages and wine. We sit at a table in an area of withered grass with tumblers of cheap red. The tumblers already show fingerprints and maybe lip prints.

Mary looks left and right. 'I need the loo.'

'Loo?' Jozsef asks. When I translate he says, 'Tell her to go in the bushes. Anywhere. It's free. It's airconditioned.'

'Jozsef says take one of the paths into the woods,' I tell her.

Jozsef watches her disappear. 'Some woman,' he says. He rubs his cheek that has almost lost its redness. 'And some spirit.'

'Maybe you shouldn't have…' I don't finish the sentence.

'Listen, here's the difference between us. In the same situation you would have used words. Talk, argue, explain. I used actions. As a baby, my mother said, I wouldn't let go of her tit. If she tried to get me off I didn't cry – you would have – I clung on and bit even though I didn't have any teeth. You see life as a novel, words. I see life as a film, action. That's what life in the police has taught me, years as a dumb cop on the street, more years as a useless fraud inspector, and now as a threatened defender of the constitution. Action gets people's attention. So I didn't tell them I was delivering a girl to their boss, I showed them her finest assets. Get an eyeful of that, boys. They were convinced because I showed them. Also…' He takes a thoughtful mouthful of wine. 'Something I've learned from Adel. Life is an opera. The plot is ridiculous, even a tragedy is laughable. We put on fancy dress. We sing and strut and are bad actors. But the audience is hooked.'

With wine Jozsef is mellowing into a more reflective mood, words not actions.

'Mary is the same as you. She hasn't lived through the accursed forty years. So I called her the Virgin Mary and showed off her tits – who was harmed? I made up a story but I wasn't lying, not dirty lying. There are good lies and bad lies – understand? We used to lie – I am talking about the old days – we used to tell good lies when it was necessary to survive. That was a good lie I told to Goenz's thugs.' He takes another swig of wine. 'Under the old regime you learned to scheme and twist and you did it with a grovel if the other person was big in the Party or with a smile if he was just a pen-pusher. Sometimes you did it with a snarl that meant: I don't care because I have a secret power you simply don't know about. But you didn't do that often because maybe the other man had his own secret power you didn't know about. Reality was part of our education. Bazil, you don't want to face reality but you're going to have to.'

There's a rusty iron table between us and Jozsef puts his elbows on it to be closer to me.

'Eva is not screwing Goenz – got that? But they want you to believe she is. They didn't want you to come to Budapest and now you are here and digging out the dirt they are jumping this way and that. They are not professionals. Oh, they may be spies and government officials but they are behaving like amateurs because they are stepping out of their comfortable lives into a different situation. Even when they hire professionals they behave like amateurs.'

'Then why was I told Eve is screwing Goenz?'

'Because it is one of those beliefs that everybody holds dear: sex can explain anything. So finally they tell you it is a big sex scandal and that needs to be hushed up. If you were an ordinary husband you might accept that but you're a reporter. Will you spill the beans? That must be keeping them awake at night. Maybe in the end they'll decide you can't be scared off so they'll kill you.'

I don't know what to say to this.

'But this British diplomat screwing a Mafia boss – that is the bad lie they are telling you. I imagine these people scratching their heads, wondering what to do, until someone says – Hey, let's hit him where it hurts, the sex thing, he'll slink off back home. It is not true. We got into the house and you saw Goenz's bedroom. There are none of her things there.'

'Hello boys, have I given you long enough to talk about my boobs?'

Jozsef looks to me so I explain what boobs are.

'They impressed Goenz's thugs, no question,' Jozsef says. 'But you have many fine points. When I lift my gaze to your face I can see a whole opera playing. I think it is Carmen I see – fiery, passionate, eyes that go flash. Do you have gypsy blood?'

'How much wine have you boys had while I was gone?'

'Phhh.' He blows out his breath. 'Living with Adel I have picked up her ways.' He shakes his head. 'Only some of them I assure you. I was telling Bazil that having been in Goenz's house we can be certain Eva is not his partner in bed.'

'Yes, no fruit in the house. She's not living there.'

'Is this the female perspective?'

'In the fridge there was beer and salami and pickles – men's stuff. Men don't think of buying fruit, women do.'

'I can always learn,' Jozsef says. 'No apple, no temptation. Think how much easier life would be if the Garden of Eden had had no fruit.'

'Also there is none of her clutter?'

'Clutter?'

'Woman's stuff. There'd be some of her things around. You know – hairbrush, lipstick, knickers. She may work there but she's not sleeping there.'

'So if it's not sex…' Jozsef says.

'Money,' Mary says. 'Money or sex, what else is there?'

Jozsef looks at me. 'Well, is she interested in money, lots and lots of money? You know her. Has she always longed for diamonds and fur coats and Paris for dinner?'

If Eve had wanted money she'd have been a banker. There was no excitement in that. But I could never see the excitement in being a diplomat either. I can't work it out. But she wasn't interested in money and I shake my head.

'Not money, not sex. So there has to be something else.' He takes his time lighting a cigarette. 'For me the accursed forty years had a hidden blessing. I was just an ordinary cop, I hadn't become…' he leans forward to whisper the word '…constitutional. Crimes were mostly banal. More interesting crimes like corruption were negotiated

175

into a settlement. A lowlife like me would hear a whisper about Agriculture Minister Kisfaludy's son getting a post at the Washington embassy. What was that payment for? Because he had found out about General Lanyi using army trucks on his vineyard? What I learned was that I had to become a psychologist when I was looking for a motive. Take that subdivision of crime known as the confidence trick. In the true con each believes he is getting something out of the other though unlike other bargains there is always one who is sadly disappointed. What we have here is a con. Eva offers something, Goenz gives something in return. Who is conning who? What is the con?'

'And you have the answer?' I ask.

'It's in my head somewhere. Or out in the wide world. I'll find it. Or you will. Or she will.'

Our tumblers are empty and I go to the shack to get refills. We could do with something to mop up the alcohol so I ask for sausages. They come with generous dollops of mustard on the plates and hunks of bread. I'm given a metal tray as battered as the shack and I manoeuvre my way back to our table.

'Where is Mary?'

'My experience of women,' Jozsef says, 'is that there is what they say they are doing and what they are actually doing so I can't tell you. She waved her little camera at me and said she was going to take some atmosphere shots. I hope that doesn't mean she is hiding in the bushes over there to immortalise the two of us together.' He raises his glass. '*Fenékig*! And you've brought lunch too.' He takes a bite of sausage. 'Good mustard.'

We eat in silence for a few moments. Jozsef wipes his fingers on his handkerchief then produces Eve's address book, flipping through the pages.

'Certain names I recognise. Here is Alonzac, Commercial Counsellor, French Embassy. He likes the Capella club for the transvestite shows... Franklin is at the US embassy... Koever... You are in here too, Potter, address in Oxford in case she forgets... Urbaniak... Van Doorn...Mainly the addresses are in Budapest, some in England. I could pursue them, I suppose, if I have nothing better to do. Let's see what help her appointments diary is.'

He opens the diary. The first week of April shows two meetings in banks, lunches and dinners in restaurants. The second week is blank except for the 8th which has a doodle of a house and next to it the letters: DD, MM, T, SW. Jozsef turns back to early weeks. The diary has a week to a page.

'Travel arrangements, restaurants, banks, also names that mean nothing to me,' Jozsef says 'There are a lot of restaurants. It is their style not to eat at home. Gundel's, well, foreigners have heard of Gundel's and the prices reassure them they're getting top treatment… a dinner at Fatal because of the name, they'll never believe it back in Philadelphia… places off the beaten track… here is Kisbuda Gyöngye. Nobody will notice who you are cosying up to there.' He turns back another page. 'More of the same. Restaurants have similar initials. We have to assume they are the initials of people.'

'There is no GG.'

'Maybe Gyula Goenz was at all of them so she didn't note it down.'

'Or it is a code.'

'Odd the doodles she made.'

'She never used to,' I say. 'I doodle, little geometric patterns, arrows, whorls, palm trees, cocktail glasses. She told me it was the mark of a daydreamer, a lazy man.'

'A wifely remark.'

Together we study the doodles and a pattern emerges. A restaurant has a wine glass, a flight has an aeroplane with propellers, once a steam train chuff-chuffed to Vienna, the Ritz in Paris has a building with frills for gutters. And then during the first three months of the year there are doodles with no appointment written in, round faces, smiley faces but with downturned mouths and slits for eyes as if dust was blowing in them. My finger rests on one of the faces.

'Maybe those are the days she sees a lover,' Jozsef says.

'And doesn't smile about it.' There is something familiar about the dates. 'Where is that paper I gave you.'

Jozsef delves in a pocket and produces it. He smoothes out the wrinkles. And there we have the connection: the dates on the sheet of paper hidden in Eve's flat correspond with the unsmiley faces in the engagement diary.

'So?'

'As you say, so,' Jozsef replies.

The corner of a photograph has edged out from the engagements diary and Jozsef slips it out.

'Eve,' I say. 'And Goenz.' I am less positive about Goenz because his expression is different from the angry face of the television news. No, it has to be Goenz, if only for the arm that is round her shoulders. Bed or no bed, it is a possessive gesture. Two other men are in the line-up. Goenz is the smart businessman in suit and tie but these other men wear rough work clothes. They are standing by the side of a truck, one of the leviathans that thunder along Europe's highways. The side panel has the company name: EXROMFRUCT. The address is simply Bucuresti – Romania. Beyond the truck is a light aircraft, not a sleek Cessna business jet but the kind of single engine runaround people fly for the fun of it. On the fuselage is painted H – GYU. Jozsef turns the photo over. On the back Eve has scribbled: 'At the schloss. Ion and Octav brought me lovely peaches.'

Jozsef looks beyond me then closes the diary and tucks it with the address book and sheet of paper with dates into an inside pocket.

'I think your Mary has bad news for us.'

She crashes down into a chair and has a long drink of the wine.

'Bloody bushes are full of sex maniacs.'

'What happened?'

'Some pervert jabbed his hand out at me and shouted some rubbish. He nearly got this in his balls.' She lifts a knee.

Jozsef's face seems to squeeze in imagined pain. 'I never realised today was my lucky day. All I got was this.' He rubs his cheek.

'It could be your T-shirt,' I say.

She looks down where the swell of her breasts distorts the message.

'Where did you buy it?' Jozsef asks.

'Some funky little shop near the hotel. I got it when Baz left me on my own yesterday.'

'Maybe next time you should take Bazil with you when you go shopping.'

'What does it say?'

'*Save a pig. Eat a vegetarian,*' I say.

'Love it,' she says.

Jozsef has lost interest in this. His mobile phone has beeped and he is staring at the message on the screen.

'That's been quick. I suspect Goenz's boys reported to their boss and he has got on to my boss. My presence is required at once at the office. It doesn't say that I should arrest myself but I think that is what it means. I have consulted my conscience – am I working for my boss or am I working to defend the constitution? My conscience orders me to work somewhere else this afternoon.'

A second beep announces a new message.

'If this is my boss...' But he stops 'From Adel. Maybe she's repacked her bag.' But he reads the message and his eyebrows shoot up. 'Lenin talked about "useful idiots". It turns out my cousin is a useful idiot. Someone has responded to your TV performance last night. The police in Kecskemét took the message and someone there deserves a medal for persistence. He rang the TV studio and they couldn't help so he rang police headquarters here and they couldn't help with Bazil but they said they used to employ a Jozsef, now working elsewhere, but if it is urgent why not try his home number. Maybe Jozsef Fazekas can help.'

My parents were Budapesters and my knowledge of what is outside the capital is small. Shameful but there it is. Lake Balaton I know. And I have visited Eger, where Bull's Blood is bottled.

'Where is Kecskemét?' I ask.

'Over there.' He waves in the direction of the bushes. 'Beyond those crows.'

'They're pigeons,' Mary says.

'A detail.

'Is it far?'

'Well,' Jozsef considers his answer, 'we're not walking.'

For a few minutes we are quiet, in itself something of a miracle, enjoying the sun and sipping the wine. It feels almost as if we were on holiday, a world away from cares. Jozsef shares a thought.

'I would judge this a second glass wine. The first glass tastes terrible. With the second glass you don't care. If only there was a way of getting to the second glass without having the first.'

His head turns aside at the sound of motorbike engines. They have stopped by the hut, two men, leathers and helmets, and they pause astride their machines, looking round, before getting off. They get tumblers of wine but don't find a table to sit at, they stand and drink and glance our way.

Jozsef leans forward. His jacket falls open so I can see the pistol in its holster.

'Mary, you must sit in another chair.'

'Why?'

'Because if I must use my gun I don't want to have to shoot you out of the way first.'

Mary stands up but before she can change her seat Jozsef has launched into a full blooded angry tirade at her at the top of his voice. Mary freezes.

'What's he saying?'

'Well.' It is a time for diplomacy. 'He was saying that if it is true that men's brains are located in their balls, where do women keep theirs? His language may not have been quite so philosophical.'

'Charming,' she says. 'Ok, mister, does this give you any idea?'

Mary gives the top of her body a vigorous shake. It used to be one of the fascinations of childhood, how giving a bowl a jolt would set the jelly wriggling and trembling and reforming its surfaces. It is the same with the lovely Two Boobs.

From the hut there are shouts of laughter and looking over we see the two young men raising their glasses in salute to Mary.

'Thank you,' Jozsef says. 'I could not hope for such a bravura performance. You have just proved those two young men are full of the joys of spring and are not Goenz's scouts.'

'Why do you think Goenz would send men here?'

'I don't think he would send men here. He doesn't know where we are so I think he would send men everywhere. But not those two.'

The feeling of spring has passed. Jozsef has work to do: the Kecskemét link to follow up, Goenz's headquarters to find. Mary and I? She catches my eye. Perhaps the feeling of spring hasn't passed.

CHAPTER 15

The afternoon sun is climbing the wall above the bed. We have dozed and thought of ordering room service tea and then thought that would mean dressing, at least one of us. So no tea. My thoughts drift to tea cups. And Jozsef. Adel has come back. Have they had a frank and open exchange of views. I imagine shouting. Is there a collection of chipped china kept for her to throw? Does Jozsef duck or catch? Stupid drifting thoughts, half asleep.

My mind slips to Moira, my first wife. Why? No idea. You are supposed to remember the good times, let the bad times fade away. But the good times have slipped from my memory and it is the end I remember. A Sunday afternoon, winter light coming through the window, sitting across the kitchen table from each other. There seemed nothing to say. Her face had gone grey and all I could see was her mouth set like a slash of red barring the way. In the end she spoke: 'That's it then, isn't it.' As last words go, those will never be famous.

My eyes flick to the patch of sunlight on the wall. It hasn't moved. No time at all has passed. Or I am dead.

I fix my eyes on the sunpatch to catch it moving. I blink and when I look again it has jumped to a corner of a print that Ibis thinks is just right for this hotel in Hungary. The print shows a wine cask – in Burgundy, the caption says – a tun, is that what I mean? Two fat and jolly monks sit at a table in this cellar, quaffing wine from goblets. I realise suddenly that I have been hiding my fear from myself. Those monks enjoying their wine by candlelight take me back to this afternoon and drinking wine at that shack in the scrubland outside the city and Jozsef leaning forward so his pistol catches the light as he watches the two motorcyclists who have arrived. I think of the warning his boss gave him. I think of Pal Pokorni raising his hand and pointing it like a pistol between my eyes. I think of the two toughs who whipped out their guns when we met them in Goenz's house. I think of West leaving in a rush from Eve's flat and his strange posture in the car as if he was sticking a gun in Eve's ribs as she drove.

I have been treating this like a story I am chasing up for the *Oxford Herald*. I am mired in something way beyond my normal job. Forget *Under the Carpet*. This is *In Your Face*.

The sun has jumped to the top of the monks' heads. In this sort of painting monks always have bald heads with a circular fringe of hair. A tonsure, right? It looks like a halo that has slipped down to rest on their ears.

My eyes close.

'Shit. What bastard is this?'

It's not a knock at the door but the telephone that's woken us.

'Aren't you going to answer?'

'I haven't got any clothes on,' Mary says.

'It's the telephone,' I point out.

'And I don't know anybody here. You know your wife, that poncey diplomat whatever his name is, your cousin Jozsef. So you answer it.'

I get up and pick up the phone and look down at Mary. She raises an eyebrow and purses her lips in a kiss as if this is the moment to play games. I turn away from her.

'Hello.'

Silence.

'*Szervusz*,' I try, though Hello is more common.

Click.

He's hung up. He didn't want to speak to me. Why didn't he? If it was a wrong connection why didn't he say sorry? What... my mind goes into a spin. I turn back to Mary.

'We've got to get out. NOW. Get dressed. Get moving.'

'What?'

'They didn't want to speak to me. They were just checking I was here.'

'You mean if I'd answered...'

'Get your fucking clothes on.'

May's never heard me swear before. She is out of bed in a flash.

'I can't find my bra.'

'Just get a sweater and jeans on.'

How long have we got? If they were in the lobby below, thirty seconds. I hear a muttered curse from Mary as the zip on her jeans catches pubic hairs.

'Shoes,' she says.

'Carry them. Passport, wallet.'

She grabs her shoulder bag. 'OK. Hold it, camera case.'

It's a small aluminium box. She picks it up and we are at the door. I open it, listen, hear the sound of the lift, push her out, close the door.

A sign on the wall shows a green stick figure with flames at his heels running towards the emergency exit. We run that way. We reach the door to the stairs and it opens away from the corridor and we are through as we hear the lift stop and its door slide open.

The door to the emergency exit has a powerful spring. I hold it back a fraction so it doesn't bang shut, long enough to hear a knock on what I think must be Mary's door. I want to have a peep, just so I would recognise them another time, but I know what they'll do. Before they force an entry they'll look both ways down the corridor to check it's all clear. I don't want them to see me.

Shoes on, we run down the stairs and go to reception. We are checking out and I ask for our bills. Why does it take such an age? How long before the baddies come after us? After I've paid I say casually that we have decided to go to Vienna and I ask about trains. No problem, the receptionist says, just turn up at Keleti station. There's always a train waiting.

Outside Mary says to me, 'I didn't know we were going to Vienna.'

'Disinformation,' I tell her.

I've read the spy novels.

So that is the great escape. We set off at a brisk walk and at the corner I look back and see no one coming after us. Briefly I wonder what the baddies will do. They'll get into Mary's room – I don't know how but they will – and see the chaos and signs of flight. And then? Telephone the boss? And then? All I know is that we have lost everything except the clothes we are wearing and our passports and Mary's camera bag. Checking into a hotel without luggage just makes the receptionist suspicious so we spend time getting a couple of small suitcases and clothes for both of us. We take a taxi to the Intercontinental because it is good to have a hotel porter carry your luggage in. We have a room on the sixth floor with a view across the Danube to Castle Hill. Mary stands by the window and could have been admiring the view.

'You know, this time last week I was a simple girl, earning my keep on a provincial newspaper, wondering which fella I could bum a drink off. And now…' she turns to look at me. 'Life with Potter.'

I make a face at her: sorry, don't blame me, I don't know how this has happened, *c'est la vie*. That sort of expression.

'I better ring Jozsef,' I say, 'give him our news.'

I have his mobile number and his home number and there is no rational explanation why I chose to see if he is at home. I find myself counting the rings. Answer, you bastard, get out of bed, get off Adel, just reach out a hand and pick up the phone. I am about to give up and try his mobile when the ringing tone stops. No one speaks. God, I have had this already.

'Hello? Jozsef? Who's there? I want to speak to Jozsef Fazekas.' I break off to listen. I can hear breathing. No, it's mine. *Jesus*, what's going on? I think back. Did I speak in English? No. My voice belts out, 'Stop playing games, this is urgent.'

'Who is that calling? Who wants to speak to Jozsef?'

It's not Jozsef who's answered, it's Adel. Her voice is shrill. She sounds too hysterical to recognise me.

'Adel, this is Bazil. I need to speak to Jozsef urgently.'

'You! You bastard! It's all your fault. If he hadn't been sniffing round your affairs and your whore of a wife…'

Her voice is cut off in full flow. She's not hung up. A hand has been clamped over the mouthpiece and I doubt it is hers.

'Adel? What's happened?'

'Who is calling?' This time it is a man's voice but not Jozsef's. 'Why do you want to speak to him at this time?'

'What's wrong?'

'Who are you?'

'I'm his cousin.'

'What is your business with him?'

'Who am I speaking to? Why is Jozsef not there?'

'Where are you telephoning from?'

We are getting nowhere. I shout into the receiver, 'For God's sake, Adel, what's going on?'

I hear voices arguing and a crash as something is knocked to the floor. Then it is Adel on the line again. 'You bastard. It's because of you Jozsef was shot this evening.'

An A&E unit is tucked in a side street behind the American embassy. I got the address from Adel after a protracted struggle. Believe me, getting milk from a donkey would have been easier because she was convinced I would bring a trail of killers with me.

There is a bay for ambulances and glass swing doors for staff and visitors. A policeman standing inside steps forward and pats me down and doesn't say a word. This is a hospital so where is the smell of disinfectant? Instead a hint of cigarette smoke hangs in the air. At the reception desk I state my business and show my passport and wait while a phone call is made. Another burly policeman appears who pats me down again.

'He's already done that.' I nod my head back at the man by the door.

'Got to do it again. Regulations. Maybe he passed you something.'

'He's your colleague, for God's sake.'

'These days you can't trust anybody.'

I don't protest because he's right. Think of Jozsef's boss.

I'm escorted up a broad staircase to the first floor and we turn right. I can tell which is Jozsef's room because there's yet another cop sitting on a chair beside the door. His body and neck and pointy nose remind me of Mr Toad. He puts down his magazine but the effort of standing up is too much for him.

'This is allowed? You are certain?'

'Yes. He's been searched.'

Innocent me. I thought he meant did the doctor approve.

Beds in hospital are high off the floor so nurses don't have to bend too low. Pillows prop Jozsef higher so that when I perch on the visitor's chair he looks down on me. I can't see any bandages and there is no drip bottle.

'You're all right?' I ask.

'Hold up a finger.' His scowl is in place. 'Go on, do what I say.'

I hold up a finger and he peers at it.

'Better.' He hasn't lost his growl either. 'Mild concussion, that's all. On a par with a Sunday morning hangover. Perhaps a...' He raises an imaginary glass and tilts it towards his mouth. '...would do the trick.'

His eyebrows look hopeful. I shake my head. I let my eyes wander round the walls and up at the light fitting in the ceiling.

'You're catching on fast,' he says. 'A facility like this in a place like this, so close to the US embassy, well, the microphones may still be in place. But who would bother to listen now? That's no career for the thrusting young entrepreneurs of our police force.' He pulls a face. 'Here's a true story, or trueish, or at any rate true in spirit. Following a Fourth of July party – understand, this was during the accursed forty years – a Marines guard from the US embassy was stretchered in here after collapsing in the street. There was a strong smell of booze on his breath. "What's he been drinking?" the doctor asked. "Whiskey and Coca-Cola." Bearing in mind the diplomatic storm if anything happened to the American, the doctor informed the political commissar. "How much did he have?" "Apparently a whole bottle," the doctor replied. The commissar curled his lip and wrote a report to his superior. "Inform our comrades in Moscow that there is little to fear about the stamina of Yankee fighting men. They are weak specimens knocked out by a single bottle of Coca-Cola."'

He sinks back into the pillows, closing his eyes for a moment.

'They came to get me,' I tell him. 'Maybe the same people who tried to get you.'

He opens his eyes and fixes them on me while I tell him what happened and what hotel we have moved to.

'You can hardly fault them,' Jozsef says. 'You are to blame coming to Budapest, digging the casket up in the cemetery, going on television, nosing around Eva's flat and leaving your coat there. And Eva is to blame for getting into this mess and pretending she's dead. And that British diplomat is to blame for lying to you. Also I am to blame for sticking my nose in. Probably your friend Mary has her share for sticking her assets out and getting all the men staring at her. We are all to blame. We can each point the finger at someone else. We are all victims. That is the modern way.'

His face contracts with pain, his eyes screwing up tight.

'What happened to you?'

He scowls at me.

'What happened to me? You happened, that's what. You are a danger to life and freedom. So is your wife if she is still your wife. I have caught the English disease and I shall write to your Queen about it. If I catch it again it may be a fatal dose.' He sinks into some region of despair then rallies. 'I am all right, just fatigued and with a chainsaw in my head. There must be a spy in my office. Maybe it's young Szolt who has a pony-tail and scratches his arse and fiddles with computers. I know the type from the old days, earning promotion by ratting on his colleagues. It could be someone else though there's not much choice. We're a very small outfit, almost smaller by one. In my experience it is best to trust no-one. I was working with certain files when I ran out of inspiration.' He makes the familiar drinking motion with his hand. 'So I went out to pay a visit to the bar which a wise city planning authority has decreed should be only fifty metres from our front entrance. They were waiting for me, two of them. Someone must have whispered that I was working after hours. They both fired, more or less at once but I wasn't making notes. One was the kind of shot that gives pheasants hope. I think his bullet went into a tree. Fortunately his comrade was an excellent shot or I might have bled to death on the pavement. He hit me here.' Jozsef places a hand over his heart then reaches out towards the bedside cabinet. He winces and pulls back. 'You open it.'

In the drawer I find Eve's appointments diary and address book that Jozsef lifted from the study in Goenz's house. A hole is chewed right through the address book, chunky leather covers and all, and three-quarters of the way through the diary.

'That seems,' I turn them over in my hand, 'an extreme way to stop you checking on Goenz's movements.'

Jozsef's mouth twitches, a hint of a bleak smile.

'Those tales about the horrors of trench life in the First World War? And the miracles? You'll have read about them. An enemy sniper shoots a soldier but his life is saved because the bullet buries itself in the Bible in his breast pocket. Remember? Those were tucked inside my jacket. They were my Bible. If that gunman hadn't aimed with such precision at my heart…' He lays a hand on his chest. 'I was thumped backwards and my head hit the kerb and I was knocked out. No, not knocked out, I was dead. If they didn't run away but came to check, that is what they would have thought.'

'Who were they?'

'Do you know, I completely forgot to ask their names. Careless of me.' He sighs. 'If you haven't brought me a bottle of whisky I suppose you haven't brought cigarettes either.'

'Not even a bunch of flowers.'

'Save the flowers for my funeral.'

'But you're going to live.'

'So they tell me. But doctors forget what it's like in the big wide world. That's twice today I've had guns pointed at me. And even at home I have to dodge flying crockery.'

'Adel was hysterical when I telephoned,' I say.

'Hysterics is what Adel does best. She's been taking lessons at the Opera. She was hysterical here until I told them to take her away because she was making my headache worse.'

'She'll be all right. She has some sort of police guard.'

'What Adel needs is someone to guard her from herself.' He touches his head, searching for a bruise, wincing. 'That bump on my head may have got my brain working. I have been searching and searching for where Goenz can have gone, our files, then our secret files, Interior Ministry, Land Registry. I found his house in Uri utca but not where he is hiding now so I have decided I have been looking in the wrong places. I must get access to the President's Archives.'

'I haven't heard of the President's Archives.'

'Of course not. It is where they buried the past, all the worst secrets from the accursed forty years. Think of Hungary as a marriage that lasted forty years despite one partner stumbling again and again. If you want the marriage to continue – Hungary to continue, the Magyar people and its institutions to keep going – it was necessary to develop selective amnesia. The past had to be buried. That is why the President's Archives exist. The files, the tapped telephone conversations, the forced confessions, the closed trials, the secret reports, the bad lies and bribes and dirty compromises were chucked in there and the key turned in the lock.'

A certain slowing and darkening in Jozsef's voice makes me think he sees a parallel: his country, his marriage. In his mind he sees lies and battles and betrayals both public and personal. He sighs.

'I shall have to go in on tiptoe.'

'Even though you work for the Office for the Constitution?'

'Yes.'

'And your Cosmic pass?'

'The President's Archives are not part of the known cosmos.' He glowers at me or maybe just at the prospect ahead. 'It will be like a poker game and all I have is a pair of twos in my hand. It is a question of bluffing but don't worry – poker is a very Hungarian game.'

Is this bravery? Or bravado? Does he feel it is his family duty to help me? In the knit of his eyebrows I read anger. He is my cousin and we have this in common: bloody-mindedness at the violence and corruption and trickery as it unfolds round us.

'Is that fat oaf still sitting outside the door?'

'He was reading a Superman comic when I came in.'

'Tell him to get off his arse and find my clothes. I can't go out dressed like this.'

Jozsef pulls off the sheet to show what looks like a nightdress or possibly an Egyptian *galibeyeh* like Eve's.

You've read the spy books. You'd be as nervous as I was leaving the hospital. Is someone following me? I wander a bit. I stop abruptly and turn back. I peer at reflections in shop windows. I hang about in doorways. I do this until I get bored. I haven't the least idea if anyone is on my tail. How could I? It's evening and there are lots of people about, couples, threesomes, home-going office workers, lone men, men astride motorbikes at the side of the road speaking on mobile phones. Take your pick.

I am in Erzsebet körút. Before that it was named after Lenin. At shoulder height on the building beside me are two paler marble slabs where Vladimir Ilyich's name used to be. He has been erased, a historical error, denied he ever existed just as were millions of others who were murdered in his name. I wonder if the slabs which had the street name have found a resting place in the President's Archives. I have no doubt Jozsef will gain access but I wonder how.

* * *

From a face we learn many things, from a back only one. Is this a piece of old Magyar folk wisdom? One of my father's pearls?

We had dinner in the Intercontinental restaurant and now we are in our room. We have undressed and I am lying on the bed and looking at Mary. She has perched on the dressing table stool and is facing the wall. What do you learn from the wall, Mary?

'What is going on, Baz?'

'What do you mean?'

'What do I mean? Don't you see? There's you and me, but there's also Eve. She's everywhere, influencing everything we do. She's here between us now, in this bedroom.'

She stops. In the dressing table mirror I see her eyes have attached themselves to me, waiting for me to respond.

'If you are married to someone, once loved someone...' I begin and stop. What do I know of love, of Eve? My emotions are a tangle of barbed wire but I try again. 'I thought Eve was dead and I mourned her. I discovered she was alive. Bit by bit I found how she had tricked me and what she had done seemed wicked.' I hack through the barbed wire, trying to avoid rips and bleeding. 'I wasn't the husband she wanted. Or expected. Or needed. So she left. In some way I failed her.' Beyond the barbed wire is the minefield. Short sentences are safest. 'She's in danger. I've barged in and made it worse. So I owe her. I have to help. Don't you see?'

I don't know what she is seeing. In the mirror her eyes seem to have shifted from me and fixed on a distant horizon.

Finally she says, 'So you owe her.'

The way she says that makes me feel like a shit.

She swings round on the stool to face me. 'You don't owe her. It's not your fault, Baz. You haven't failed her. She's not wicked either.' She's contradicted every regretful thing I've said and she's not finished. 'It's just the usual bloody mess we make of things. You go blundering on and make it more of a mess. You're not Philip

Marlowe, you're Bazil Potter, you're a reporter, a hack for God's sake. And you're not Sir Galahad so why do you go on? You're up against the Mafia and they've tried to kill Jozsef and they've come after you so what is it for? Tell me, Baz, why?'

Reason, motive, explanation – what can I say? Because I picked Eve up one Sunday morning outside a cinema, because I married her, because I let her slip through my fingers? I feel I owe her and that isn't enough for Mary and I shake my head. In some strange way my confusion impresses Mary.

'Maybe you're a shit but you're an honest one.'

She switches off the dressing table light and comes to lie beside me.

'You're straight,' she says. 'It's just you find yourself in this mess you didn't create and your stubbornness takes over.'

She reaches out and turns my head this way and that, looking for something in my face: sincerity, determination, some great moral plus. Finally she turns my head so I am looking directly in her eyes because she feels she wants to unburden herself of something.

'I've fucked a lot of men. Do you mind?'

I am not expecting this. What do I say? What does any man say?

'For good reasons? Bad reasons?'

'Both. Sometimes for no reason at all.' She releases my head. 'But the thing is you have been more strict. Focused on Eve. And it's hard for you to let go.'

'I think,' I say though I haven't had the thought until this moment, 'it's because of my parents. They escaped from Hungary with the memory of all the tanks and machine guns and everything else that was pointed at them. The danger brought them close, forged them together all their lives. Now the guns are being pointed at us.'

'So danger makes us cling together.'

'That has to be part of it.'

She wriggles so her skin rubs against mine.

'There's too much bloody psychology flying about these days,' she says. 'You can't even tie your shoelaces without being told you never escaped your mother's apron strings.' She runs a finger along my lips. 'Just hold me, Bazil.'

I put my arms round her and hold her tight. I can feel the life in her, her breathing, her heartbeat. We lie very still but in a while her hands start to explore.

CHAPTER 16

'What bastard is this?'

For once I am the one who has muttered this but I know who it will be. I leave Mary in bed and pick up the telephone.

'Hello.'

There is a pause while I hear the rasping of a lighter.

'Listen, we're in business. The President's Archives are a black-mailer's dream. Among many other treasures I found…'

Jozsef makes me wait. He makes me ask. 'Come on, Jozsef, it's too early in the morning to be a sadist. What did you find?'

'El Dorado,' he breathes.

'Stalin said that he who is not for us is against us,' Jozsef says. 'When Kadar became our leader, naturally as a true Hungarian he saw the world through the other end of the telescope. Kadar said that he who is not against us is for us. You can translate.'

We are in Josef's old VW Golf, the colour of grass that has lain under winter snow. I am in the back, Mary is in the front next to Jozsef. He can see me in the interior mirror but I notice how his eyes slide to the door mirror to check whatever is overtaking. We are driving along the embankment and I can see across the Danube to where the camera caught Goenz and Eve, and Pal Pokorni asked about the Mafia families getting cosy.

Busy with my thoughts I have taken too long to translate so Jozsef tells Mary in his growling English, 'Stalin said: if you are not for us you are against us. Our great Hungarian leader said it differently: if you are not against us you are for us. All right, I have a question for you.' Here Jozsef lays his hand on her knee for extra emphasis. 'If you are neither against the system nor for the system, what are you? Hm?'

'I would say…'

'Yes?'

'A person who is neither for nor against the system has found something more interesting.'

Mary returns his hand to the steering wheel.

'Such as?'

'Being a secret policeman like you,' she says.

Jozsef speaks to me in Hungarian, 'She is not so stupid. You chose well, my cousin.'

'I haven't chosen her.'

'Then maybe she has chosen you.'

'What're you two fellas saying?'

'You should have my job,' Jozsef tells her. He pauses to look at a truck coming up behind us. It is loaded with beer crates. 'I have people with no name telephoning me to tell me to stop sticking my nose where it has no business. My boss makes me stand in front of his desk while he tells me to stop. Two men waiting outside my office use bullets to tell me to stop. I am sure you know what that means.'

'If you knock the system,' Mary says, 'the system will drop on you from a great height and flatten you.'

'That is why we leave Budapest today so that when the system falls on me I am somewhere else.'

He lifts both hands from the steering wheel like some magician unveiling his latest trick.

'Kecskemét,' I say.

'Yes, you'll meet the man who saw you on television. And then we will go a little further.'

Is that all Jozsef is going to say?

'You've found Goenz's hide-out?'

'I believe so.'

'In the President's Archives?'

'Yes.'

'How did you get in?'

'In the end it was not difficult. My neighbour is what I would call a little strange. He keeps bees in his back garden. So last night I went to see him and borrowed the mask he wears when he is taking honey from his bees. I told him it was for a special masked ball we were invited to. Why did he frown? Didn't he believe me? Was he worried what kind of party it would be? I stood there, filling his front door, until he fetched an old mask. It had a tear which he had mended with sticky tape but that didn't matter. So this morning at five o'clock I went to headquarters. This is a good time because the people who have been on duty all night are no longer very sharp. I went to the small room it is necessary to pass through to get to the President's Archives. A policeman is on duty there, usually asleep. I am wearing the bee mask so nobody will recognise me and I carry some cans of spray and I hold a clipboard. The clipboard is essential because it means you are on official business. It went like this. Me: Unlock the door. Guard: It is forbidden. Me: It is the termite inspection. Guard: You cannot enter. Me, looking at the clipboard: It was inspected five years ago. Guard: It is not permitted. Me: It is not the archives I inspect but the floors and ceilings and any wooden shelves. Guard: You cannot come in. Me: Where were you five years ago? Guard: Pécel. Me: You must have had a lovely time, on the street on Saturday night, rounding up drunks. You could easily go back there. Your choice. Now open up and lock the door behind me because this can be lethal stuff. And I waved a can at him.'

'So he let you in?' Mary says.

'Yes.'

'You make it sound easy,' I say.

'You couldn't do it. You haven't got the attitude.'

We have passed a sign to the airport which has what looks like a child's drawing of a plane. I see Mary's head turn that way and then her eyes squeeze shut to block out temptation.

'So this hide-out you've found – is that where Eve is?'

'Maybe. But I must get out of Budapest and I have no better idea and it is a sunny day.'

For a while no one speaks. We are on the motorway going south and as Budapest drops behind the traffic thins. Mary squirms round to face me.

'What are you thinking?'

'I left Eve's flat in a hurry and was hiding behind bushes when Eve and West came out and set off in a great hurry. Eve was driving, West beside her. His body was in a twisted position while he looked out, as if he had something stuck in her ribs.'

'Like a gun?' Mary says.

'Like a gun. Maybe she drove to this place Jozsef found. Maybe she had to.'

'All right,' Jozsef says, 'this is how it seems to me. Eva is not sleeping with Goenz. Eva is not sleeping with that British diplomat. She is doing something else. Does the diplomat speak Hungarian?'

I think back to meeting him at the restaurant with the bicycle hanging over the bar and his problem with the waiter.

'No.'

'I have been told that Goenz does not speak English. Eva speaks both. So her job – part of it anyway – is to interpret.'

'So West is corrupt?'

'Have you any other explanation for all his lies and why he sticks a gun in Eva's ribs? He sees the evidence of you being in her flat and he decides she is double-crossing him. That seems logical. But because you were told Eva was Goenz's mistress your emotions got in the way and you couldn't think logically any more.'

So what has Eve been doing? Pushing emotions aside, thinking logically, it has to be more than being an interpreter.

We are crossing the great central plain of Hungary. People say it is featureless from horizon to horizon but it is not flat. It is a prairie that rises and falls like a gentle swell on the ocean. A car is overtaking us, barely overtaking, hardly pulling ahead at all. Two men are in the front seat, heads turned to peer in our car. Even the driver is leaning over the wheel, head angled round for a better look.

'Shit.'

We are just passing an exit road as Jozsef brakes and hauls over the steering wheel to the anguish of the traffic behind. The car that was level with us dwindles into the distance. Our old Golf bounces over a strip of waste land before joining the exit road. A church and a village lie a couple of kilometres ahead on a rise of land but Jozsef pulls over in front of an isolated farmhouse. A fenced enclosure holds geese that stretch their necks and shout defiance at us. Jozsef twists in his seat to look behind us.

'What are you looking for?' Mary asks.

'It's because of those men in the car who stared at us. The old policeman in me warns they might have been given my licence number and maybe they had friends in another car following behind us.'

'Jozsef,' she says and waits until he looks at her. 'In England I often have men in cars look at me. I don't think men in Hungary are different.'

'Maybe they were admiring your balcony. Maybe I'll win the lottery next week. Maybe Adel will bake me a cake. But the world is full of people who believed in maybe and were disappointed. Sometimes they were fatally disappointed.'

He lights a cigarette. From the way he inhales deeply I know he is angry.

'We live in a bad world.' He pauses. It is his opening announcement, like a headline. 'Every part of the world is bad. Bad in Africa where the tyrants steal elections and the tribes kill. Bad in South America where the generals wear more medals than they have wars. Bad where the mad Muslims fly planes into skyscrapers. Bad where the Pope says women must produce more babies even if they cannot feed them. In some countries the houses fall down because the builders steal the money. In other countries parents sell their ten-year-old girls to be whores. Or sell their boys to old men from

Germany. And everywhere there are bad men who make bigger weapons to kill more people and sell them to countries where they have no money for hospitals or clean water. You still awake?'

Mary could have willed herself into a coma. She is staring ahead through the windscreen.

'This is not some great discovery of mine,' Jozsef says. 'Everybody knows it is true. In my country I would say we are very good at being bad. Maybe we have a divided heart, part of it from Asia, part from Europe. We have bad leaders because the two halves don't make a whole. The Turks come in and it takes centuries to make them understand they are not welcome. The Nazis come and we join them. Bad. Then the Russians come to fight the Nazis so we join them instead. More bad. The Russians decide to stay and everything goes from bad to worse until the people say no. Bazil's father, my father, the whole nation, we say enough is already too much. You have seen the graves in Kerepesi. My father died with a rifle in his hands because he wouldn't take any more. It needed a few more years but finally we got rid of the bad old leaders. And what do we have? The bad new leaders. The politicians who lie, the bankers who steal, the Mafia who kill and corrupt. We have Goenz and a hundred other Goenzes. What do we do? Do we give them the keys to our houses and say, *please help yourselves to what you want and take our women while you are about it*? Or do we say *no*!'

Jozsef smacks the steering wheel.

'I am not brave like my father but I am angry. I say no.' Again he slaps the wheel. 'That is why I am here today. So if you want to get out and walk back to England, do it now.'

Nobody speaks. Nobody moves.

Jozsef doesn't return to the motorway but continues into the village. It is strung out along the road which swells into a square. A church occupies one side. The rest of the square is made up of a butcher, a grocery, a children's playground, a post office and a café. Jozsef looks at his watch.

'Our meeting in Kecskemét is at 11.30.' He produces a map and finds where the town is. 'We're going to be too soon.'

'Why did we leave so early?' I ask.

'Because I wanted to get out of Budapest. The air there is no longer healthy.'

I point to the café. 'Coffee would be good.'

But Jozsef has other ideas. He drives past the church and draws up by the entrance to the cemetery. The wooden gate has swollen in the winter weather and he gives it a kick and then a harder kick which sends it flying open with a thud.

'In Hungary we understand the power of a boot,' he tells Mary except his explanation is in Hungarian. 'The Janissary's boot, the Nazi boot, the Red Army boot have left their footprints all over our history.'

'What's he saying?' she asks.

'What he is saying,' Jozsef switches to English, 'is you even have to fight your way to your own grave. Come, we walk a little among the dead. Anyone who sees us will think we are searching for a grandfather, say hello and goodbye to him. What I am going to show you is not what is written on a tombstone. I am going to show you what is *not* written here.' He slaps his hand against a pocket.

'Showing you something that is not there is one of Jozsef's special tricks,' I tell Mary.

Jozsef ignores me. Looking round at the rows of graves, his eyebrows lift. 'First, because we are in a cemetery, I tell you a Hungarian joke, all right?' He glances at Mary but does not bother to wait for her approval. 'Zoltan is on his deathbed – cancer of the sewer – when a truly wonderful smell drifts upstairs. With his final strength he gets out of bed, struggles down the stairs and crawls into the kitchen. There on the table are dozens of *pogácsa*, his favourite cheese pastries. One last treat, he tells himself and reaches out a hand. "Don't touch," his wife screams at him. "Those are for after the funeral."'

As if some nervous itch has been scratched, Jozsef nods and leads the way to an imposing family vault at the east side of the cemetery. Though he links arms with Mary as a family mourner, I feel it is me he is speaking to. He bends down to inspect the lichen-covered inscription carved into the stone.

'Erkel, given name Imre, his wife Margit, also two daughters and a son. Yes, I know him.'

'Jozsef,' Mary points at the headstone, 'he died in 1871.'

'Not him personally, but his type.' He pats her hand in reassurance. 'He has money – just look at the miniature cathedral he is sleeping in. His wife is by his side to keep him company in his long rest. She still has a nagging tongue so he has his mistresses for fun, here and there and over there.' He swings round to point at three graves at random. 'His children are with him; see, they are buried here too. What about his bastard children? He has taken care of them also. They cannot be called Erkel, that is forbidden. But if you know their names you can find their final homes here. You see I know him because he is the same kind of man as Münnich: the system changes, the men of power never do. In just the same way Münnich has taken care of his bastard wolf-child Gyula Goenz. You object that this is a fantasy of mine. No, it is my understanding.'

Jozsef smiles. It is not the smile of someone who sees a joke, rather one who foresees some future reckoning. He gestures with his head for me to come closer. Whereas before he had one map, now he has two. He waves one in the air.

'This map you have already seen, the map is for general public use. Look, here is the *autópálya* we drove down until those men stared in our car. Here is Kecskemét where Bazil will meet the man who saw him on television. We hope that the mystery of the hand that was in Eva's car will be explained. After that there is another journey we must make, though it is not too far. We will drive down here, along this road, but then there is a puzzle. You see these small towns – Bugac and Kiskunfelegyhaza? With Kecskemét they form a small triangle and the map shows nothing inside. Maybe you think it is like the desert, a Hungarian Sahara, empty, dead, nothing but dry earth, not even a camel. During the accursed forty years that is what you were meant to think. All right, you say, so there were secrets there, some big secret, or some small secrets, but all hidden in this space. No, it was different, different in a Hungarian way. You may not know what a secret is but at least you know that something secret exists. In the People's Republic of Hungary there were certain places that were nothing, not even secrets, they didn't exist at all, they were zero. I have read that the idea of zero was an Arab invention, or possibly Indian. Maybe we Hungarians got there first.'

Jozsef gets out his cigarettes and in lighting one just naturally looks about. Seeing no figures crouching behind the tombstones he unfolds the second map, a photocopy.

'So what I am going to show you is not a secret. You are seeing something that does not exist. Do you understand? Like zero is not a secret, zero is nothing.'

Mary frowns at the photocopy, then at Jozsef. 'Are you saying this document in your hand – '

'No no no. There is no document. My hand is empty. Why don't you understand? Can you imagine you are Hungarian?'

'I'm English.'

'So does a Hungarian Mary exist?'

'No.'

'All right, if you do not exist, does this photocopy exist?'

This is a trick question. Mary frowns. It's a childish game but Jozsef is frowning right back at her. 'No,' she says.

'Excellent. Now you understand Hungarian logic. This photocopy that does not exist is a map of the same area. Look – Bugac, Kecskemét, Kiskunfelegyhaza. Follow the road south from Kecskemét. Here it turns east and crosses the railway line. Now it gets interesting. A small road branches left and enters what is a blank area on the public map. This little road goes straight except for a tiny loop. What does it go round? An old mine? A small hill? Some holy grave? I don't know. Yet. Then the road goes straight again until it ends at this group of buildings. It's too small to be a village. If you believe bad things you might say it was a prison camp. Or maybe it is a place for mad people who are sick with the wrong political thoughts – fresh air and barbed wire could make their thoughts better. No.'

Jozsef stops to look at me, then Mary. He takes a pull at his cigarette. He is an actor making certain we know he has reached a dramatic high point.

'The truth is that it was the country estate of Ferenc Münnich. Let us call it a reward for helping destroy our fight for freedom in 1956. My father paid for this house with his blood.'

Jozsef pauses but we don't speak.

'When Münnich died the house passed to his bastard son Gyula Goenz. This is what I learnt this morning in the President's Archives. I made this photocopy though why there is a photocopier in the President's Archives is one of life's mysteries.'

Jozsef drops his cigarette and grinds it under the heel of his shoe with noticeable savagery. You don't have to be a great psychologist to grasp the symbolism. You were responsible for my father's death, that shoe says, also you tried to have me killed, but today it's my shot. I can feel it. So can Mary.

'Why hasn't it been put on the map now?' she asks.

'That is another story. *Viszonzas*. Explain to her.'

'In communist days,' I say, 'people got by on favours: you scratch my back, I'll scratch yours. The old boy net.'

'Not just during the accursed forty years,' Jozsef says. 'It never went away. It is how Goenz and his kind operate. The people who used to have power, the old ruling class, their sons and daughters, they know each other. Everything can be arranged. It is so much less messy than democracy. You think it cannot happen once communism collapsed? Why not? It happens everywhere. I have read about your country and certain ministers in the government who accepted money in brown envelopes or weekends in Paris. And newspaper editors being sweet with important politicians. Even the police being helpful. Is no different here. They are in bed with each other.

You touch me here, one says, and I'll touch you there. All right? You understand?' He rolls his shoulders like a wrestler and takes a deep breath. 'So now we go. We have a meeting in Kecskemét.'

The photocopied map has vanished. Maybe it never existed after all. Jozsef turns and walks towards the gate.

'I'm drowning,' Mary says.

'What do you mean?'

'Words words words. A tsunami of words. Do all Hungarians talk like that?'

During the accursed forty years you were careful what you said. When the old order changed it was as if a dam was breached and all the forbidden thoughts and emotions could flow free. Do I try to explain?

Jozsef turns. 'Come on, we should hurry now. We mustn't be late.'

CHAPTER 17

As we drive into the centre of Kecskemét a car pulls out from the kerb, freeing a parking space. Jozsef brakes.

'Why did he do that?'

'It was a she,' Mary says. 'She's finished shopping so she's going home.'

'Just as we arrive.'

'You think that is suspicious?'

'It's as if we were expected and they want us to park right there. Is anybody watching us?'

'About fifty people,' Mary says. 'Plus the drivers behind. They are beginning to wonder why you don't like the parking space.'

Jozsef angles the car into the space and cuts the ignition. He checks his watch.

'Now this is what we do. Mary, you will get out first and go into the square. It's a market so there is a lot for you to look at. You are a tourist so it is natural you take photos. Then Bazil and I get out and go the same route. You must not look at us. The man we are meeting is very nervous, worried for his life I would say. He says he will be watching us. If he is doubtful about anything he will not meet us. So you must follow a long way behind and stop to take photos of the many interesting buildings. Bazil is going to meet the man in a museum. It is natural that a tourist like you would visit a museum but you must not come too soon because I think anybody walking in is going to frighten him. You can photograph the outside of the museum and when the man leaves you can photograph him.'

'What does he look like?'

'He looks like a man. All right? Now go.'

Mary gets out of the car and I take her place in the front seat. Jozsef and I watch her disappear past a group of schoolchildren and into the square.

'She is a fine woman,' Jozsef says. 'Maybe she will marry you.'

'That's a stupid thing to say. I hardly know her.'

Jozsef lights a cigarette. 'She would make a good third wife. You marry the first time in hope, the second time in desperation, the third time in resignation. Me, I have married three wives in one marriage.' He sighs. 'All right, she is far enough ahead so we go.'

It turns out the square is not a single square but several run together. We pass beds of winter pansies and tulips that are no more than tufts of leaves. In the centre are lines of stalls selling peasant rugs, books, balloons, clothes.

'He said we must wait here.' We are in front of a stall of wooden carvings – wild boar, deer, bears, eagles with spread wings. Jozsef gestures at the display. 'It is for the German tourists. You see old men with sticks reliving their youth. Heinzi, isn't that the building we were in when the Russkies rolled up? *Nein, dummkopf,* we were dug in over there.'

'This man I'm meeting – did he give his name?'

'Zsigmond. That's what he said on the telephone. Just Zsigmond. He's scared which is why he hasn't come forward before.'

'What is he scared of?'

'What's he scared of? Shitting his pants. That is why we wander through this market and look at the stalls while he hides and watches there are no bad men about. Also he wants to have a look at you in real life. He says that sheet you sat in front of made you look like a police suspect.'

'It wasn't a sheet.'

'Don't start contradicting him.'

'What does he do?'

'He didn't tell me.'

'He sounds to me like another crazy.'

'Oh, he is crazy all right or he wouldn't have telephoned. Another thing I picked up from speaking to him, questions make him even more nervous. Come on, we can move on now.'

We cut diagonally across the square, heading towards a forbidding church. We pass more stalls selling hunting knives, dried apricots, wooden chairs, fox pelts. Next to the church is a pinkish building of municipal pomp. Other buildings give an architectural history lesson: baroque, romantic, art nouveau.

'Now we must wait here two minutes more.'

Here is a great stone compass laid into the ground, arrows pointing to towns all over Hungary. We wander round it. Tata, Gyor, Sopron, Nagycenk… hello, Paris was never part of Hungary. Jozsef would explain that this is a Paris that does not exist. I wonder where Mary is, if she can see us, what she is photographing. What did Jozsef call her? A fine woman…

'All right, let's go. We walk through to the next square slowly then carry on straight ahead fast so if anyone is following us they would have to hurry. That is what Zsigmond said.'

We wait at traffic lights, cross over and take a right turn, then a left and pass into the courtyard of what must once have been a large farm, now engulfed by the inner suburbs. A sign says it is a craft museum. We don't go into the building but head for a concrete and wood bench where a man is sitting. A bicycle is laid on the ground beside him. I remember that at the traffic lights a cyclist pedalled past us.

'Do you have a match?' Jozsef asks.

The man runs his tongue over his lips. 'Yes, but I have no cigarettes.'

'Here, have one of mine.'

'That brand is too strong for me.'

How spies greet each other, I think.

Jozsef holds out the packet. The man looks down at it, then towards the street, then at me.

'You are Bazil,' he tells me. 'I recognise your head from the tele-vision. Don't you realise that if I can recognise you…' He doesn't finish the sentence. 'Listen, I will enter the museum now and go right to the last room.' He points. The building is L-shaped and the room is the furthest but with windows overlooking this courtyard and the entrance. 'After two minutes you will come in. Tell the woman at the desk you are interested in the furniture and she will direct you and leave us alone.'

He picks up the bicycle, wheels it to the door, locks it, casts a last glance round and disappears inside.

'My name is Zsigmond,' he begins, 'and I am not here.'

The beginning defines him: no social niceties, no other name because he is terrified, no existence after this encounter. We are in the last room of the museum, a long display area with a central table and chairs as if for a board meeting. We are standing near a window looking out over the courtyard. Jozsef has angled himself into a corner of the bench. His face is tipped up to the sun. Smoke from his cigarette hovers above him like a cloud of gnats.

'Who is he?'

'Jozsef? He is my cousin. His father and my father were brothers. His father is buried in the Heroes section at Kerepesi.'

'I mean what is he?'

'An inspector.'

'Of police?'

'A special kind of police. To do with upholding the constitution, ensuring the integrity of the state.'

'You mean a secret policeman.' Zsigmond is still peering out.

'He is not very secret, is he, out there sunning himself like a lizard.'

'On that television programme you said to contact the police. Why didn't you give your own phone number? Were you too frightened?'

'I was cautious.'

'I am frightened, you see. For months I have not spoken about this. It was just hearing you talk about your wife…' He doesn't finish. 'I tell you my name is Zsigmond, but my other name…' He dismisses the other name with a wave of his hand. 'Also you do not need to know where I live. It is safer.'

'Safer? What do you mean?' Is this the reporter in me reawakening, sniffing after a story? Or the snivelling panicky animal concerned for its own survival?

Zsigmond stares at me. 'Why do you ask?'

'Am I in danger here?'

His face twists in a frown. Jozsef said: he does not like being questioned. 'Of course. So am I if anyone sees us together. We shall sit down. No, don't take that chair. It is one of the museum exhibits, made by Palatkas. He is famous. Well, he is famous if you collect farmhouse furniture.'

We sit at the central table, Zsigmond taking the end seat so he faces the archway we came through and, if he turns his head to the right, he can check outside in the courtyard. I sit at right angles which gives me a different view of his face. Now the thing is this: we judge someone we have met for the first time by how they speak and dress and look, and Zsigmond's face has the unfortunate look of an East End gangster. A white streak down the skin of his left cheek – is that a knife slash? His mouth has a twist to it. One eyebrow has a piece missing and the stitch marks are still visible. It is the face of someone who has walked down a dark alley at the wrong time.

I don't stare wide-eyed but Zsigmond has noted my inspection. He says, 'I drive an ambulance. When it is an emergency, say a car crash, minutes are important. So maybe I go through a red light or drive on the wrong side of the road. That is how I met a lorry carrying a load of gravel. I ended the day not driving the ambulance but lying in the back of one.'

He glances away at the window. Jozsef is standing but only in order to settle himself more comfortably, stretched out on the bench with his feet draped over a wooden arm.

'Forget that accident,' Zsigmond says. 'That is not why I am here. It's about your wife and the hand that was found in the car in the river. You think it was not her hand?'

'At first I thought it had to be. But now…' I make a vague gesture, encouraging him to speak.

'Last December was when the car went into the river?'

'Yes.'

'Then listen to me. Last December there was an emergency – not in Budapest, here – and my ambulance was called out. There is a little train that goes from here to Kiskovos and Kalocsa where they grow all that paprika. The railway is only narrow gauge, no express trains run, but there are dangerous level crossings with no gates. I was driving the ambulance and with me was Istvan who has medical training. Actually he wanted to be a doctor but he had problems.'

Istvan's problems bring a frown to Zsigmond's face and he shakes his head.

'Ten, maybe twelve, kilometres outside Kecskemét we came to a level crossing with a train stopped just the far side of it. Men were standing around and there was a group of women weeping. A man was sitting on the ground, the train driver. It was twenty minutes, maybe twenty-five minutes, since we had been called out but he was still shaking. Then I saw the body.'

Zsigmond leans forward. I thought it was to whisper a secret but he just bows his head. After a pause he goes on.

'Or what was left of it. Head and shoulders were on one side of the track, legs on the other, something in the middle. Istvan had a flask of brandy – actually that is part of his problem – and we both had a drink from that. Police arrived just after us and they questioned the train driver. The person was lying on the track, the driver said, and he couldn't stop in time. He said there was nobody else about, and there was no car, no bicycle, no horse, just this person a long way from anywhere. There was no official photographer but one of the police had a mobile phone and he took a photo as a record of the scene.'

He makes another pause.

'I thought about it later and it seemed to me the police were very casual, as if they had decided from the start that it was a suicide. Or even before the start, if you follow me. Istvan and I had to gather the body parts together to put in the ambulance and we could tell it was a woman. We took her remains to the hospital so a doctor could sign a death certificate – Unknown Female – then we took her round the corner to the mortuary. We were given forty-eight hours off duty to recover. This is normal policy after something so terrible.'

Zsigmond gets to his feet but it is to walk to the end of the room, bow his head against the wall and put his hands behind his neck with his fingers kneading the muscles. A minute passes, possibly more, before he turns back. I am following Jozsef's instruction: no questions.

'I had two days off work. The first afternoon I was telephoned at home by the pathologist. Did we bring all the body back? Of course. Nothing was tossed in the ditch? No ditch. Or slipped down a bank? The land was flat. A hand is missing, he said, the left hand. I heard nothing more that day or the next and then I was back at work. It was busy – it is always busier in the weeks before Christmas – and I tried to put the handless corpse out of my mind. But I read a piece in the newspaper, just one paragraph, about a woman aged in her twenties or thirties, no papers, name unknown, address unknown. Tests showed she was a heroin user. She had been hit by a train at a level crossing. That made it sound like she was walking over the tracks, though the driver said she was lying on them. No mention of a missing hand.'

He goes to the window to look out at Jozsef, then leans against the wall. I have to turn my chair to see him.

'A few days later I was having coffee with my colleague Istvan and he told me something. He drinks too much, sometimes in bars, sometimes in clubs. Well, he went to the Crazy Mouse Saloon and – '

'The Crazy Horse Saloon?' Perhaps I didn't hear correctly and Kecskemét was inspired by Paris.

'Crazy Mouse.' Suspicion comes into Zsigmond's eyes and a

frown deepens the lines in his forehead. No questions, I remind myself. 'The girls put on little masks with whiskers and they have tails strapped on behind. Nothing else. That is what I have heard. Istvan said some man came in and asked where Sisi was. He was drunk and kept shouting, "Where is Sisi? I want Sisi. I don't want any of these sluts." It is not clever to shout out something like that even if the girls are from Serbia and Romania and Vietnam. After two minutes the man was thrown out. Then Istvan – so he said – ordered another drink and asked the barman, "Tell me, who is Sisi? Is she special?" Oh yes, indeed she was special. Istvan is a regular customer and the barman knows him well. He beckoned Istvan closer, no, closer.' Zsigmond leans towards me, gesturing me in with a hand. His breath is hot in my ear. 'The barman's voice was a whisper, nearly drowned by the music. "Sisi was the girl on the railway line."'

Abruptly Zsigmond straightens up and looks away to the archway to the next room. We have just a glimpse of a figure vanishing behind a display panel.

'Who was that?'

'I couldn't really see.'

'Was it a man?'

'Possibly it was a woman.' But Zsigmond is not reassured and is pushing back his chair. Bloody Mary, I saw her, camera raised, before she stepped out of sight. Of all the stupid…

'I'm leaving,' Zsigmond says. 'You stay here two minutes so we are not seen going together.'

I am being cheated of the end of the story. 'The girl from the Crazy Mouse…' Zsigmond is already walking away. 'If it is Sisi's hand, how did it get in my wife's car?' He has reached the end of the table, slipping away from me. I am losing my only link to Eve and the mystery of the hand. I'm on my feet with my own hand stretched out, someone begging.

He stops, then comes back. 'Listen.' He is murmuring for my ears only. 'That girl who was run over by the train was already dead.

I'm talking about Sisi, the whore and heroin addict who worked at the Crazy Mouse. There was no public enquiry but in a hospital you hear things. Her hand had been cut off before she was put on the tracks. Kecskemét is not a bad town but you have to ask yourself why it was hushed up after that little paragraph in the paper.'

He glances round but Mary is out of sight.

'Why was there no murder investigation?' he asks. 'Why was there no medical examiner's report? Why was the hand of a prostitute cut off? Why do the police not raid the Crazy Mouse Saloon where the girls wear no clothes and you can buy any drugs you want? Why?'

He pauses. His eyes dart all over my face, his Adam's apple bobs up and down and when he speaks his voice has dropped from a murmur to a whisper.

'Because the Crazy Mouse is owned by Goenz. Heard of him? Gyula Goenz. He is a crook. The Mr Big of all the Mr Bigs, so it is said. He lives not far away.'

I stand at the window and watch him leave. He unlocks his bicycle and wheels it towards the entrance. Jozsef sits up from his bench and I think says something. Zsigmond has his head down and ignores him. He is a frightened little man who has used up his stock of bravery speaking to me.

'I got him,' Mary says. 'I got one of him frowning, his face all clenched up. Scarface Zsigmond. You know, his cheek with what looks like a razor slash? With his face screwed that scar has the line of a woman's hip. You want to have a look?'

'He saw you,' I say. 'You scared him off.'

'You found out what you wanted, didn't you?'

'Maybe there was more.'

'Well, fuck you, Potter.'

We are in a café on the edge of the central square. Mary stomps off down the alley of stalls.

'She's a fine woman,' Jozsef says, watching her. 'Plenty of spirit.'

'She could have ruined everything.'

'But she didn't. You found out where the hand came from. We know it is all Goenz's work. If he went to all that trouble, it shows how important he thought it was to have Eva working for him.'

Jozsef has ordered beers and has a drink.

'You are English and correct and think we should do something about the girl Sisi. So listen to me. There will be no body to exhume. It will have been cremated. If there was an autopsy, the report will have been lost or shredded, or the computer will have gobbled up the file and got indigestion.'

'You can't be certain.'

'With Goenz involved I can be certain. Suppose you go to the Crazy Mouse. They will never have heard of Sisi.'

'But the other girls...' I begin.

'The other girls will think of what happened to Sisi and develop collective amnesia.'

'Suppose I go to the newspaper.'

I get no further.

'Here comes the great British reporter to tell them how to do their job. They did print something – all right, only a paragraph – it just wasn't worth following up. Some tart takes an overdose and goes under a train, yawn, yawn. You bang your fist on the desk and insist that Goenz is involved. Goenz? You said Goenz? They go very still and hold their breath, thinking of their families and mortgages, then shake their heads. They mutter about proof and libel laws.'

I feel I am being beaten into a corner. 'The police?'

He drinks some more beer though it seems to leave a sour taste in his mouth. 'What's the missing person's name? That's their first question. Sisi? Sisi who? Show us the body. The body is cremated. Except, they point out, you say the hand wasn't so show us the hand. The hand has vanished. So it will go. They'll lean back in their chairs and shake their heads in pity at your story. I am not saying the local police are in Goenz's pocket, I'm just saying they don't act on every madman who comes in with a tale of a hand in a car in the Danube taken from a woman a train ran over but can produce no evidence.'

* * *

'I must go on,' Jozsef says, 'because I would betray my father if I stopped.' He takes a mouthful of beer. 'You must go on because you feel your wife has betrayed her marriage or her country or maybe both.'

He finishes his beer.

'I know the British have something of a tradition of betrayal. But…'

He shakes his head and gets up.

'Have you thought,' Jozsef says, 'that she may have sacrificed her marriage?'

Jozsef disappears, mobile phone in hand, to make calls out of my hearing. Mary hasn't returned. I wander until I find a public phone. I can't remember when I last spoke to my editor but I get put through to Dodo.

'Where's his lordship?'

'Out.'

'What's his mood? Stormy?'

'Worse. Circulation is down. Advertising is down. You're away. Two Boobs is away. Pip and Anna have pulled sickies. One of his Thai girls has gone home.'

It's odd how personal details find their way around an office.

'Poor Dexter, down to his last Thai girl. Did he say where he was going?'

'He didn't even glance at me when he left. From the look on his face I'd say he was having an argument with himself and both sides were losing.'

I try Dexter's mobile number and I'm on the verge of giving up when he answers.

'Because the phone is in the locker in the bloody changing room and I had to get off the exercise bike.' Is Dexter out of breath? His voice is hardly more than a murmur.

'You're at a gym?'

'It's called FastFit. It advertises itself as being for the time-poor. Where the hell are you?'

'Kecskemét.'

'That's in Hungary, right?'

'South of Budapest.'

'You're touring the country, having a nice holiday, pretty girls, good food.'

'The hand that was in Eve's car definitely was not hers. It was taken off the corpse of a dead whore.'

'Let me get this straight. You fly a thousand miles at my expense. You don't file a single story. There are no photos. All you find out is that the hand in your wife's car belonged to someone else.'

'This afternoon we are going to visit the Mafia boss. That is my cousin's idea.'

There is a pause that stretches into a silence, not a complete silence because I can hear distant echoing voices and what I think is the hiss of running water.

'Dexter, are you taking a shower?'

'I've turned it on.'

'Why? And why are you whispering?'

'I had a visit from the Special Branch last night. I believe there are two of the specials in Oxford and I had both of them come to my house. The senior one announced he was Superintendent Beckett, built like a mountain and I'm not. They went straight to my study as if they already knew the lay-out of the house. They wanted to see my appointments diary so I asked where their search warrant was. Oh, we could get one, sir, no problem, sir, but we appreciate the willing cooperation of the public. I asked on whose orders they came and Beckett answered: London. London's a big place. Who in London? Scotland Yard? Foreign Office? MI5? At this stage, said Beckett's sidekick, we would prefer to just say London. They wanted to know about you. I said, Just a minute, the Special Branch is concerned with terrorism so are you saying that Bazil Potter is suspected of terrorism links? It was Beckett who answered: At this stage we would prefer not to say. I didn't like the way he repeated the phrase *at this stage*. They wanted to know what you thought you were up to. Makes three of us, I said. They said you were crashing round like a dodgem car and had no idea of the significance of what was going on.'

Dexter stops speaking. In the background I hear male voices, then the slamming of a door.

'So what is going on?' I ask.

'Good question. I wanted to put an end to this interrogation so I got up from my chair. That was a mistake because Beckett got up too and he towered above me. There is a field of energy around a big man – do you know what I mean? – and when he is a policeman that is transformed into menace. I took a breath and said my piece. I told them it was a newspaper's duty to dig out the facts and that was what you were doing and I would be the judge of their importance.'

'Mr Valiant-for-Truth,' I murmur.

'What?' But Dexter has heard me all right. 'Mr Feeble-Mind, more like. The sidekick began some bleat about security and the national interest and I said politicians always drag out the national interest when they've tripped up. Beckett took a couple of steps so he was very close and I could feel his strength. I think I could take offence at that, *sir*, he said, I really could. I might even decide you are obstructing the police in the performance of their duties. I wouldn't like you to have that impression, I said, so what would you like me to do? Pick up that nice telephone on your desk and have a word with Mr Potter, tell him you are calling him home. There is one problem with your idea, I said. And what is that, sir? He has changed his hotel, I don't know where he is staying, I cannot telephone him.'

Dexter stops. All I hear is the hiss of the shower.

'Did they believe you?'

'Coppers never believe anything you tell them. It's part of their DNA. Even if what you say is true. But in case they call round again, just don't bloody tell me where you're staying.'

He cuts the connection.

'Did these two callers at your editor's house wear police uniform?' Jozsef wants to know.

'I doubt it. You don't.'

'Did they show identity cards?'

'You two boys are leaving me out again,' Mary says.

'What I am saying,' Jozsef tells her, 'is that police don't threaten journalists, not usually. It makes journalists stubborn. They forget their feet walk in the gutter every day. Instead they lift their heads and gaze at the stars. They remember the ideals they started out with, finding the truth, exposing lies and corruption. Just like your new and good friend Bazil. So I was just wondering if they were police at all.'

'They could have been police,' I say, 'but moonlighting.'

'Ah.' Jozsef nods. 'That is certainly possible.'

We are driving through the outer suburbs of Kecskemét. Mary is sitting in the back. Maybe that way we don't get so many men staring at us. That is what Jozsef said. Mary is leaning forward to speak to Jozsef.

'Moonlighting cops,' she says, 'that sounds very like you.'

Jozsef lifts a hand off the steering wheel in an airy gesture. 'Well, we are cousins.'

CHAPTER 18

Jozsef is not lost. He is making up his own way as we go. It's how he approaches life.

'This is Goenz's turf, so we tiptoe.'

He avoids the main road as we leave Kecskemét and sets out on a tour of the suburbs. Raw new housing pokes into vineyards and fruit orchards. Nobody is about. The houses look abandoned except for one woman hanging washing out on a line between two trees. She turns her head to watch as we drive past. She has a small white dog that barks and chases us away.

'Map is no good here,' Jozsef mutters, 'not the public map, not the map that doesn't exist.'

He plots his route like some old navigator crossing uncharted waters, stopping the car at junctions to peer at the sky and let the sun guide him. Finally we rejoin the main road and head south.

The back seat confines Mary and she edges closer as if she could join us.

'Jozsef, it's time you shared,' she says.

'What part of me do you want to share?'

'Don't be cheeky. Tell us where we're going, what is going to happen, what we do, Plan A, and when that runs into trouble Plan B, everything. Or at least something. Are you going to arrest the whole gang? Have a shoot-out?'

Josef thinks a few moments, to decide what to say or how to put it in English. 'I am one man, middle-aged, fat, with pains in my body and my head. My job is not to fight. I do have a gun, you have seen me use it, but only on a lock that was refusing to cooperate with a protector of the constitution. Naturally I use legal methods in my work although sometimes it is necessary to look at the meaning of the word legal from a different angle. Before my cousin came I had no interest in Goenz. He was a gangster, certainly, but I can feast on gangsters every evening on American TV shows. It was my cousin who awoke my sleeping interest and now I know that Goenz has a darker side. His Mafia gang controls a lot of crime here but there is more. He is involving foreign diplomats, spreading his activities to other countries, corrupting our bureaucrats and almost certainly foreign ones too. Bazil has met one in London. What was his name?'

'Lovegrove,' I say.

'Well, he won't be the only one. Police in Oxford and if Oxford maybe other cities. Goenz is like a virus, spreading through the body. He is turning our police bad, even the head of my own organisation. Maybe he has links to Moscow, to the Kremlin. Putin likes to spread trouble in the West. I have a good friend in the police in Bucharest, a *comisar*, an ethnic Hungarian who is always happy to speak his native language with me. I have consulted him about the paper that Bazil found hidden in Eva's apartment. He says it is very simple: the column of figures and letters are the licence plates of Romanian trucks. I have no friend in Belgrade but I imagine it would be the same for Serbia too. So I think we can add serious smuggling to Goenz's other crimes and that probably involves the corruption of customs officials here and in Romania and in the rest of Europe and in England.'

In my own slow-witted way I have got round to thinking this.

'If Eve wasn't with Goenz for sex or money…' I say. 'If she wasn't working for Goenz… she had to be spying on him.'

'Well,' says Jozsef, 'she was *pretending* to work for Goenz. In order to do that she had to die. Her car was sacrificed in the Danube – that was well thought out. And this morning we have found out where her hand came from.'

'But what can you - Jozsef Fazekas, all on his own – do about this?' Mary insists. 'Goenz is powerful. He's got all these thugs.'

'I know, I know.' In a reflex action Jozsef touches his head.

'What are you getting into – getting us into?'

'That's a good question.' He drives a while in silence. 'If it is possible we are going to have a look at where Goenz lives.'

'And then?'

'And then I will think of something.' After a while he adds, 'Goenz must be stopped.'

'And Eve?' I say.

'Goenz must be stopped. I just said that.'

We turn off the main road on to something the public map insists does not exist. There is no gate but a sign planted in the middle of the lane means we have to drive half off the tar to pass. The sign reads: TILOS. This is No Entry and something more. It is PROHIBITED, an echo of the all-powerful state, as if the accursed forty years were still marching on, warning private citizens to back off. Or else. The road is narrower but in good condition and stretches ahead across the plain.

'Somewhere there has to be a gate,' Jozsef says. 'Don't think you are free to come and picnic. Somewhere there will be guards and guns, maybe dogs.' He is driving more slowly now. 'Watch out for security cameras at the side of the road.'

Mary is staring out of the side window at a fire-blackened cottage. It is built of stone and brambles with a skeleton of roof beams missing their tiles.

'What happened? Where did everyone go?'

'Away,' Jozsef says. 'Or…' He jabs with his thumb at the ground.

Mary swings round to keep the ruined cottage in sight. 'There's something, a cat, a black cat, on the roof timbers.'

As I watch a crow lifts off and flaps away.

Jozsef is staring ahead. 'Soviet generals liked land like this. More than just liked, they *loved* land like this. Shall I tell you why?'

'Go on,' Mary says.

'Smooth slopes and gentle dips and bare plains were what they dreamed of.'

'You make it sound sexual,' Mary says.

'It was.' In the mirror Jozsef's eyes are on Mary. 'Women didn't appreciate their big guns but here they could play with them. Line them up, one hundred guns, two hundred, start shooting at first light and shoot all day. When night comes have a bottle of vodka, go to bed, dream of shells sighing through the air as they find their target. Next day they make advances and their big guns did it again. They gloried in conquests. This land just lay down in front of them.'

'Wow,' Mary says..

'The enemy was not shy, hiding behind rocks or in caves, making secret attacks.'

'Ambushes,' Mary says.

'It is why the Red Army did not know what to do in Budapest. I am talking about 1956. We, the Hungarian people, were the enemy. Their tanks came down empty streets, someone ran out of a door with a petrol bomb, then he was gone. My father shot from a window, very high, and the Russian soldiers didn't know where he was. Their generals had no skill for this kind of fighting. Look at Chechnya. They came to Grozny, the enemy was everywhere and nowhere. Their only plan was to destroy the city, street by street, until there were no buildings left for the enemy to hide in, and they called that victory.' He straightens his shoulders and rolls his head. 'I am talking too much. Why do you say nothing, my cousin?'

Some people talk. Some stay silent. Tension takes us in different ways.

'On the map that doesn't exist,' I say and wait.

'What about it?' Jozsef asks.

'It shows this road going straight except for one blip. Possibly it was a hill, you said. Is that it? Not much of a hill.'

On this rolling great plain some quirk of geology has heaved up a knoll of giant boulders. The road aims straight at this hillock and then has to curve round it. Why? Why build a straight road across a flat plain so that it has to make a detour? I let myself be distracted by this. In the days before cars, horsemen could aim at this point, I decide. Outlined against the sky the boulders look like a balcony thrust towards the road. It's a perfect look-out point. Men with binoculars could lie there. Men with rifles could lie there. Jozsef slows right down. We can see no one.

Jozsef drives off the road. He bumps over rough land and stops where the car is hidden by low-sweeping branches of trees. 'Walnut trees,' he says. 'I like walnuts. Maybe the Turks had a camp here. The Turks liked walnuts too.'

'Were the Turks here recently?' Mary asks.

'As recently as three hundred years ago.'

'Great. Thanks, Jozsef.' She grips the seat belt where it runs between her breasts as if she could haul herself out of some morass. 'Three hundred years ago the Turks maybe camped here. But they're not here now.'

'We kicked them out. It may take a long time but in the end we do the right thing.' He takes a breath. 'I want you both to stay in the car while I go and have a little look.'

We watch as Jozsef scrambles between the rocks, his arms swinging wide like an old wrestler.

'He doesn't speak in sentences, does he?' Mary says. 'He speaks in paragraphs.'

Jozsef is smoking a cigarette but pauses before the top to drop the butt and grind it out with the heel of a shoe. He gets down on his hands and knees to crawl forward.

'What's he doing up there?' Mary asks. 'Searching for walnuts? He talks about walnuts and we're going after the fucking Mafia. Christ, I had no idea. Dexter has a lot to answer for, I tell you.' She turns her head towards me. 'You leave a lot to Jozsef, right?'

I smile and then I frown. True, I explain to her but only in my head. It is his show and his country. All I've got is a bit of Magyar blood in my veins. It's his Office for the Constitution, his President's Archives, his Mafia. Agreed, it is my wife but it's his boss who is mixed up in it. It's his big problem. True, all true. But there is more and I can't escape that. He is my cousin whose father died with a rifle in his hand while my father rowed to safety. Do I feel some guilt about this? Am I trying to repay some debt I don't owe? So I come with him on this hare-brained journey but I defer to him and – yes – leave a lot to him.

'He who must be obeyed wants us,' Mary says.

Jozsef is peering ahead with his left elbow angled in front of him to keep his balance while his right arm arcs through the air, an urgent summons. He turns his head once to check we are coming. As we get close he raises a finger to his lips then gestures to us to keep low. We crouch at his shoulder and peep between boulders. Now his finger points below.

'We were wise to come off the road,' he says.

Ahead is a high metal gate. A mesh fence with barbed wire angled at the top stretches out of sight in either direction. A hut by the gate is built of creosoted planks with a tiled roof. A round metal chimney shows wisps of smoke. But the hut and the fence are dwarfed by the sweep of the view.

'The *puszta*, the great plain,' Jozsef says, 'but a very special part of it.' He clutches Mary's upper arm. 'Everything you see – everything - was given to Goenz's father Münnich for his help in crushing our fight against the Russians. It's what I read in the President's Archives.'

'Jozsef, it is my arm you are crushing.'

He doesn't hear her.

'There were notes of a meeting in the Kremlin. This is what I read.' Jozsef has a special voice for this, the leaden delivery of a party hack dictating for hidden microphones. '"In recognition of his great service to the people and to speed the inevitable triumph of the glorious working class and according to the historical truth of Marxism-Leninism and the something of something else..." I forget the exact words but even what I don't remember is the truth anyway. It was always like that when a very bad lie was being made up. "Comrade Ferenc Münnich will be appointed Minister of the

Interior, also Minister of the Armed Forces. In addition, to reward his outstanding courage and strength etcetera etcetera, he will be given Kishegy in the district of Kecskemét, its land and its buildings, for ever." Kishegy means Little Hill, where we are now. When you have sold your country, isn't it right that you keep a piece for yourself? Now lift your eyes along the road.'

He lets go of Mary's arm to point but we have already seen the Kremlin's gift. A kilometre away, more or less, is what Jozsef on the telephone had called El Dorado. I don't know why I imagined some Mad King Ludwig *schloss* set in the middle of the great plain. What we see is a substantial country mansion, two storeys. Most likely it has a half dozen bedrooms, a kitchen with a revolving spit to roast a baron of beef, a dining hall with a stuffed bear's head snarling above the fireplace. The doors and windows are outlined with timber and the plastered walls have been given a mustard coloured wash. There are sheds, cottages for servants, barns for farm equipment. There seems no sign of life except smoke from a chimney.

'You brought your camera case?' I ask.

Mary nods.

'The pee-wee peeper?'

She nods. 'I'll fetch it.'

Every trade has its jargon. Around our office a telephoto lens is called a pee-wee peeper. It's what the paparazzi used when they were stalking Diana. The paps hid in the bushes, waiting to catch the Princess of Wales in a compromising moment. Princess of Wales, dubbed pee-wee. Poor woman.

From the aluminium case Mary brings out a tripod with telescopic legs. 'With a seriously long lens it's a must-have,' she says, 'or you get camera shake.' She screws the pee-wee peeper lens on the camera, then snaps the camera on the tripod.

Jozsef points at the sun. 'Will the lens, you know, flash towards the house?'

'No, it's coated.'

When she extends the lens it's as long as her forearm. Kneeling behind the tripod she tilts the lens sharply down, fiddles with the focus and takes a couple of shots. Then she swivels the camera up so the long lens points at the mansion like a rifle. She clicks and adjusts, clicks and adjusts.

'Is it OK?' Jozsef is unexpectedly subdued in the presence of someone else's technical skill. 'You get the picture all right?'

'See for yourself.'

The image on the viewing panel is bright and sharp and startling in its close-up detail. We see the hut as a whole, then a window.

'Just a minute,' Jozsef says. 'Go back.' He studies the hut again. 'There is no telephone wire.'

'Is that important?' she asks.

'Someone comes to the gate. The guard must contact the house, say who it is. The house says, "Let him in," or "Go away," or "Shoot the bastard." But maybe there is a radio.'

Mary shows the window again. There is a seated figure made ghostly by reflections off the glass.

'Is he reading?' Jozsef asks himself. 'I think he is holding a magazine. If it is one man, he reads. Two men, they smoke and they talk. Football, girls, going to town and getting drunk. But I think he is not talking. One man. Maybe.' Jozsef takes a cigarette, changes his mind and stuffs it back in the packet. 'Ah, the house. Not so much detail as the guard hut.'

'It's a kilometre away, Jozsef.'

'Yes. Big aerial on the roof. Münnich will have spoken to Moscow with that. Useful for Goenz too. No bars on the windows but there will be alarms. You have another one of the house? Now I see curtains are closed on two windows upstairs. What do you think?'

He has turned his head towards me, not because I am his cousin but because it is Eve who could be upstairs and he is being delicate about it in the presence of my lover. No, I have that wrong. Delicacy is not in his nature. He thinks I'll know whether Eve takes naps before lunch.

'It could be a couple of Goenz's men.'

'Curtains closed in the middle of the day?'

'They could have been on duty all night.'

'Maybe.'

'Or it is Eve locked up.'

'I prefer your first idea,' Jozsef says. 'Too many men mean too many guns in the house. Stop! Stop! Look at that. It is Goenz with a telephone.' Mary has moved on to a shot of another window and Jozsef leans forward with urgency as if he could snatch Goenz from the frame. 'Gyula Goenz. My father died fighting his father. Now we meet. Do you know what Gyula means?'

'No. No, of course not.' She clicks onto another exposure.

'Of course not. It is our history, not yours. When the Magyars arrived, the first true Hungarians, a *gyula* was a big military chief. Münnich looked at his bastard son screaming in his cot and chose that name. And Gyula Goenz has turned out to be a fighter, though possibly not the way his father intended. I must be careful. Just a minute. Do you see what I see?'

'It looks like stables,' I say. 'I don't think Goenz would put a guard on his horses.'

The viewing panel shows what looks very like a stable block, a long low single storey building with six doors, though whether they divide in the middle like stable doors it is impossible to tell. Outside one door a man sits on a chair, his legs crossed. His hands are resting on something on his lap. A gun?

'So who is he guarding?'

Jozsef and I look at each other but don't answer.

'Eve?' Mary says. 'You going to snatch her? How're you going to do that?'

'For the moment my ideas bank is empty,' Jozsef says. 'Do you have a plan?'

'Jesus,' she whispers and wraps her arms round her chest as if a blast of cold air has hit her.

Seconds pass. None of us speaks. Then, as one person, we turn.

* * *

Sometimes things happen too fast. Events crowd in like a speed-ed-up film but it is your brain that has slowed. What's happening? What do I do? Until now we have focused on the guard hut and the distant country mansion. The images on the viewing panel were our world. Nothing else existed. Now our attention widens.

We can see them. Can they see us? Jozsef tucked the VW Golf away behind branches, still winter-bare but good enough camouflage. We are crouching behind boulders. A truck is coming along the same road that we did half an hour ago, the road that doesn't exist on the map, guarded by the Prohibited sign.

'If we keep still…' It is one of Jozsef's maybes, but he doesn't finish the sentence. Maybe they won't see us.

There are two in the cab and the sun is in their eyes. The driver is staring straight ahead at the road; his mate has his head cocked as if he could peer past the rocks that make up Kishegy. The truck vanishes then reappears beyond us, stopping at the gate. A guard comes out of the hut, opens the gate and waves the truck to go through. The driver's hand appears out of his window in a lazy salute like royalty acknowledging a patriotic crowd and drives on.

'What name was on the side of the truck?' I ask. 'I couldn't make it out. It wasn't EXROMFRUCHT.'

'Look at this,' Mary says. We peer at the viewing panel which shows the rear of the truck as it was passing though the gate. INTERSPEZIONE is in red capitals. There is the licence number and an international disc RO.

'Romania,' Jozsef says, 'like many of the others on that list from Eva's apartment.'

We look up to watch the truck. The road divides, one way down to the stable block, the other way to the country mansion. The truck moves slowly round a turning circle and comes to a halt just beyond the front entrance. Nothing happens. We stare and wait and then the doors of the cab open and the driver and his mate jump down. A movement catches our eye. The door to the house has opened and a figure comes down the entrance steps and walks towards the truck.

Click.

Mary takes a step aside so Jozsef and I can look at the viewing panel. Jozsef elbows me out of the way so he can peer closely.

'Could be.'

Mary and I crowd in to see as Jozsef's stubby finger taps the man who has come out of the house. In the snatched footage Pal Pokorni shot in Budapest Goenz was dressed as a businessman. This is a country squire wearing a sheepskin tunic, dark trousers and boots.

'Move over,' Mary says. She makes some adjustment and clicks again. 'There.' Now the focus is on the man alone.

'Goenz,' Jozsef says. 'Same face as his father. They say that Münnich liked his food. Goose liver and *ciganpecsenye*. Fat neck, cheeks like a pig.'

Click.

The three men are standing together. Goenz is shaking hands with the driver.

Click.

Goenz is slapping the driver's back.

Click.

Goenz is shaking hands with the other man.

'Good. Very good.' Jozsef straightens up and claps his hands together. There is an urgency about him as if a decision has been reached. 'Bazil, we must hurry.'

'Hurry? Do what?'

'Where are you going? What's happening?' Mary says. 'Fuck's sake, what about me?'

Jozsef considers her and gives a little shake of his head: this flower of English womanhood, how her language slips.

'You must stay here.'

'Baz, I don't want to be stuck alone on this fucking hill.'

'I need Bazil to come with me. He has to hold the gun. I need you with your camera to record the evidence.'

'Who's he going to shoot?'

* * *

As we reach the car Jozsef stoops to pick up one of last year's walnuts. He tosses it in the air a couple of times.

'Do you play cricket.'

I screw my face up. Me with a gun? What does he mean? 'Jozsef...'

'You must have played cricket when you were young. The English invented all sports – tennis, football, cricket, rugby, golf. Inventing is one thing, getting sweaty is another, so they left it to lesser nations to play and win. But when you were a boy you threw a ball.'

'Of course.'

He hands me the walnut. 'Throw this walnut.' I stare at him. 'Go on.'

I feel the weight of the nut. It is not heavy and won't travel far. I hurl it at a tree trunk in front of the car. To my surprise I hit it.

'Excellent,' Jozsef says. 'I'll keep the pistol. You will have another role.'

'What have you planned?'

Jozsef has climbed in the car and started the engine. He waits for me to join him, reverses, then makes for the road and heads back the way we came.

'All generals have plans. They sit around tables, well away from the front line, argue, have a shot of brandy and draw arrows on maps. We advance here, we go round the enemy this side, the enemy counter-attacks, we draw him into our trap, we win. Of course, the generals on the other side are also sitting round a table, having a shot of brandy, drawing arrows on maps. Don't they teach them at training college that war is chaos? Next day when the battle starts it is always different and the plans are useless.'

We bump over the rough ground towards the road.

'I have a plan for the beginning. After that...'

He says no more.

CHAPTER 19

We are driving back along the long straight Prohibited Road and I am thinking of the man beside me. Jozsef is honest. Or as he would put it, he only tells good lies. He is real, in Dexter's view of the world, but without Dexter's agenda and five-year plan which has become a three-year plan. He has no dark side like West. Whatever Jozsef does, he does for a reason. Sometimes the reason is not obvious but it's there. When we met at the Statue Park and he gave me the tour of the fallen communist titans it was to end up with Münnich, Goenz's father, and show Goenz was a bastard with connections. At the cemetery this morning he treated us to an imaginary tour of a nineteenth century patriarch, and it was to show us the type of man Münnich was and how he had taken care of his bastard son.

So what was the purpose of making me throw a walnut?

I have a plan for the beginning. After that…

The plan includes me in the way a circus includes trapeze artists, tightrope walkers, lion tamers, a human cannonball, clowns and a master of ceremonies. I know who the MC is. But my part? That's what makes me edgy.

Just before we join the main road Jozsef checks the mirror again. Nothing behind us. We skirt the TILOS sign and turn right towards Kecskemét.

'There's a café a couple of kilometres back,' he says. 'Do you remember it?'

'No.'

'A cop always notices where he can get a drink. I thought journalists did too.'

'We don't have time for a drink,' I tell him.

'We have time for a drink because I have a telephone call to make and I don't want to use my mobile,' he says. He checks the mirror again. 'What do you know?'

'You mean about this whole business?' I ask. When he doesn't answer I say, 'I know what you know.'

The answer seems to impress Jozsef. 'Excellent. The longer you are here, the more Hungarian you become. Give nothing away except cigarette smoke, and you don't smoke. Incidentally, have you noted that Mary has stopped smoking?'

'How do you know she smoked?'

He takes his right hand off the steering wheel and wiggles two fingers. 'Nicotine stains but she hasn't had a cigarette all day or yesterday. You know why? Because of you. You don't smoke. You don't want to kiss an ashtray.'

True. Mary hasn't had a cigarette since she has been with me. Why hadn't I taken it in?

'She is serious, Bazil.' He glances at me. 'All right, I'll tell you what I know. I know two gunmen tried to kill me. Someone whispered to them I was working late and they were waiting for me. I know my boss told me to leave Goenz and you alone. I know I got an anonymous call telling me to keep away from you. I know that at the President's Archives the custodian gave me a straight look and rested his hand on my wrist as I was reaching for the files. "Are you sure this is wise, Jóska?" he asked. "You look tired. Wouldn't a holiday in Phuket be better for your health?" Obviously Cuba is no longer the fuck-and-forget island of choice any more. This is a man who worked with me in the old days when I was in the national police. "You saved my life once," he said. "Maybe I should save yours." You know what struck me? It wasn't just what he said, it was the way he said it, his voice a murmur like the old days because of hidden microphones.' Jozsef prods a stubby finger at the roof of the old

Volkswagen Golf. 'I've never been good at taking advice so here I am.' He glances again at the mirror. 'Your turn. What do you know?'

It sounds like a children's game but Jozsef has his reason.

'I know I wasn't meant to come here. A BBC tape was destroyed so I wouldn't have evidence that Eve was alive, a Foreign Office man tried to browbeat me, my house was broken into and my passport stolen. I know the hand was taken from the cemetery after I told West I would have tests carried out on it. I know my editor has been offered bribes and threatened if he didn't call me back to England. I know baddies came to the hotel to get me after they had shot you. I know Eve was making a list of dates and licence numbers of trucks from Romania and Serbia. Well, you know all about that.'

'You see,' Jozsef says, 'when we put it all together it shows a criminal network that stretches across Europe. It involves smuggling – drugs, arms, whatever is profitable – and it involves crooks, diplomats, bureaucrats, customs, police. It is something big enough, profitable enough, to protect at any cost. Tell me, are you going to write all this up for your paper?'

'Could be.'

'Do me a favour,' Jozsef says. 'Give me a different name.'

'I mightn't need to.'

'Why not?'

'My editor will show it to the lawyers and they will have a heart attack.'

'Why.'

'Libel.'

'Oh that,' he says, as if it is nothing.

He slows down and turns off the road and comes to a halt. The café looks much like a small house. It has a sign featuring a bunch of grapes and last year's vine leaves over the door. A shiny BMW is parked at the side of the building and Jozsef sits staring at it. He says nothing and there seems no point in my asking why we aren't going inside. Finally the café door opens and a grey-haired man and woman come out and drive away.

'All right,' he says.

I'm sitting at a window table in the café, nursing a beer and a hard roll with salami. There is no public telephone here but the owner has let Jozsef use his own. Jozsef walks over to my table and sits down.

'Has the Romanian truck passed?'

When I shake my head he picks up his beer and takes a long swallow.

'I have spoken to the army, or rather the Ministry of Defence in Budapest. I asked the girl on the switchboard how many stars does a general have on his epaulettes? What? How many stars etcetera? Four, she said. Then I want to speak to a general with five stars. To punish me for my cheek she put me through to a Colonel Babits who is in charge of a battalion of filing cabinets. I told him who I am, told him I need his urgent help, but his brain had gone on military manoeuvres. So I made up a good lie. Colonel Babits, I said, a truck has smuggled arms into our beloved homeland, terrorists are planning an attack so you better do something about it. He found a map but Kishegy isn't marked. How can our army invade another country when it can't even find its way round our own? Can you believe it?'

'Yes.'

'Actually, so can I. All right, helicopters, I told him, helicopters can follow a road. Take the road south from Kecskemét etcetera etcetera. The turn-off is marked TILOS but don't believe it. It's where Goenz has his country estate, Goenz, bastard son of one of the communist old guard. In that case it's political, he told me, so it will need the minister's signature. Provided the minister is not too busy. Lunch, golf, mistress, the minister has a full life. Colonel Babits has spent his entire career waiting for a proper war so he's not about to break sweat over this. That was Plan A.' Jozsef sighs. 'Never mind, we move on to Plan B. Zsigmond is riding to the rescue.'

He takes a bite from his salami roll and looks at it in some surprise.

'Zsigmond?'

'Zsimond, this morning, drives an ambulance. You remember?'

'Of course. He scooped up the whore Sisi from the railway tracks.'

'I rang the hospital, said I had an accident to report, was Zsigmond there because he knew the railway crossing. Maybe this is our lucky day after all, he had just reported for duty. So Zsigmond is coming. He's our way into Kishegy.'

'You have a plan.'

Jozsef tilts his hand back and forth. 'A plan... Plan is too finite a word. I prefer what the Pentagon would call a scenario. Possibilities, flexibility, nimble footwork, prayers. Above all, prayers.'

'Tell me.'

'I will.'

But Jozsef, normally so free with his talk, lapses into silence. When he is good and ready he'll tell me.

A brief mystery of time. You'd swear that five minutes waiting at the level crossing had stretched to five hours. But when the ambulance comes into view it brakes to a halt in a split second. Zsigmond and a colleague bustle out in a flash and then time goes back to its normal pace. They have gone rigid, staring at the gun in Jozsef's hand. I'm not going to point it at them, Jozsef said, just let them see it so they know we are serious.

'We meet again,' Jozsef says to Zsigmond, 'and so soon.'

Zsigmond nods his head three or four times. The scar on his cheek, so like a razor slash, has gone whiter. The corners of his mouth turn down.

'My wife warned me I was a fool to telephone after that television appeal. "Don't get mixed up with corpses," she said, "or you'll end up one yourself." "Roza," I said to her, "Roza, my whole life is mixed up with corpses," but she got angry. "This is not a joke," she said.' He nods again. 'She was right.'

His colleague's head is turned to peer along the tracks in search of another handless corpse. 'We were told there had been an accident.'

'You must learn patience,' Jozsef says. 'It hasn't happened yet. What's that you've got in your pocket?'

'What? It's nothing.'

'It's not a gun, is it?'

'No. It's nothing, I tell you.'

'Too big for a cigarette packet. Perhaps I'll just…'

'Get off. It's only this.' He pulls out a flask. 'I carry it for emergencies.'

'All things considered,' Jozsef says, 'I think this is an emergency.'

So there we are, an ambulance and an old VW Golf by a level crossing, four men standing about as if they're at a hunt meeting, shunting a flask of brandy from hand to hand, one of them holding a pistol. This is not life as I have known it in Oxford. Jozsef realises he still holds the pistol and tucks it under his jacket.

'We're all pals now, aren't we?'

'We're on duty,' Zsigmond says. 'We can't spend all day here swigging *palinka*. Why did you call us out?'

The sound of a car approaching makes us all turn towards the road. The car is coming not from Kecskemét but from the direction of Kishegy. It stops and the driver's window winds down.

'What's happened? Has there been an accident?'

'Don't worry, nothing is wrong.' It's the man with the brandy flask who speaks. He has had a couple of shots and everything is sunny.

The man's gaze passes over us all. We are a puzzle to him. 'You're sure there's nothing I can do?'

'It's a false alarm, that's all.'

As the car drives away I say, 'I remember you, you're Istvan.' His name has suddenly popped into my head.

'How do you know me?'

'That doesn't matter,' Jozsef says, turning back from watching the retreating car. 'The fact is we do know you. You came here the day that whore's body was mashed by the train. Her hand was missing which meant she was already dead when she was put on the tracks but you never reported this to the police.'

'Are you trying to blackmail us?' Zsigmond frowns and the bite out of his eyebrow twists into something like a Q. 'We'll just drive off. You wouldn't dare shoot.'

'Who mentioned blackmail?' Jozsef growled. 'Suppose I threatened to let Goenz know you told tales about the corpse; that would be blackmail. Or rather the truth.'

There is silence while Zsigmond and Istvan consider this.

'I believe we understand each other better now,' Jozsef goes on. 'What we want is to borrow your ambulance. Goenz has this man's wife prisoner in his estate. We are going to drive in and get her.'

'I'm not going in,' Zsigmond says. 'Not into Goenz's estate. I don't care what threats you make.'

'Good. I wouldn't want you along, just your ambulance and your jackets. You follow behind in our car and when we get close you turn off the road and wait for us to come back. You'll find a friend of ours there, a professional photographer. She's got her lens pointed at Goenz's property so there'll be a record of what happens. Do either of you speak English?'

'No.'

'No.'

'She doesn't speak Hungarian so you'll have something in common. You won't understand each other. Also you'll all be scared.'

I scribble a message to Mary on a page torn from Jozsef's notebook. *These two men are on our side. Jozsef and I are going in to rescue Eve, but I don't know how. Keep taking photos. If it all goes wrong or you think someone is coming to get you, escape in the Golf. Love. B. XXX*

I want to say more. I want to make sense of my emotions. I want to work out why I am trying to rescue the wife who abandoned me. I want to explain in two sentences why I have to stay with my cousin but I don't know what those two sentences are. I am desperate to touch Mary but all I can do is underline *Love*.

The red tops of the ambulance crew are tight across our chests. We are in the front of the ambulance and they are waiting in the Golf. Jozsef turns the key in the ignition, then turns it off.

'Are you up for this? Are you sure?'

'I married her.'

'That was in the past. This is now. Eva cut you out of her life and now you've found someone new. Why are you being such a gentleman about it?'

'If it was Adel, you'd do your best to rescue her, wouldn't you?'

Jozsef takes his time lighting a cigarette. 'That's a tough one. Adel goes and comes back. But if I heard she wasn't coming back unless I rescued her...' He thinks a moment. 'In the end...' He shrugs. 'You're my cousin and I worry because you haven't lived here. We learnt different things here, how to survive, how to get on, how to get out.' Jozsef's face has a puzzled frown. 'Maybe you want to scoop Eva up and put the clock back to earlier in your marriage.'

I shake my head.

'You can be in your coffin at the graveside but you can't put the clock back, not even by two seconds. Only God can do that. I can't remember who said that.'

'Sounds like an atheist to me. They're always bringing up God.' He draws on his cigarette and blows out a lot of smoke. He gives his head a little shake to clear away the frown. 'All right, down to business. There are no microphones here so don't worry.' He points at the ambulance roof. 'Tell me – have you ever killed a man?'

Have you ever killed a man?

Have you ever killed a man?

The question echoes inside my head.

Have you ever killed a man?

Jeremy Paxman would ask the question fourteen times.

Have you ever killed a man?

At the *Old Hag* I have a desk, a computer terminal, a telephone, a view of Dexter's office. When Dodo passes my desk she gives a little wiggle of her bum, just to let me know she's a woman.

Have you ever killed?

This is an alien landscape I am getting deeper into.

Have you?

Jozsef is staring at me.

'Good God, no.'

'Ever shot at one?'

'Of course not. It's not common in England.'

'Have you ever fired a pistol at a target? Let's be honest here – have you even held one in your hands?'

'No.'

For a moment Jozsef squeezes his eyes shut, then he rallies. His pistol is tucked inside his trouser belt and he slips it out.

'I thought you said you would have the pistol.'

'True. But suppose I am killed. Then it will be your turn with the pistol. All right?'

I say nothing. What's the point?

'The first thing to learn is that a pistol is not a weapon until the safety is off. Until then it is useless except to impress an ambulance crew. So I'll slide the catch. Now you have a weapon. Lesson number two – it's still useless unless you are prepared to shoot. Bazil, you've got to understand this. If he can, Goenz will kill you. More than that, every single one of his men wants to kill you. They came to your hotel after they shot me because they wanted to kill you. Don't think you can be a decent English gentleman and play by the rules. There are no rules. Shoot first. Aim for the stomach – it's a big area and it hurts. Or shoot him in the back – that'll surprise him. Do you understand?'

'I understand.'

'Will you shoot first before they get the chance? It's my life at risk too. Do you promise?'

'I promise.'

'Do you swear on my father's grave?'

'Yes, Jozsef.'

He glares at me. He's not satisfied.

'Say it. Say you swear.'

'I swear on the grave of your father.'

'Keep the pistol hidden until you need to use it. Of course you may not have to use the pistol.'

I am numb. Can I do what Jozsef asks in cold blood? Can I look in a man's face and see his terror and then squeeze the trigger? But there is worse. He hands me something out of the bag he brought from the car.

'Do you know what it is? *Careful.*'

It popped out of my hands and I fumbled to catch it before it fell on the floor. Whatever it is feels slippery. No, my hands are.

'What is it?'

'A stick grenade, Soviet manufacture. A souvenir from 1956 but I'm told it most likely still works. Everything else they made was crap but they made good weapons. It's a small bomb, think of it like that. Pull out this hook and you have eleven seconds until it explodes. Or is it seven? I hope it won't be necessary but there are times... all right, you can keep it from exploding by pressing down on this lever. When it does go off it will blast everyone within a radius of fifteen metres, so don't drop it, not unless you are an Olympic sprinter.'

This is it, my two-minute initiation into soldiering.

'Do you feel sick in your stomach?' Jozsef asks.

'Don't you?'

'When I was an ordinary cop – before I landed this nice, safe, easy job – I had to go into a stinking tenement in Köbanya one night and arrest some hoodlum. He'd mugged a foreigner, stuck a knife at his throat and robbed him. Unfortunately he chose the wrong foreigner, a Soviet diplomat, so we had to mount a full scale assault on his flat. As I remember it we had half a dozen cars round the building, sharpshooters hiding behind the rubbish bins.'

'You were going to storm the apartment block?'

'I was. I was given the honour of going into the flat first. I wasn't going to mess about knocking on the door, I was going to shoot out the lock and run in with my pistol leading the way. Except I found the door wasn't locked. Strange you think, but who dares to rob a robber's flat? I took a deep breath and offered up a prayer. Be good to me, O Lord, or at least kick the other bastard in the balls. And yes, I felt sick in my stomach.'

Jozsef turns the ignition key again, drops the cigarette out of the window, gives the other two a wave and gets going.

'But what happened? You went into the flat?'

'I had to. Stupid oaf had got drunk and passed out on the bed. Power of prayer, right?'

Maybe, I think.

Why an ambulance? I'd asked. Who queries an ambulance? he'd asked in return.

The drive from the level crossing goes mostly in silence. I sit with the gun in my pocket and the grenade jammed between my shoes to keep it safe while the ambulance bounces over cracks in the tarmac. Like any soldier – as I pompously labelled myself – going into action I brooded on what lay ahead and by what crazy route I had got here. My life has so absolutely changed I feel I must be a different person. Last week I was living in my non-des res in a provincial city in England, I worked at the *Old Hag*, I wrote Under the Carpet about the petty sins of Oxford Council, its politicians and its servants. I had a pint or two at the Temporary Sign with Josh, I put up with the ribald jibes of my workmates – mainly female – with good humour, I looked at the first three chapters of the Great Novel and buried them in the desk drawer again, I dusted photos of Eve. That was it. My life. And now?

We pause below the boulders and walnut trees while Jozsef jabs a hand out of the window to show Zsigmond and Istvan where to hide the car. I look up but there is no sign of Mary.

'I said to your friend earlier: if she wanted to get out and walk, that was the time. I say the same to you now. After this there is no turning back.'

Jozsef's eyes hold mine.

'Well, cousin?' he asks. The compassion that sometimes comes into his voice surprises me. It is like the gentleness that soldiers can show before a battle.

I thrust my hand in the jacket pocket. 'Just checking the safety is still in the off position.'

'Good, very good.' Jozsef nods and slips in the clutch. 'I'll do the talking.'

No change there.

You leave a lot to Jozsef, Mary said. It's not a question of leaving it to him. Jozsef reaches out for it as his right.

We take the curve round the boulders of the little hill at a lick and head for the gate at increasing speed as if Jozsef is intent on crashing it. At the last moment he stamps on the brake pedal and brings us to a halt so violent the grenade breaks loose. I am scrabbling on the floor for it while Jozsef mutters curses at my clumsiness and the guard appears out of the hut and stumbles and recovers.

'Shit's sake, didn't you see us coming? Why didn't you open the gate?' Jozsef is leaning across me to shout out of my window.

The guard is dressed in army surplus clothing of camouflage trousers and tunic. As he stands up straight his hand goes to the pistol holstered at his hip. Oh God, if he draws that… but he is checking it is still there.

'Who are you? What are you talking about?'

'Who are we? Are you blind? What does it look like?'

'What do you want?'

'To bloody get in. What do you think? Don't they tell you anything? They ring up from the big house, say it is an emergency, they should tell you to have the gate open. Now move.'

Jozsef's tone of voice brings a frown to the guard's face and his hand drops towards the handle of his pistol, pure reflex. It's starting, I know, the nightmare.

'If he starts to draw the gun,' Jozsef murmurs, 'shoot him. There's a big key ring on his belt. So then you must get out and open the gate.'

When he pulls the pistol out of the holster… no, that'll be too late. The moment his hand touches the butt… I'll shoot. No hesitation. No discussion. No gentlemanly warning. My pistol is out of my pocket. I can feel the safety is off. Don't look at his face. Don't see him as a human being. Aim at the broad expanse of shirt front. Two metres away. Can't miss. But he won't be dead. He'll be screaming. He'll be twisting on the ground. How do I get the key ring off his belt?

But the guard doesn't draw his gun, or try to. He is turning to go back in the hut.

'Where the hell are you going?'

The guard hesitates, then turns back to us. 'The radio is inside. Getting orders.'

'I don't believe it.' Jozsef is leaning on my knee and stabbing a finger at the guard. 'Heart attack. The big boss. Seconds count and you're going inside to have a chat. I wouldn't want to be in your shoes when they hear how you wouldn't let us in.' Jozsef extends a second finger and raises his thumb so now it is a pistol. He fires off two rounds in the face of the guard, silently mouthing *bang, bang*. The guard's eyes widen then blink. I can see his adam's apple bob as he swallows.

'You'll have to move,' the guard says.

'What the hell are you talking about?' Jozsef asks.

It's true. The gate swings outward and the ambulance has halted too close. Jozsef reverses. The guard undoes a padlock as big as his fist and pushes the gate open.

Jozsef leans across me to fire one last salvo. 'We'll be back soon. I'll give a touch on the siren and you open the gate for us to drive straight through. I hope we're not too late.'

That's how it is done. Easy as pie. Jozsef could talk his way into Fort Knox. And out again with a sample tucked under his arm.

'Has he closed the gate?'

I look back.

'Yes.'

We are driving down the road to the house.

'Do you think Colonel Babits has got to the minister yet?'

How would I know? I glance at Jozsef. What does his face say? Nothing. Everything. He could be determined, impatient, angry, eager, scared. No, not scared, the memory of his father won't allow that. He doesn't like the silence.

'I can picture an army convoy coming down the road,' he says. 'Soldiers in the back of the trucks with their rifles pointing everywhere. They stop at the gate. "I'll just check with the boss whether I can let you in," the guard says. "No, wait a minute, I can't ask the boss. He's had a heart attack."'

Soldiers on one side, Goenz's thugs on the other, us in the middle. I don't share the thought.

'That was close,' Jozsef says. 'I thought you were going to have to shoot him.'

My hand is on the pistol grip. It's wet and slippery just like the grenade was. *Are you up for this? Are you sure?* I hear Jozsef's voice in my head. No, I am not sure. *Have you ever killed a man?* No, and I don't want to. The house is less than half a kilometre away now.

'She's not working for Goenz, is she?' I say.

Jozsef glances at me, then back to the road. 'No.'

'She was put in to get information?'

'Not by anyone in the embassy here. It would have to come from London, someone high up in the ministry.'

'Why has it taken so long?' I adopt a journalist's view: get the story, see it in tomorrow's paper. 'Why didn't she get out?'

'Long?' Jozsef shakes his head. 'It's more than Goenz. Goenz is just her way in. She has to find out about all his activities, back to his sources, on to his target country which happens to be yours. There are a lot of people she has to find out about, crooks, officials, contacts everywhere. That's what I think she's been doing. You're her husband but you're also a journalist so she cut you out. You were a risk. She put her job ahead of you. That's how I see it.'

In my guts I know that but I need someone else to say it.

'But it's just her,' I say. 'One person.'

'No,' Jozsef says. 'She is just the one person we know about. She'll have a boss in London, not that Lambswool you talked of.'

'Lovegrove.'

'Yes. Not him. But she'll have someone high up. And in Budapest, a contact, controller, maybe others. We just don't know. It's like a war and she is a spy, a single person, sent in to get information. Imagine what a terrible life she is leading. She has to prove herself, convince them she's left the embassy for some damn good reason. Money? Revenge on someone there? In the old days it could have been ideology, helping the revolution, but Goenz doesn't qualify for that. She has to be useful to Goenz. Languages obviously because he doesn't speak English. Being beautiful is a help because even if Goenz is not screwing her he can have hopes. Maybe she recruited Lovegrove not the other way round. You have to think like that to understand what she's doing and how difficult – I mean dangerous – it is being a spy at the heart of Goenz's operation while all the time...'

His voice dries up and he shrugs.

'Your friend Mary,' Jozsef pauses, 'she's up on that little hill taking photos. If you'd shot that guard she'd have it on her camera. Evidence against you. If the guard died, murder.' He pauses again. 'Lucky it didn't turn out like that. I'm hoping our luck continues.'

A hundred metres, less. The upper windows in the mansion that were curtained are now clear. Someone is coming down the steps from the front door but Jozsef hauls the wheel over to follow the track to the building that looks like stables. The big truck from Romania has parked there, obscuring half the block. Beyond the stables we can see a dandy little plane parked on the grass strip that does as a runway. H-GYU is painted on the side.

'Vanity registration,' Jozsef says. 'Could you fly it?'

'No.'

'Just a thought. Grab Eva, run for the plane, fly off to Marrakesh.'

'Why Marrakesh?'

'Do you have a better suggestion?'

'The moon,' I say.

Call it gallows humour. Jozsef's lips twitch.

'First we have to find Eva.'

He drives in a circle so the ambulance is pointing back the way we came and stops. When he switches off the engine there is silence but not absolute silence. Jozsef gives a little grunt because of the voices. They sound near but distant. No, that doesn't make sense. They're like voices from a neighbouring hotel room. I can't pick out words. The cadence doesn't sound Hungarian or English. It's more high-pitched, male, female, even child, no telling. But I would say there was an energy, a drive, to the way they are speaking.

Jozsef has stopped the ambulance so that the truck is between us and the stable block. Mary will have the long lens on us, I think. Away on the left is the big house. Has anyone observed our arrival? As Jozsef said, who queries an ambulance?

'Now we must get moving,' Jozsef says. 'Give me the pistol. You have sweaty hands, so do I.' He wipes his palms on his trousers. 'You remember, Napoleon only wanted lucky generals? Do you feel lucky?'

'I feel…' Ever since Jozsef asked if I had killed a man I have felt different, distant from reality. I am in a movie, a Western, the showdown. 'I feel numb.'

Jozsef takes a moment to stare into my eyes.

'That will have to do. Now we are going to get out and stir the wasps' nest. Pull the hook out of that grenade but hold the lever down. If I tell you to throw it, then throw it as far as you can.'

'At who?'

'Choose somebody you don't like. Now you may think this is all wrong but it is the only way: I am going to stand close behind you.'

I frown at him.

'Aren't you going to ask why? I'll tell you anyway. Goenz's men are going to appear out of the stable, out of the trees, down from the house, I don't know, but they'll come. I can threaten them. I can shoot over your shoulder but they can't shoot me because you are in the way. If they shoot you then the grenade falls and they will catch the blast. My betting is that they will understand that so there will be no shooting.'

No. I want no part of this. It should be Jozsef who holds the grenade, Jozsef who stands in front. But he doesn't give me the chance. He puts a hand on my collar as if I'm under arrest and marches me along the length of the truck and around the front and there we are, in full view of the stables. The guard is still sitting on the chair. An ambulance arriving didn't worry him. Two men - one with a grenade, the other with a pistol - suddenly appearing is different. He gets to his feet, grabbing for the rifle that's on the ground by the chair. I am almost deafened by the shot Jozsef fires by my ear. He has aimed up in the air not at the guard.

'Freeze,' Jozsef bellows. 'Don't move. Drop the rifle or I'll kill you.'

The guard goes still, the rifle is in his hand but down at his side.

'Drop the rifle. If you don't, I'll shoot you. I'm counting down. Five… four… three… two…'

The rifle clatters on the ground.

'Now unlock that door behind you. Do it. Move.'

'I'm not allowed to,' the guard says.

'You've got the key?' The guard doesn't answer. 'I'm allowing you to. In fact I'm ordering you to.'

'Who are you?'

'God. God with a gun. Now move.'

The guard nods. He understands the logic of the situation. He turns, unlocks the door, steps aside and out they come. They are running, they are screaming, they are tripping over each other, elbows jabbing, eyes wild. Then they see Jozsef with the pistol and me with the grenade and they come to a stop. Maybe there are a dozen men, four or five women, one of the women with a baby. They are Chinese. They have heard Jozsef's gunshot and now they see the gun and they don't know what to do.

'You've got to run,' Jozsef says, 'get out of the way, it's dangerous.' He tries it first in Hungarian, then in English. 'Get out. Run. Don't any of you speak English?'

One of the women says, 'I speak.'

'Get away from here. You might get killed.'

'We go England. We pay.'

'Change of plan. Run.'

'This not England. We pay fifteen thousand dollars England.'

Jozsef points towards the gate. 'England is that way. You walk. You walk across Hungary and Germany and France. You walk across the sea and *then* you are in England.'

The woman is translating some of this. There is that keening cry the Chinese have in distress when Jozsef points the pistol in the air above their heads and fires a shot. The pistol is close to my head. My eardrum is going to shatter. It cracks and then it sings. *Bang* in my ear. *Bang* doesn't begin to describe the explosion and the ringing in my ears.

Shouts, screams of terror, a wail from the baby. The group scatters, runs, towards the gate, towards the side of the building, towards the little plane.

'The grenade – you've got it ready?' Jozsef's growl joins the singing in my ear.

No time to answer. A door further down the stable block is flung open. Two men come out with pistols in their hands, followed by a thickset figure.

'The man.' Another growl in my ear.

'Goenz?'

He doesn't answer. Now two men who must be the Romanian drivers appear, see what is happening, and vanish back inside. The men with guns are yelling at the Chinese, one shoots and a figure stumbles. But Goenz is standing stock still, staring at Jozsef with his pistol resting on my shoulder. He shouts without turning his head.

'Stop it. Dezsö, Mihaly, stop.'

'This is the position,' Jozsef says. 'Listen to me.' He waits until he has Goenz's full attention. 'Goenz, I can shoot you but you can't shoot me. If you try, you'll hit this man and he'll drop the grenade and we'll be cut to pieces, you and me both. Back in Cold

War days this was known as Mutually Assured Destruction. You understand, don't you?'

It is calm, peaceful. Maybe the Chinese are still shouting but I don't hear them. One of the men with a pistol turns on his heel and starts to run. The pistol resting on my shoulder deafens me again. The man trips, lies on the ground screaming.

'Now do you understand who's in charge? You do what I say. Goenz, tell your man to be quiet. Go on, do it. Do it now.'

There is a moment while Goenz does nothing. He keeps staring at us. Jozsef, I suppose, is holding his gaze. Goenz is taking Jozsef's measure, pondering certain odds. There is a cliché: the other man blinked. I actually see Goenz blink but he goes on staring.

'Dezsö,' he says without turning his head, 'shut your mouth or he'll shut it for you.'

Dezsö does shut his mouth because there is groaning from behind clamped lips. Jozsef has put a bullet in his buttocks and Dezsö lays a hand there, blood oozing between his fingers.

'Now you, what's your name, Mihaly, drop your gun.'

Mihaly glances at Goenz who says, 'Do what he says.'

'And your gun,' Jozsef says.

'I'm not carrying. I employ others to do my shooting.'

'Do you know who I am?'

'You are Jozsef Fazekas,' Goenz says, 'some kind of security cop. My people told me you were dead.'

'You should employ better people.'

'The other one, he must be the Englishman who has changed his hotel. And his woman.'

'Chief,' Mihaly says, 'those bloody Chinks are getting away.'

'It's the closed season on Chink shooting,' Goenz says. 'Keep your eyes on these two bastards. Whatever you do, mind that fucking grenade.'

'All right, where is she?' I have had enough of holding it in, enough of the action, of having Jozsef with his pistol resting on my shoulder. 'Eve, where is she?'

Goenz doesn't answer. Not a muscle in his face moves. He simply stares.

'Where - '

'Eve is right here, Baz.'

The voice comes from behind me, behind Jozsef with his pistol too. We've been outflanked, outwitted.

It's as if a movie director had shouted, *Action*! This is the moment the world goes wild. The Chinese woman who spoke English has climbed in the cab and is trying to start the truck and there is a wheezing as the diesel engine turns over and coughs but doesn't come alive. Four or five of the Chinese have met another of Goenz's thugs, have punched him to the ground and are taking kicks at him. The wounded man is crawling back towards his pistol. The Romanian drivers come out again at the sound of the engine turning over. Mihaly is bending for his pistol. Goenz is giving an order but I don't know what it is. I turn round and see another stable door open and Eve a dozen paces away from me. West is close behind her. He is pressing a pistol to the side of her head, just above her right ear.

I hate him. I'll kill him. I have never thought like this before. A red mist swirls in my brain.

When I came over for Eve's funeral he helped with the bureau- cracy, consoled me, held my hand. He was tricking me. When I came back to Budapest last week he tricked me again and again, weaving stories, lying. Now he has discovered that he is the gullible one and Eve has been getting the evidence against him and Goenz and he is more than angry. He feels humiliated. That look on his face says it all: I hold all the aces and you are going to suffer.

'She's talked,' West says. 'It took a little persuasion so she finds it painful to walk. You had a wife full of spirit, Baz.'

Had? Why does he put it in the past?

I say nothing. West, Eve and I are at the centre, the still centre, while all around the world moves on. I am staring at West and Eve but at the side of my vision I see other things. Jozsef moves his pistol and there is a shot and a bellow of pain and rage from Mihaly. Then I see one of the Chinese men has turned back and has produced a knife and is coming up behind West, and Goenz yells, 'shit's sake, the bastard's creeping up on you.' In Hungarian. West frowns in ignorance, shaking his head, not understanding. Goenz raises his hand to point with urgent jabs and at last West turns round to look for the danger and Eve takes her chance and kicks back at him, heel up into his balls. West screams at the pain and she breaks free. She is coming to me, Eve is, hobbling, slow steps as if she is crossing the surface of the moon. She is reaching out for me, this wife who cut me out of her life, who staged her death, who let me suffer, who never took me into her confidence, who led a secret life, who never contacted me even when I came last week to search for her... step by step, her arms out... and the noise and the chaos fade away... her eyes locked on mine... counting how many more steps until she reaches me... and I am holding this stupid bloody thing in my hand and I simply toss it away so I can catch hold of her as she stumbles... she's a step away... and Jozsef cries out...

'God in heaven.'

CHAPTER 20

I'm all right now, really I am. It's late summer. Is it the worst summer since records began? They always are. But today is a perfect day. In England we don't enjoy good weather, we are grateful for it. I have come out to drink my fill of the midday sun in the Parks which are wonderful during university vacations. There are no joggers to force you off the path, well maybe a few, American graduate students and other homeless waifs.

A pond offers a welcoming bench and I sit there, basking in the warmth. I listen to the voices of girls speaking Italian and Spanish and Swedish, au pairs from the Victorian family houses of north Oxford. I hear no Hungarian and for that I am grateful, truly grateful. The sound of Magyar voices makes me catch my breath, though the clenching of muscles in my guts when I overheard Stumpf of the wild hair has faded. *Tout passe, tout lasse, tout casse.* No, for once Anon has slipped up. Time passes and everything gets better. Opening my eyes I see a pair of black swans patrolling the pond. That syllogism comes to mind: all swans are white; this bird is black; therefore it is not a swan. I toy with a bastard form of syllogism: all swans are white; this swan is black; therefore it is not black. Well, why not?

You won't have read anything of what happened in Hungary in the press, not one word. You won't have seen anything on the TV news. Nothing. It might never have happened. It took time for the truth to sink in: Goenz and West were dead, the organisation wasn't. The two Mafia clans had made a bargain and with Goenz out of the way Hamori took over. I never fully understood West's part – link to certain people in Britain?

It wasn't a story to TV news. It was all over and tidied up and there was nothing to show on the screen. Radio wasn't interested – it just seemed a small punch-up in a far-away country, yawn, yawn. But surely the national press would pounce – top diplomat killed, smuggling operation blasted, plucky British heroine loses her life, who is hiding the guilty men back in England? I rang a couple of old chums and they pricked up their ears but then another banking scandal broke and 'it's just lost traction,' as one said to me.

I tried my old friend Mike at the *Mirror* and he said he'd had enough grief from his editor about this shemozzle already. Shemozzle? Yes, Mike insisted, shemozzle. Do it under a pseudonym, I urged, and give it to the *Guardian*. It's got everything that puts them into spasm: arms, drugs, poor bloody immigrants, devious British diplomats, establishment cover-up. He *mmmed* and *aaahed* and shuffled his feet; believe me I can hear feet being shuffled a hundred miles away. It's not really my *beat*, Mike said, I do showbiz.

Hey, you've forgotten the *Oxford Herald*, you object, how about it? How about it indeed. I wrote it up, major feature, handed it to Dexter who went into purdah. One of the *great* stories, he said after a twenty-four hour delay. Got local interest, I pointed out, plus huge national importance shining out of every word. And Two Boobs got pix? he asked. Yes, yes. Well, he said, let me ponder how to handle it. Can you guess the rest? He pondered and I nagged. What are you scared of? It's the implications, he said, the legal eagles are verifying certain aspects. The hell with lawyers, I came back at him, where's your crusading spirit? What happened to freedom of the press? Dexter looked me straight in the eye, a sure sign of lying, and said, 'Trust me, Baz.' Dexter's crusading spirit was wilting fast.

Then came the bombshell. How did he fix this up without anyone having an inkling? Everybody knows that editors are devious but this took sneakiness to new heights. Or should that be lows? One morning Dexter was simply no longer there. His office had been cleared overnight. The paper came out without his oversight and the next day the truth ricocheted round the office; somebody must have told us but I don't know who. Dexter had flown off to take up a senior managerial position on – wait for it – the *Bangkok Post*. This defection stunned us at the *Old Hag*. Some said strings had been tweaked at the highest level, levers of power pulled, write your own cliché, though Dodo sniffed it probably had more to do with the Thai girl who had flitted back east. It fell to Josh to coin Dexter's epitaph: Feckless but not fuckless.

So you never read a dicky bird about this in the press.

In a fury of late nights I have knocked it into book form. It's all there, the clumsy lies, the dirty tricks, the scummy details, the explosive ending, the crassness of sending my wife – my late wife – alone into the heart of darkness. Editors may be chicken-hearted but publishers are made of sterner stuff. Maybe, as Jozsef says.

By the way, Jozsef is all right now. So am I, really I am. It's just that a number of curious things have happened.

One was the disappearance of Dexter to the steamy delights of Bangkok. Another was the disappearance of my manuscript a month back when it was nearly complete. The hard disk on my computer at home had the first seventeen chapters on it and then it didn't. Computers crash, files get deleted in error, we all know that. It was only a minor hiccup because I had a back-up on a memory stick which I carried with me so I could squeeze in half an hour's work on it at the office. I had a wee chat with Sam the Smuggler across the road who agreed it was curious but hardly a great mystery. A car had been parking up the street, two men in the front doing crosswords and eating taramasalata baps from the Cypriot deli. What were they doing? 'Waiting for Christmas,' Sam replied, 'which in this case was you. To those bastards you are Santa Claus, you're the bearer of gifts, you mean promotion if they can nail you on something.' I asked if he saw them go into my house on the day my computer developed Alzheimer's. 'No,

I was making a little trip to Calais. They'd have noticed that and taken their chance.'

Another scary thing: Mary's digital camera also developed Alzheimer's. A story has added punch with photos. She had shots of West with the pistol to Eve's head, Jozsef resting his gun on my shoulder, Goenz pointing as if he's directing the action, the chaos seconds after the grenade exploded, the army swarming out of helicopters. There they were on the memory card. Then there they weren't. She was spitting curses.

About Mary... we've been together months now. As Jozsef said, she chose me. I no longer try to puzzle out why. I just know I would have gone to pieces without her.

I try not to think about what happened at Kishegy that afternoon but there are times when my mind slips the leash and goes bounding back. Nothing I can do about it. My mind prowls down trails of its own. It never gives me a full coherent narrative. It's more like some experimental film with jump cuts and flashbacks and zooms and subliminal stuff and tricksy editing to confuse you. I saw a counsellor at the Warneford and she said that even ten years down the line it could hit me. Certain prisoners who survived Japanese POW camps, she said, could never obliterate their experiences. Even now they couldn't bring themselves to get into a Nissan, never mind that the cars are made in Sunderland.

This is what happened. This is what happened, I think.

I threw the grenade. Eve was stumbling towards me. I wanted to take her in my arms, I wanted to protect her, the grenade was in the way so I chucked it. Just like that. A reflex, not thinking. The Romanian truck was starting to move and the grenade bounced from its windscreen. Jozsef saw it. He's not built to be a runner but he scrambled round the other side of the truck. It sheltered him.

The grenade bounced off the windscreen, yes, arced in the air, fell to the ground. When it exploded...

No, I'm skipping. West saw it and was grabbing for it, actually reaching down, desperate to hurl it away. It exploded. Nothing was left of his arm below the elbow. His neck and his head… no, I can't describe that. Killed instantly. The Chinese man coming for him with a knife, also dead.

And this is the thing, the bloody bastard thing. Eve was a step away from me, not even in my arms, I was bending down, reaching out for her, when the grenade exploded. Her back took the full force of the blast. Her body shielded me. She died. I killed her.

I killed her.

I k…

What happened after that tumbles through my head. Goenz lay twisted on the ground. I have an image of Jozsef standing over his body, pistol in hand, aiming down. So I assume… but I never asked. Goenz's father brought in the Red Army that killed Jozsef's father all those years ago. Let's say Jozsef was settling the account.

There was a roaring, in my head, in the world. Helicopters. A lot of noise. Soldiers going about their business are not quiet. Nor are the wounded. I lost consciousness or I have lost my memory. Actually I don't want any more of it to come back. Don't ask me to recall it.

While I was still at the Intercontinental Jozsef came to visit me. I was drawing breath before returning home. Mary was acting as nurse but Jozsef sent her out to get a bottle of booze.

'What do you want?' she asked.

'Something with alcohol,' he growled.

After she'd closed the door he produced a small tape recorder from a plastic carrier bag. I noticed how taut the skin was across his cheeks. His eyes seemed flattened in his face.

'This was in the stable room where Eva had been. A couple of the gang were there – Mihaly and I forget the other's name. West throws in a couple of questions but mainly it's Goenz. There's a kind of controlled fury to him but…' He looked up as if searching for the right words. 'Well, sometimes it's not controlled.'

Jozsef broke off to frown at the recorder. He was sorry now that he'd brought it, I could see that.

'You know that Goenz and Hamori were getting together? We questioned one of the survivors at Kishegy about the people smuggling. Hamori was going to be handling it so this was the last truck that would pass through Kishegy. I imagine Eva felt under pressure to find out as much as possible.'

'Why did Goenz make the tape?'

'I don't know. Hamori wasn't present so maybe Goenz made the tape for him.'

He went quiet.

'Listen, if you've brought the tape, you have to play it. Otherwise why bring it?'

Jozsef held my eyes a long time and I didn't blink. So he put on headphones and played some of the tape to himself, frowning all the time, fast-forwarded to a spot he thought was all right, or at any rate not awful.

Yes, dates and licence numbers, of course I did.

It was Eve, I knew it. But the voice was hoarse as if she'd been shouting at a football match.

So all this time…

She broke in. *All written down. Yes. Ever since I started with you.*

Names? Goenz asked.

Of course.

Shanghai?

I was proud when I worked out that Green Tea was Zhang.

Shit. How about Izmir?

Yes.

Patras? Brindisi?

Mmm.

Kishegy? Why are you smiling? Bitch, I'll –

There was a cry and Jozsef stopped the tape.

'He was beating the soles of her feet. Bastinado. The Turks used to do it when they were here. Long ago.'

* * *

That is the last time I heard her voice. She smiled in a situation like that? I always come back to that, puzzling over it. There were dimensions to Eve quite beyond me. I don't think I could ever have been enough for her.

Sometimes, remembering that cry, I have to take a walk, long and hard, until the sweat comes. But I'm all right now.

Here's another curious thing. Remember Lovegrove, Cyril his first name, lank and anally retentive Foreign Office mystery man? I was only a few days back in England when I was summoned. His obscure club, Curzon Street, near that gambling casino. The young man he called 'Grey' was in the room but Lovegrove told him to wait outside. So, there would be no witness.

'You're an extremely lucky fellow,' Lovegrove said.

This was a sort of softening up statement, setting the tone for our meeting. My left arm was bandaged because I'd had bits of metal removed from it. Shrapnel I suppose you'd call it, named after a British general. Not a lot of people know that. I lifted the arm, was about to say the dressing would be off next week, but I closed my mouth.

'Lucky because it has been decided on the highest authority,' he said, 'and bearing in mind all the circumstances, not to initiate legal proceedings against you.'

I looked at my bandaged arm, then looked at him.

'You killed two British citizens,' he went on, 'both of them, as it happens, in the service of Her Majesty. But it is to be recommended that no further action be taken. You used a hand grenade which is not something that can be bought legally. Clearly you were engaged in grossly criminal activities. Two lives taken – British, I mean, the others are not our concern – but you have been let off. Consider yourself damned fortunate, Potter.'

Count to ten while you wonder where to begin.

'But West...'

He raised a hand.

'It is a condition of dropping criminal charges that you never talk about any of the events to anybody, never mention any names.'

'So how do I explain this?' I raised my arm. 'Opening a can of worms? Eve was tortured. West watched, maybe gave a hand.'

'I'm warning you, Potter, just a word of caution. If you try to cause trouble you *will* be prosecuted for breach of the Official Secrets Act. Remember you signed it when your wife joined the service.'

'I did no such thing.'

Lovegrove lifted a geriatric leather briefcase from the floor, thumbed through documents, and drew out a sheet of paper with the royal crest, lion and unicorn enjoying foreplay in Eve's words, and *Dieu et Mon Droit* at the top.

'Looks like your signature to me.'

All swans are black. Some swans are blacker than others.

Jozsef paid a flying visit to Oxford. He came alone.

There is an old Jewish joke that Jozsef had changed to fit his situation. 'You haven't asked how Adel is,' he said to me. 'So how is Adel?' I said. 'Don't ask,' he said. He was in Oxford for what he called a short weekend.

'Isn't the constitution safe if you're away longer?'

A wonderful smile that had never been in his repertoire transformed his face. It was like the sun hitting Mount Rushmore.

'I've got to get back because I'm due in court on Tuesday,' he said. 'Witness for the prosecution at my ex-boss's trial.'

'What's he done?'

'Messed where he shouldn't have messed.'

'Anything in particular?'

'What are you? Some kind of lawyer suddenly?'

'He has to be charged with something,' I point out.

'Subverting the constitution,' Jozsef says. 'There are deposits in his bank account that come from Luxembourg and before that Switzerland and before that Istanbul and before that Moscow.

Specifically, he has been bought by the Kremlin. Putin likes to pull the strings and watch his puppets in the West dance. Putin is old KGB. They never went away. They just changed their name. Putin is always prodding, looking for weakness. Drugs, immigrants, politicians out for a good time, he tries everything. Listen, you have to hit him back. Like now.'

And he had a gesture I hadn't seen before. He raised his right arm high in the air, hand clenched in a fist. He's a closet Nazi? No, he's a victorious gladiator saluting the emperor before despatching the fallen.

Mary had decided that nothing but a full-blown English Sunday lunch would do: smoked salmon, roast beef and Yorkshire, apple pie and clotted cream to finish us off.

'You two boys go out while I cook,' she said. 'You make me nervous.'

So we wandered down to the Temporary Sign where I introduced Jozsef to draught Guinness. I bought the first round. Come to think of it I bought the second round too while Jozsef brought me up to date with everything that had happened after I left and I told him about the problems I was having: Lovegrove, Dexter prevaricating and then doing a runner to Bangkok, break-ins, computer and camera wiped.

'The trouble is I can't tell if it is the good guys screwing me or the bad guys screwing me.'

'That is the modern dilemma,' Jozsef said.

I frowned.

'I can't write this story,' I said.

In my voice I could hear the echo of a boy protesting to his mother and stamping his little foot. Jozsef could hear it too. He rubbed his knuckles along his chin as if it was tender from a punch.

'You can write it,' he told me.

'I can't. They'll find a way to stop me.'

'You can write it,' he said again, more force this time. 'You'll find a way.'

Jozsef stared at me, Jozsef my cousin, the cop, the killer, the cuckold, the survivor.

All right. I took a deep breath. 'This is a true story. Only the facts have been changed.'

Jozsef's smile was slow to come but worth the wait.

'Isn't that the Hungarian way?'

Jozsef pronounced Mary's lunch superb. Afterwards he produced a bottle of *barackpalinka*.

'We drink this the Hungarian way,' he said, 'until the bottle is dry.'

So I sit on the bench in the Parks, not brooding but reliving. In a way, Eve and I showed more love to each other at the end than we did during our marriage. I think I tried to serve her, to show steadfastness even when I knew it was finished. Mary seems to understand this, even salutes me for it. With my face turned up to feel the life-giving warmth of the sun and my eyes closed to other distractions, I say: this is my epiphany.

There's a sixth sense that warns of danger creeping up on us, isn't there. What vibrations do our nerve endings pick up? What electrical charges? What mental wavebeats? Also it can alert us when a loved one approaches. I open my eyes as Mary comes round the pond and we smile at each other at the same moment. Often I think of this miracle: that I used and abused her in Budapest, went blindly after Eve, left Mary knitting socks (as she calls it) and yet here we are in the sunshine. I asked her about this, why she put up with me, why she didn't scratch my eyes out or spit in my face and she smiled.

'Love,' she said. 'It's wonderful or it's a con. What do you think?'

Josh has spoken to me about 'this love business', as he calls it. He says it has been noticed round the *Old Hag*, the change in me. What change, Josh? Hard to pin down, an openness, a steadiness, some said a maturing. And Dodo says I no longer have the journalist's eye for a deadline, I take a longer view. I just believe I am fortunate to be alive. I take time to ponder that.

I was working this morning. For my sins the new editor, a no-nonsense Brummie whose eyes are not lifting towards the big smoke, has kept me writing *Under the Carpet*. It simply has not been possible to go with Mary to the clinic. She comes to a halt and beams down at me, still standing.

'So how did it go?' I ask.

She's just had a scan, you see. She lays her head to one side, still smiling at me.

'Come on. Why are you holding back?'

She lays a hand on my shoulder to steady me. 'It's twins,' she says.

'Twins?'

She nods.

I see the nod but still don't quite take it in. 'Really? Really really really?'

She nods again.

'Twins. Well I'm buggered.' For a moment, words desert me. A little cloud is sailing across the blue sky and I imagine I can see someone's face in it. Not my mother beaming, not my father clapping me on the back, not Jozsef's scowl turning sunny. Is it Eve's face? But it is gone before I can decide.

'You did say twins?'

Me having twins, I think. Then: *no, her, you stupid man*. I lay my head against her belly as if I can already pick up the heartbeats.

Two babes.

About David Brierley

David Brierley was born in Durban. He moved to Canada, then England and back to South Africa all by the age of thirteen. Travel and curiosity about different countries is deep in his nature. After Oxford University, he taught at a lycée in France followed by work in London advertising agencies. Once his career as a novelist was established, he moved to France. As well as writing, he was a prison visitor. Together with his wife Jill he created a garden that won first prize in a regional competition. Now back in England, they live near Bristol in a small market town whose name – Chipping Sodbury – always raises a smile.

Safe House Books is an independent British publisher of spy fiction which is reviving quality espionage for a new audience.

Printed in Great Britain
by Amazon